THE
MASTER
OF
AYSGARTH

THE
MASTER
OF
AYSGARTH

◎◎◎◎◎◎

MARGARET MAYHEW

HAMISH HAMILTON
LONDON

First published in Great Britain 1976
by Hamish Hamilton Ltd
90 Great Russell Street London WC1B 3PT

Copyright © 1976 by Margaret Mayhew

SBN 241 89531 6

Printed and bound in Great Britain by
REDWOOD BURN LIMITED
Trowbridge & Esher

For my mother —
with love and gratitude

CHAPTER I

In the summer of my eighteenth year I went to live at Aysgarth
Hall. Set down on paper in a single sentence it sounds a simple
enough event, but behind those few words lies a story of momen-
tous upheaval in my life.

For the previous two years I had lived in genteel poverty with
my mother. We rented furnished rooms in a tall, gloomy house
on the edge of Clapham Common. It was respectable but
drearily shabby and depressing and poor Mama found it insup-
portable. We had been used to far better things in the days before Papa died and she was never able to reconcile herself to our
sadly reduced circumstances. Once we had lived in a gracious
white house in Regent's Park. There had been fine furniture, servants at every hand, expensive clothes, jewels, smart carriages,
and a life of comfort and elegance. And when we tired of London
there was a large estate in Hampshire for our country retreat. In
fact, I infinitely preferred the periods spent away in the country.
I had two ponies of my own and three friendly brown and white
spaniels and I was happiest of all when out riding across the
fields with the dogs lolloping along beside me. There at least it
did not matter a jot that I was gauche and plain and quite incapable of making the sort of amusing and witty conversation that
came so naturally to my mother. I could talk to my horse and to
the dogs without any fear that they would find me dull and un-
sophisticated. My mother, on the other hand, found the country
unutterably boring and only tolerated Hampshire when the London season was dead. It was far too quiet, she declared, and
there were too many tedious trees and fields everywhere, to say
nothing of the mud. And, as for the horses in the stables, she
considered them stupid, dangerous creatures.

Of course, I was a great disappointment to her. Mama was one of the most beautiful and brilliant hostesses in town. She was tall and exquisitely graceful with heavy gilt-colored hair and deep blue eyes. Her invitations were anxiously sought after and wherever she went she was surrounded by admirers, all dazzled by her charm and vitality. Beside her I must have appeared a very timid and plain little mouse. I had not inherited any of her famous beauty, being short and rather too thin with dark, straight hair and a sallow complexion, and I found it impossible to make the sort of amusing small talk that might have allowed me some success in smart society. When Mama launched me with one of the most glittering balls of the season I was a dismal failure. I did not sparkle or shine in any way and but for her unflagging efforts in ensuring me dancing partners, I should certainly have spent my evenings as a miserable wallflower.

"If only you would try a little harder, Alice," she would urge impatiently as the season progressed and I had still not attracted a suitable husband. "Sometimes I think you'd sooner be left to molder away down in the country with your books and all those muddy animals. Heaven knows what I've done to deserve such an unrewarding daughter."

"Leave the child alone," Papa would reply, defending me as always. "At least she's some brains in her head even though I'll admit she's no beauty. She's done well with her studies—fluent French and German and more history than I'll ever know!"

Surprisingly, he understood how I felt and I was grateful to him for that. He was a tall and floridly handsome man who enjoyed their gay and extravagant style of life quite as much as my mother. He had a generous and easygoing nature that made him very popular with everyone.

But my studies were of little importance to Mama. To be clever was merely a handicap in her opinion since it could make a man feel foolish or even inferior. "Always pretend you know nothing," she advised me firmly.

I was anticipating our departure for Hampshire with pleasure and relief when suddenly Lord Alfred Witherspoon appeared on the scene. He had just returned from a tour on the Continent and Mama, swooping on him like a bird of prey, exerted herself so charmingly and persuasively that before long I found him my constant partner at every dance and, later on, a house guest in

Hampshire. Within a few weeks we were engaged and Mama began delightedly to plan a brilliant wedding, while I was left to reflect soberly on a future to be shared with Lord Alfred. He was, of course, a very eligible young man and also perfectly amiable but he could talk of nothing but the latest society gossip in a high-pitched, affected drawl, he had an irritating laugh that sounded like a donkey's bray, and he was the vainest man I had ever met. I watched him admire himself in every available looking glass—his protuberant blue eyes sliding constantly toward his reflection to pause and admire, smoothing a crease here and flicking a speck of dust there, before continuing his monologue of tittle-tattle. When I look back on that time now, I wonder how it was that I ever accepted his proposal or, just as puzzling, why he wished to marry me in the first place. But then I have forgotten the sheer force of my mother's will and the fact that I had never expected to love my husband, or even necessarily to respect him. Mama had taught me from the nursery that both feelings were unlikely and, as she pointed out with her usual candor, it was a far better match than I had any right to expect considering my plainness and lack of wit. As for Lord Alfred, I think perhaps he saw me as the perfect foil for his own image—the colorless little peahen beside the dazzling, dandy peacock.

It was a few days after we returned to London for the new season that Papa shot himself. He was found dead in his study one morning, his pistol in his hand and a letter left on the desk before him. And, after that, a grim and terrifying tale of reckless gambling, mountainous debts, and disastrous investments came to light. The scandal was appalling: many friends were owed huge sums of money without hope of repayment and even the beautiful white house and the estate in Hampshire had been mortgaged to the maximum. There was nothing left.

The shock broke my mother. It was as though the very light of her spirit had been snuffed out forever. Perhaps she might have rallied in time if it had not been for the callous cruelty of her former friends. The scandal and disgrace of debt and suicide had finished us in society and we were shunned and ignored by all the smart people who had once been so eager for her acquaintance. The fulsome admirers called no more at the house in

Regent's Park and no gilt-edged invitations or extravagant bouquets of flowers were delivered to our door. Lord Alfred had written asking to be released from his pledge and although Mama ranted furiously against him, I certainly could not find it in my heart to censor him. The truth was that the fact that I was no longer obliged to marry him was the single comforting thought for me in those dark days. As creditors continued to harass us, increasingly Mama took to her bed and the doctor diagnosed a complete breakdown. It was left to me to sort matters out as best I could and at least I had one ally in the well-meaning, if somewhat bumbling, person of Mr. Pendleton, the family solicitor.

Joseph Pendleton was a kindly old man who was deeply distressed by our situation. He did his utmost to help but could do nothing to save the gracious London house nor the Hampshire estate. Everything had to be sold to meet the debts that pressed on us from all sides: the houses, the carriages, the jewels, the beautiful furniture all went. My ponies were auctioned and the three brown and white spaniels destroyed. We were left with a tiny capital sum to live on and Mr. Pendleton himself found us the furnished lodgings in Clapham.

He shook his white-whiskered head sadly over our new home. "I'm afraid that dear Lady Chell will find it very difficult to adjust to such a change in circumstance. It is all going to be a great trial for her."

Like most men he had long ago been completely captivated by Mama's beauty and charm and his concern was chiefly for her. Not that I bore him the slightest ill will for this; I was perfectly used to being overlooked and because I managed to preserve a reasonably calm exterior no doubt he felt that I had been less affected by the tragedy. In fact the memory of it was to haunt me for the rest of my days. I grieved deeply for Papa and my mother's fragile state of health was a constant anxiety to me. On the rare occasions when I could persuade her to leave her bed she would lie for hours on a couch near the window, not speaking but staring blankly up at the London skies. She seemed almost unaware of her surroundings, and considering their pitiful drabness, perhaps this was just as well. She grew steadily thinner and paler, her skin took on a gray, papery look, and her once luxuriant gilt hair grew dull and lank. In late spring she caught a cold which no amount of careful nursing on my part could cure. She began to cough and the cough grew steadily worse as the weeks went by until her whole body was convulsed by the violent spasms which seized her and the pathetic sound of her rasping breath filled my ears night and day. Once, as I sat as usual beside her bed, she opened her eyes for a moment and spoke in a faint, exhausted voice.

"Whatever will become of you, Alice," she whispered. "No one at all will want you now."

I made some soothing reply but later on admitted to myself the truth of her words. My chance of marriage had gone forever, just as everything else had been lost to us.

Mama died that summer. The doctor was a conscientious man who did what he could for her, but finally she slipped peacefully away one July dawn into a world where our downfall and disgrace no longer mattered. At the end I know that she was thankful to go and the thought comforted me. I resolved to try and remember her only as the beautiful and vivacious woman she had once been and to forget the gray and wasted creature who had coughed her life away in those dreary lodgings. Not one of her society friends had visited her during her long illness and the bitterness I felt against them would be carried with me to my own grave.

Mr. Pendleton and I were the only mourners at the funeral. Mama was buried in the corner of a quiet graveyard in Clapham on a cool and windy summer day. The black veil I wore blew wildly about my face as I stood at the graveside and watched the plain wooden coffin being lowered into the ground, and the sorrow I felt for my mother was now also tinged with the apprehension I felt about my unknown future, alone and friendless in the world.

M.. Pendleton shared my anxiety and evidently felt some responsibility for me. He accompanied me back to the empty lodgings and paced up and down the room, giving little worried tugs at his short, white beard.

"My dear child," he said kindly, "we must think what is to happen to you now. Were my late wife still alive I should be happy to welcome you into my own house, but as it is, my bachelor chambers would be quite unsuitable. . . ." He shrugged his shoulders hopelessly. "Is there no relative or friend of your parents who might take you under their wing?"

"None," I replied. "My parents were both only children and we have no friends left since Papa's death. But there is no need to be concerned about me, Mr. Pendleton. You have told me that there is still a little money left, even after paying the doctor's fees and the funeral expenses, and I can perfectly well find a post as a governess or companion with some family. I'm quite well educated, you know, and I shall be able to look after myself."

But he refused to be calmed. "I'm afraid the money will not last you for very long now, my dear, and although I've no doubt you would make an admirable governess it is not at all what your dear mother would have wished for you. I feel she has left you in my care and I shall not rest until a suitable solution to the problem is found. We must think hard. . . . Surely you have godparents at least, my child?"

"I believe I have a godfather who lives somewhere in Yorkshire but I haven't heard from him for years. I think Papa quarreled with him for some reason when I was very young and they never spoke to each other again after that. I had almost forgotten he existed."

Mr. Pendleton was looking delighted. "Ah! I knew we should find the answer eventually. What was his name, my dear?"

"Mr. Miles Metcalfe. I still have a volume of poems that he gave me inscribed with his name."

"Excellent!" Mr. Pendleton rubbed his hands together with enthusiasm. "I shall find out his address in Yorkshire and we shall write to him at once."

"But I should much prefer you to do nothing of the sort. He has heard no word of me for over ten years and I have no right whatever to approach him now."

"Nonsense, my dear. He made certain promises on your behalf at your christening and now is his chance to keep some of them and to make up for all the years he has neglected you. The name Metcalfe sounds familiar to me and I fancy he may well be one of the big landowners in Yorkshire. I shall write to him today and acquaint him with your unfortunate circumstances. No gentleman of honor would wish his goddaughter to be left penniless and bereft in the world and I'm confident that I shall receive a favorable reply. I shall let you know as soon as I hear from him."

When Mr. Pendleton had gone I sat alone in the silent room and considered the prospect unhappily. I had no wish whatever to impose myself on a stranger who might take me into his house only out of a reluctant sense of duty. My experience had taught me to mistrust and doubt people and there was no reason to suppose that my Yorkshire godfather and his family would be any less condemnatory of my father's disgrace than London society. I did not want to spend the rest of my days as a poor, despised dependent, sitting mutely in some dark corner and hoping for the occasional kind word.

I tried hard to remember what my godfather was like but could only recall a vague impression of a big man with a deep, booming laugh who had swung me high into the air above his head when he had visited our house in Regent's Park long ago. I remembered that his beard had tickled my cheek when he kissed me and that I had thought him a rather loud and alarming person. I could recollect nothing about his wife except that she had seemed very quiet and colorless beside him. And why, I wondered, had my father and he quarreled so bitterly? Money must be the reason and very likely my godfather was owed some enormous sum that I should never be able to repay. I should be hopelessly, humiliatingly in his debt forever and it was not a fate that I relished one bit.

With an effort I put the matter from my mind, hoping that Mr. Pendleton would be unable to trace the Metcalfe family and, even if he did succeed, that my godfather would refuse to have anything to do with me. Mr. Pendleton would be dismayed but I should, at least, remain independent of charity. I occupied myself with the task of sorting out my mother's few clothes and belongings. She had little left and most of it I gave away to the parish poor, keeping only three cherished mementos of her: a black japanned trinket box and a cut-glass scent bottle that had both stood for years on her dressing table, and most treasured of all, a heavy silver locket given to her long ago by Papa. Inside its elaborately chased case were two exquisite, miniature portraits of my parents—face to face behind their oval glass and looking eternally youthful and carefree. I put the locket round my neck, fastening the stiff clasp with difficulty, and resolved to wear it always.

More than a week passed before Mr. Pendleton returned, looking smugly pleased with himself.

"Your troubles are over, my dear," he declared, and produced triumphantly from his pocket a letter he had received that morning from Mr. Miles Metcalfe. It had been a simple matter, he assured me, to trace the family—they were well known in Yorkshire and had lived at Aysgarth Hall, near York, since the twelfth century. Mr. Metcalfe—clearly an honorable gentleman in Mr. Pendleton's confident opinion—had answered his letter by return and his reply, as I could see for myself, was everything one would have wished. The elderly lawyer held out the letter toward me, oblivious of my lack of enthusiasm.

I took the piece of paper reluctantly and read the black script that scrawled carelessly across the page. The acknowledgment to Mr. Pendleton was brief, the sentences curt, and the writer's meaning unequivocal: I was invited (in fact, commanded) to pack and leave for Yorkshire immediately to make a new home at Aysgarth. The signature at the end was clear and very firm and looked as though it had been penned by a man accustomed to instant obedience; he would see no reason why I should be anything other than grateful and relieved to accept his offer.

I turned away from Mr. Pendleton, pretending to be still perusing the letter while my muddled thoughts whirled round in my head in hopeless confusion and indecision. I could see the good sense of such a plan and appreciate the apparent generosity of my godfather, and yet, I still shrank instinctively from the idea. The North was so far away, the Metcalfe family complete strangers, and Mama's friends had always spoken of Yorkshire with a shudder. I had often heard how cold and bleak it was—full of wind-swept moors, grim, gray houses, and dour, humorless people.

Mr. Pendleton spoke again. "Well, how soon can you be ready to leave, my dear?"

I swallowed. "I'm not certain that I wish to go at all."

His faded blue eyes goggled at me in disbelief. "Not want to go? What are you saying, Miss Chell? Of course you must go. You have no alternative!"

He stared at me in consternation, and then, calming himself with an effort and seeing the genuine distress in my face, he took my hand gently in his own and spoke more kindly.

"I can understand something of your feelings, my child, but, please believe me, that this is the wisest step to take. Your best hope for the future lies in the North. Few people in Yorkshire will have heard of your family's tragedy and from his letter your godfather strikes me as an honorable man. I'm sure he will do his best for you."

Honorable enough, may be, I thought unhappily to myself, but the cold, brusque tone of his offer did not seem to augur a very warm welcome to his home. However, I reasoned, nothing could force me to stay there if I did not wish, and families would require governesses as much in the North as in the South. I could always find employment in Yorkshire if need be.

"So you will go?" Mr. Pendleton persisted.

"As you say, I have little choice."

He sighed with relief and mopped his brow with a white silk handkerchief. "Just for one moment, Miss Chell, I thought you were going to behave very foolishly . . . and after everything was settled so satisfactorily."

I felt rather churlish and ungrateful toward him when he had exerted himself so diligently on my behalf, and I guessed how thankful he would be to be relieved of the responsibility he felt for me. A penniless, orphaned girl of eighteen must have been a grave embarrassment to an elderly widower.

"There seems no reason why you should not leave almost immediately, as Mr. Metcalfe instructs," he continued happily, and consulted a small notebook taken from his pocket. "There is a stagecoach leaving the Black Swan in Holborn for York the day after tomorrow—I have all the details here. If you can be packed and ready I will arrange for a seat inside for you and escort you to the coach myself."

He looked at me earnestly. "I trust you are in full agreement?"

I nodded and he smiled benignly at me and patted my hand. "A wise decision, my dear, a very wise decision. I assure you that you will never regret it."

"I do so hope, Mr. Pendleton," I said quietly, "that you are right."

And so it was that early one July morning in the year 1832 I found myself boarding the stagecoach for York. As promised, Mr. Pendleton conducted me from the Clapham lodgings to the Black Swan Inn himself, partly from a kindly courtesy and partly also, I think, because he did not trust me not to change my mind and stay in London. The courtyard at the inn was crowded with people and alive with bustle and noise. I stood for a moment, dazzled and bewildered by the color and life of the scene that met my eyes at the Black Swan. A cacophony of sounds seemed to whirl and eddy round me as I stared; the throng pushed and jostled me. A serving maid, hot and harassed, hurried by carrying a full tray of ale and weaving her way skillfully through the crowd. I stood back to let her pass and instantly bumped into a large leather portmanteau that was being carried through behind me. The blow all but knocked me off my feet and tilted my bonnet askew on my head.

"Sorry, miss!" One of the two porters, perspiring under his heavy load, grinned at me as I recovered my balance and retied the bonnet ribbons firmly under my chin. He had such a pleasant, jolly face that I smiled back and watched with interest as he and his partner staggered on with their burden across the cobbled yard toward the stagecoach. It was a huge and impressive vehicle—towering high above our heads, its green paint and massive red wheels glinting in the sunshine. The doors bore the sign of the Black Swan and the words *London* and *York* were lettered in gold on the foreboot, with the coach's name, *Quicksilver,* written below, and beneath that in smaller letters, the word *improved.* Improved in both comfort and safety, I fervently hoped, as I looked apprehensively up at the tottering, top-heavy pile of luggage being stacked aloft on the roof. The outside passengers had already taken their seats on the top, and although the day was fine and warm, I was thankful that Mr. Pendleton had insisted on paying the one guinea necessary for a seat inside. At least I should not be obliged to travel the four days to York without cover or shelter and clinging precariously to a hard, wooden bench high above the ground. The four bay horses were stamping impatiently at the cobbles as though anxious to begin the long journey and the coachman, fat and weather-beaten, with strong and capable-looking hands, was gathering up the reins and settling himself in his place.

Mr. Pendleton plucked anxiously at my cloak. "Come along quickly, my dear. We must hurry."

He handed me up into the dark and poky interior of the coach, fussing and fretting all the while. Was I comfortable? Could I see out? How fortunate that I had a seat facing forward since he had heard that traveling backward could give one a *very* disagreeable sensation. I tried my best to reassure him and to give the impression that I was perfectly comfortable. Unfortunately, the truth was that I was miserably cramped for space and my three traveling companions looked a decidedly alarming lot. My neighbor was a large and blowzy woman whose gross bulk had oozed across the seat to occupy most of my share as well as her own. She wore a tight purple gown and a straw bonnet garnished with enormous red feathers, and as I took my place beside her, she gave me a hostile glance and spread herself even more, so that her elbow dug painfully into my ribs. A rank, sour odor emanated from her, pervading the stuffy air inside the coach and mingling nauseatingly with the even stronger smell of ale and brandy that hung about the man opposite me. He was also enormously fat and had the rough clothes and ruddy complexion of a farmer. He was slumped heavily in the corner, eyes shut, mouth sagging open a little, and breathing deeply. His neighbor was a thin, sour-faced man with a gray skin and hollow, mean eyes, who sat in stiff silence, ignoring me completely as I settled myself as best I could. Suddenly the fat man opposite me stirred, and staring at me with fuddled, bloodshot eyes, he gave me a long, coarse wink. I looked hastily away from him and was dismayed to find that there was so little space between us that my knees were actually pressed against his, and no amount of experimental shifting this way and that could avoid some physical contact with him. At last I resigned myself to the situation and saw with relief that he had shut his eyes once more and begun to snore loudly. With luck, I thought, he might sleep most of the way to York. It was hard not to think of the days when Mama and I had driven out in our smart little phaeton, bowling in stylish comfort through the park; but there was little point in dwelling on such memories. That time was gone forever.

An ostler slammed the door shut; the coachman blew his horn loudly and we lurched forward, the horses hoofs clattering noisily on the cobbles as the coach swung out under the big archway into Holborn. I caught a last glimpse of Mr. Pendleton's white-whiskered head bobbing anxiously among the crowd we were leaving behind, and despite my efforts at self-control, the threatening tears spilled over from my eyes and ran wretchedly down my cheeks. I was never to see Mr. Pendleton again.

◎◎◎

I shall remember that journey to York as long as I live. For four long days I sat squashed and nauseated in that stifling little box as we jolted and swayed northward across England. The coach would creak slowly and ponderously up the hills, the horses straining in the shafts, and then, once at the top, would rattle madly down the other side at breakneck speed, the trunks and boxes dancing a frenzied tattoo on the roof above our heads. We hurtled through peaceful little villages, the coachman blaring a long call of warning on his horn at our approach, and scattering children, dogs, ducks, chickens, and everyone and everything from our path. Bystanders were spattered with mud as the huge wheels churned through ruts and puddles, and old crones gaped openmouthed from their cottage doors. A thatcher looked down on us from his roof-top perch, a blacksmith laid down his hammer and came out of his forge to watch us go by, and a laborer stopped in the middle of sharpening his scythe to stare as we rumbled past him. And once we were held up for miles by a flock of sheep that streamed slowly before us in an impenetrable white and woolly mass. The old shepherd plodded along behind them, stubbornly deaf to the coachman's shrill blasts on the horn and violent abuse.

Soon after leaving London it began to rain—a cold, drenching downpour that continued relentlessly for the following three days. Cramped and uncomfortable as I was inside the coach, I thanked God that I did not have to ride outside on the cheaper seats. At least I was dry and warm whereas the passengers perched above us were exposed constantly to the merciless wind and rain. I remembered hearing horrific tales of people traveling outside on stagecoaches on bitter winter journeys, who had arrived at their destinations frozen to death—rigid, icy corpses still clinging in grisly desperation to their seats.

Our nights were spent at country inns along the route and these, at least, were mostly warm and cheerful places with good food and comfortable rooms. It was bliss to exchange the jolting and jarring of the coach for the still softness of a feather bed and no amount of noise could have kept me from sinking instantly into the deep sleep of the exhausted traveler.

The further north we progressed, the less pleasant became the scene. The land was scarred and blackened by coal pits and there was a grim, bleak look about the countryside which contrasted dishearteningly with the pretty green lushness of the South. The villages were now gray, joyless places where hand looms rattled ceaselessly in dark stone cottages and dirty children played listlessly in the dust—thin, pale, and hollow-eyed. And yet there was beauty too. We passed peaceful medieval churches sheltered by tall oaks and elms and saw many fine mansions standing in rolling park land, and there were vast fertile fields of ripening wheat and barley.

Our long journey had taken us through Cambridgeshire, Huntingdonshire, and Lincolnshire until finally, one morning, we crossed the county border into Yorkshire. It was still raining, and as I peered out of the coach at the wet and wind-swept landscape, my spirits sank. The fat farmer opposite me, however, suddenly stirred from his usual drunken stupor to lean forward excitedly, pressing his fleshy knees hard against mine. For once, though, he ignored me and gazed out of the window, his coarse red face alight with pride and pleasure.

"Take a good look at that, lass," he advised me earnestly. "That's Yorkshire out there and 'tis the best place on earth!"

"Your home is in Yorkshire?" I asked politely.

He turned his head to stare at me. "Where else would it be, lass? There's nowhere in the world to touch it, I told you."

His opinion did not seem to be shared by my neighbor, who sniffed loudly in a disparaging way. She had said almost nothing to me throughout the whole journey, but now she remarked venomously: "If you believe him, then you're a fool. You'd do best to catch the next stage back to London. It's a miserable, cold, dull place and I shan't stay a day longer than I have to!"

And she heaved her plump shoulders emphatically.

"A barbaric county," agreed the other man sourly. "It has none of the comforts that I am accustomed to in London. They seem to live in the past, you know, and know nothing about progress."

Fortunately the Yorkshireman either did not hear them or chose to ignore them. He continued to stare raptly at the passing landscape as we rolled northward.

It was evening before we came to York, and as we covered the final miles, the gray skies cleared and a pale sunlight emerged from behind the clouds. The countryside had become noticeably softer and pleasanter with hedgerows full of wild flowers and green woods and fields, and my heart lifted a little as at last we approached the ancient walls of York. The beautiful minster rose majestically behind them, its pale stone turned to gold by the rays of the evening sun. This, I thought, was how weary travelers had first glimpsed the city for hundreds of years—a glorious, gilded citadel of the North, and they must have felt as awed and thankful as I.

The coach slowed down and rumbled into the city through the arch of Micklegate.

"They used to stick people's heads on poles on top of the gateway in the old days," remarked the Yorkshireman with relish. "It was a sort of warning to everyone to behave themselves. Pity they don't still do it, I say."

The thin man shuddered. "Barbarous!" he muttered to himself, and looked unhappily out of the window as we followed a narrow, cobbled lane that wound into the very heart of York.

When at last the coach turned into the courtyard of the Black Swan in Coney Street and drew to a halt I could scarcely believe that I was alighting from it for good. The inn was almost as noisy and busy as its London counterpart and I waited only to see my battered portmanteau safely lifted down from the top of the coach before hurrying into the sanctuary of the Black Swan.

It was far too late to hire a conveyance to Aysgarth that night, and in any case, I felt too weary to face a further journey until I had rested my stiff and aching body. There had been no time to advise my godfather by letter of my arrival and as I sat alone in the parlor later that evening I found myself wondering what kind of reception would await me the next day. Would I be welcomed warmly or with a chill and perfunctory civility that would relegate me instantly to the role of despised dependent? What sort of man, I wondered desperately, was my godfather?

The landlord of the Black Swan was a genial and friendly man who had treated me with great courtesy and kindness, arranging a room for me that night although the inn was very full. When he paused to inquire after my comfort I asked him casually about Aysgarth Hall and the Metcalfe family who lived there.

He looked at me curiously. "I've heard of the place, miss, of course. It's one of Yorkshire's big, old houses—built hundreds of years ago and lived in by the same family ever since. It was a very grand sort of place once, I believe, but it's a bit run down from what I've been told. Bit of a mess, so they say. Money troubles if I remember rightly."

"Do you know anything of Mr. Metcalfe?"

He shrugged his burly shoulders. "Not too much. I've heard he's an odd sort of man nowadays—very solitary and difficult since the accident."

"Accident?"

He looked surprised. "Surely you know about it, miss? He had a bad fall from his horse in the hunting field a year or two back. Tragic really—he used to be a very active man. The fall left him a cripple."

Before I could ask him more, the landlord was called away to attend to another customer and I sat in stunned dismay, appalled at the news he had given me. I had now learned that my unknown godfather was a crippled and impoverished recluse who lived in a decaying mansion in the wilds of Yorkshire. I wondered what Mr. Pendleton would think of my prospects for the future now?

I slept badly that night at the Black Swan in York. The next morning, with great trepidation, I set out by hired post chaise for Aysgarth.

CHAPTER II

The following day was sunny with a clear blue sky and a light breeze. I had dressed that morning in my most presentable gown of plain green muslin with a turndown collar, a close-fitting bodice, and a full skirt that swept the ground. It was far from being the latest mode but it was reasonably becoming and suitable for the occasion. I had long ago made the discovery that elaborate frills and fussiness did nothing whatever to enhance my undistinguished looks; the simpler the style, the taller and better I looked. I had put on my best bonnet of fine straw with a mentonnière of cream lace and green ribbons to tie under my chin, and as the hired post chaise sped along the cobbled street that led out of York, I felt ready to face the unknown.

The post chaise was a great improvement on the stagecoach. The carriage was well sprung and rode smoothly, and the cushions inside were thickly padded. It was luxurious to ride along in such comfort with the whole seat to myself, and not to be squashed mercilessly into a corner as I had been on the stage. There was a large glass window before me, in the front of the vehicle, and I could observe the passing scene with ease instead of having to crane forward and peer out sideways as before. I could also see the postilion, who drove the carriage by riding the horse on the left of the pair. He was a jaunty young man with hair cut short, a round hat, and a brown jacket of good cloth. As we bowled along at a smart trot he turned round to me every so often with a smile that solicited my approbation. With some justification, I decided, for apart from the smoothness of the post chaise, the countryside we passed through was extremely pleasantly composed of wooded dales, rolling fields bounded by mossy dry-stone walls, and clear, shallow streams where the cold water ran fast over a bed of glassy pebbles and boulders. It was a wild, untamed landscape compared with the orderliness of the Hampshire countryside I had known as a child, and yet, there was a serene and compelling beauty about it that made me remember the quiet pride of the fat Yorkshire farmer for his native land.

We stopped at Ripon for refreshment and a change of horses. It was a peaceful old town with narrow, winding streets and a picturesque market square, and the inn was a friendly and clean place. Despite the warning of the Black Swan landlord, I began to feel quite optimistic about my destination. When everything had been so pleasant since setting out from York surely Aysgarth Hall could not be as bad as he had intimated.

We journeyed on deep into Wensleydale, twisting and turning along lonely lanes with the green slopes of the dales about us. Middleham Castle loomed before us—a massive ruined shell from the Middle Ages—and we skirted its gray walls before climbing steadily uphill toward the open moorland that lay ahead; an infinite expanse of misty, purple heather with black crags etched against the skyline. The gentle shelter of the dales fell away behind us as we slowly ascended the steep road. There was the occasional isolated farmhouse and sometimes a shaggy, slender-legged sheep would bound from the path of the post chaise to resume its steady grazing almost immediately, and once or twice a curlew or lapwing would flutter indignantly into the air before us, emitting its eerie, plaintive cry. I saw no other signs of life on that final stage of the journey.

It was dusk when we came to Aysgarth. We had been following a half-overgrown lane that crossed the lower slopes of the moors when a sharp right-hand bend downward plunged the post chaise into the dark gloom of a beech wood. The postilion slowed the horses to cross a narrow stone bridge over a stream and then, almost before I was aware of it, he had skillfully swung the carriage into an open gateway. It was now so dark under the trees that I could scarcely see more than a few yards ahead but I had seen enough of the stone pillars on each side as we passed through the entrance to know that they were cracked and crumbled and that the iron gates hung crooked and rusty from broken hinges.

Even the smooth post chaise was no match for the potholes

and craters that abounded in the long driveway that led down-hill through the trees. I was bumped and jolted around on my seat while the postilion made desperate efforts to steer the horses round the roughest patches. When at last the house came into view my worst fears were instantly realized.

It was a huge, rambling, gray stone building with castellated turrets at each end, dark, mullioned windows, and clusters of tall chimneys. It was clearly a very old place and one glance as we drew near was enough to detect unmistakable signs of decay and dilapidation. The slate roof sagged badly in the middle and there were many tiles broken or missing altogether; window-panes were cracked and masonry moldered greenly with damp and neglect. Weeds choked the gravel sweep in front of the house and the steps leading up to the big front door were broken and moss-covered.

The postilion seemed anxious to be gone and I could not blame him, considering the gloomy atmosphere. He had lost his cheerful grin and hurried to help me down from the carriage and unload my portmanteau. As soon as I had paid him he sprang quickly onto the horse's back, and urging the pair into a fast trot, had soon vanished up the drive into the darkness of the trees. I stood alone at the foot of the steps and looked apprehensively up at the blank windows above me. There was no light anywhere or any hint of habitation, and the only sound was the raucous caw-ing of hundreds of rooks in the tall elms that surrounded the house. They swooped above the roof tops in the darkening sky, flapping their black wings and croaking discordantly to each other.

Nobody came to the door and I could not stay outside all night, so after a few moments, I screwed up my courage and mounted the steps to ring the bell. Its iron handle was so stiff with rust that I had to tug with all my strength before I could move it, and then I heard the hollow jangle of its bell echoing somewhere deep inside the house. For a while nothing happened and then, at last, there was the noise of shuffling footsteps, the rasp of heavy bolts being drawn back, and the big oak door swung slowly open to reveal a tiny, elderly man dressed in a shabby butler's uniform. He looked very frail and confused as he stood staring down at me in astonishment.

"Good evening," I said with far more confidence than I felt. "I'm Miss Alice Chell. My godfather is expecting me I believe."

"Miss Chell?" He seemed completely bewildered. "You must have come to the wrong place I'm afraid. We don't have visitors any more."

He began to close the door, and picturing myself spending the night on the moors, I stepped forward hastily.

"This is Mr. Miles Metcalfe's home isn't it?"

He nodded slowly.

"Then I am not mistaken. Mr. Metcalfe is expecting me I assure you. I have his letter with me."

I drew the letter addressed to Mr. Pendleton out of my reticule and held it before him. He peered shortsightedly at the heavy black writing and the signature at the foot of the page and then shook his head distractedly.

"I'm sorry, miss. I don't remember the master mentioning you at all—it must have slipped my mind. But then I'm getting so old now that I often forget things. . . . Please come inside. Daniel Duck will carry the portmanteau in later."

He gave a little bow and stood back to let me pass through the open doorway and into the house.

I found myself in a vast and cavernous great hall, whose lofty, beamed ceiling was almost lost to view in the gathering gloom of the evening. The mullioned windows along each side let in so little light that it was hard to see clearly to the far end of the hall. At the end nearest the door there was a beautiful minstrel gallery of carved wood, projecting from the stone wall high up above me. In the center of the hall was a huge stone fireplace, wide enough to take a tree trunk; but now it was cold and empty. At the furthest end of the hall I noticed the dim outline of a grand staircase sweeping upward into the darkness.

Its size and grandeur should have been impressive, but the air was chill and musty with the smell of rot and decay, and to my astonishment, I saw that there was not a stick of furniture anywhere to be seen. There were no rugs on the flagstone floor, no curtains at the windows, no tables, no chairs, no benches, or chests; it was as bare and bleak as an empty tomb. As I looked slowly round the blank walls I caught sight of a few rusty vestiges of decoration, suspended high up against the stonework: a helmet hanging drunkenly askew, two or three breastplates, a broken pikestaff, a poleax, two crossed swords—all relics of ancient battles and all covered with a thick layer of dust and grime. And three tattered banners trailed limply from poles over the minstrel gallery, their bright, woven colors long since faded away to nothing but a flimsy network of gray threads.

As I gazed about me in horror, a gleam of light appeared at the top of the staircase and a woman's voice called sharply from above.

"What is it Unwin? Who's there?"

Beside me the old butler muttered inaudibly to himself. There was a hiss of exasperation and the light bobbed downward, descending the darkened stairs swiftly and purposefully. As its bearer reached the bottom step I saw that she was a tall, thin woman with an angular figure who wore the plain black dress of a housekeeper. Her footsteps echoed hollowly and the ring of keys she wore at her waist jangled imperiously as she walked across the stone flags toward us. As she drew nearer, I saw from the pale light of the oil lamp she held in her hand that she was plain to the point of ugliness, with a large, bony nose and gray hair drawn tightly back into a bun. Her eyes were dark and unsmiling and she raised the lamp close to my face while she examined me suspiciously.

Unwin, the butler, shuffled his feet nervously. "This is Miss Chell. The master expects her, so she tells me. She has a letter."

The woman ignored him. She lowered the lamp and said:

"Your room has been prepared, Miss Chell. Please follow me."

She went ahead of me up the wide staircase and the light from her lamp showed up the badly worn stone steps. The oak banister rail felt satin smooth beneath my fingers as I followed her upward, keeping a careful distance from her trailing black skirts. At the top she paused and spoke again:

"I'm Mrs. Silver, the housekeeper at Aysgarth. The master gave me instructions about you, Miss Chell, but we did not expect you to arrive so soon."

"I'm sorry but there was no time to send word by letter and Mr. Metcalfe wished me to leave London immediately."

"No doubt. I am sorry that Unwin should have been so unwelcoming. I'm afraid he is getting very old and forgetful."

I thought her welcome little better than the butler's but said nothing, and she walked on across a large, galleried landing and turned into one of the several corridors that led off it. The upstairs walls were as bare as in the great hall and the floors uncarpeted. The boards creaked beneath our feet as we progressed down a long, narrow passageway. The last traces of daylight filtered feebly through small windows, and without the housekeeper's lamp to light the way I should have found it hard to follow the strange twists and turns of the passage. At last she paused at a doorway, selected a key from the bunch at her waist, and turning it in the lock, motioned with her hand for me to precede her into the room.

Impossible not to gasp at the sight which met my eyes! I had been prepared for some damp, drab little cell, dismally furnished. Instead I saw a pleasant, airy bedchamber with tall windows, a high, arched ceiling, and an exquisite collection of fine old furniture. There was an oak fourposter bed with hangings of embroidered silk, a handsome wardrobe, a pretty mahogany dressing table, carved and inlaid and draped with frilled muslin, with a silver toilet mirror and two silver candlesticks on the top. In the corner was a washstand of pink marble with a set of pink and gold rose-patterned china; a small velvet chair and papier-mâché table completed the furnishings.

"What a beautiful room!"

"The master's orders," she replied woodenly. "Daniel will bring up your portmanteau presently and I shall send Thurza to unpack for you. She will also bring you some supper on a tray later; I'm afraid you have arrived too late for dinner. If there is anything else you need, she will inform me."

My greatest desire at that moment was for a friendly, smiling face and some words of cheer and reassurance, but looking at Mrs. Silver's sour and shuttered face, I knew that she could give me none of these. Where, I wondered, was Mrs. Metcalfe, who might at least have feigned some sort of welcome? And where was the master himself? Why was the rest of the house as silent and desolate as a mausoleum? No laughter could ever echo through those gloomy corridors, no merry band of musicians would play in that dusty minstrel gallery, and nobody would dance below in that cold, empty great hall. The house was moldering away and this pretty room must be a crazy delusion, as frightening and inexplicable as everything else I had seen.

The housekeeper lit the small brass lamp that stood beside the bed and departed with a brisk rustle of skirts, closing the door firmly behind her. I was left alone in the shadowy room and wandered unhappily about, trying to rally my spirits and courage, until at last, exhausted from the journey and from despair and disappointment, I curled up on the velvet chair and fell asleep.

I was awakened by a gentle knock at the door and opened my eyes in time to see a thin, waif-like girl creep shyly into the room. She wore a white cap and apron over her lilac print dress and looked scarcely more than a child. She bobbed an ungainly, awkward curtsy and stood twisting her small hands together nervously.

"I'm Thurza, miss. Mrs. Silver sent me."

She spoke in a high, little voice with the broad, flat intonation of Yorkshire. I smiled warmly at her to put her at her ease, for it seemed as though she might bolt off at any moment like a startled rabbit.

"I'd be glad of your help, Thurza," I said gently, "but, as you see, my luggage has not yet been brought up so we cannot unpack."

"But he's bringing it up this minute, miss."

"Who?"

"Daniel Duck, miss."

There was a sound of heavy footsteps in the passage outside the room, followed by a thunderous knocking on the door, which flew open to reveal a giant of a man. His hair was fiery red and wildly tangled about his face and he was dressed in a strange assortment of rough, peasant clothing. He stood in the doorway, filling it with his vast bulk, and grinning eagerly at me; and in his arms he cradled my battered portmanteau, holding it as easily as if it weighed no more than a baby. His eyes were a brilliant blue and completely vacant, and a stream of mumbled, jumbled utterances burst forth from him—all incomprehensible. I stared at him, not knowing what to do or say, and it was Thurza who gestured calmly for him to put the box down under the window. He did so obediently, laying it down as gently as if it had been made of glass, and then he shambled noisily out of the room, nodding and grimacing crazily at me. The door slammed violently and his footsteps pounded away down the corridor.

"He's quite harmless, miss," said Thurza timidly.

I swallowed. "I'm sure you're right. But he is a little alarming."

"You'll get used to him, miss," she replied confidently. "He's a bit odd in the head but he's never hurt a fly. We don't notice him really."

I took some comfort from the fact that this shy little creature was quite unafraid of that lumbering, grotesque giant, but even so, it made me wonder still more what other strange, bizarre secrets this house might contain.

"Where is Mrs. Metcalfe, Thurza? I should like to meet her soon, if possible."

"You can't do that, miss."

"Can't?"

"She's dead, miss. The mistress died eight years ago."

I stared at her, shocked. "And Mr. Metcalfe? Shall I see him?"

She twisted her hands nervously again. "We none of us see much of the master. He likes to be left alone."

"I see. And are there any other members of the family here?"

"There's Miss Eweretta; she's always out riding her horse on the moors."

"Are there many servants in the house?"

She shook her head. "Oh no, miss. Only Mr. Unwin, Mrs. Bizzy, the cook, a scullery maid, and me. And, Mrs. Silver, too, of course."

Which accounted for the dust and neglect I had witnessed. It would need an army of servants to keep the house clean.

I felt it would be unfair to cross-examine the child any further and we set about unpacking my belongings and putting them away in the big oak cupboard. There was more than enough room for my few clothes and we had almost finished when there was a strange scrabbling noise at the door. It sounded like a mouse scratching with its front paws, and presently the door opened slowly and a woman's face appeared, disembodied, round the edge: a podgy, round face rather like a dumpling with dark, currant little eyes and puffy cheeks, all framed in a starchy bonnet trimmed with cream lace.

The face spoke. "Signorina Chell?"

I nodded automatically, unable to feel any more surprise at the strange inhabitants of Aysgarth. The door opened further to admit the remainder of her body, and before me stood an elderly, very plump little woman, dressed in a fussy wine-colored gown. Frills and lace and furbelows seemed to cover every inch of her, accentuating her dumpiness. She peered at me shortsightedly for a moment and then spoke again in a birdlike trill and with a strong Italian accent.

"The contessa will see you now, signorina."

"The contessa?" I blinked at her, bewildered.

She frowned at this and drew herself up to her fullest height—which was little more than my shoulder—thrusting out her frilled chest importantly.

"The Contessa de Montefiore is waiting to receive you!"

I looked inquiringly at Thurza, but her back was turned as she burrowed busily among the contents of the cupboard.

"You will follow me *subito per favore!*"

The command was rapped out and her dimpled hand beckoned me as she left the room again. I shrugged my shoulders helplessly and followed her meekly: there seemed no point in arguing, and in any case, she had not waited for any further discussion. Her short, tubby figure was already a long way ahead of me, the light from the candle she carried flickering jerkily on the bare walls as she trotted swiftly down the passage. She moved so quickly and steadily through the house, turning this way and that through a labyrinth of passages, that I had, at times, to run to keep up with her. To lose sight of her would have meant being completely lost and yet not once did she glance behind her to see if I still followed. Who on earth, I wondered, was this illustrious contessa whose command had to be obeyed instantly? And what could she be doing in this bleak mansion in the wilds of Yorkshire?

"Come with me please!"

My guide had stopped, at last, by a doorway and whisked inside it as fast as a scampering mouse. I followed her slowly and found myself in a large room even more startling than my own bedchamber. This time, however, the surprise lay not only in the beautiful furnishings and their quality but also in the quantity. The room was crammed to bursting with exotic Italian furniture: marble-topped tables with massive golden legs, heavily carved cupboards and chests inlaid with mother-of-pearl, gilded chairs, an immense, sparkling chandelier of ruby glass, and row upon row of oil paintings, which covered the red flocked wallpaper. Ponderous swags of wine-colored velvet hung at the windows and a huge looking-glass towered above the marble mantelpiece, framed by a border of golden cherubs and garlands of flowers entwined with bunches of grapes and reflecting the whole incredible scene.

The little woman in the brown dress had vanished and the sole occupant of the room seemed to be a large, fluffy gray cat that sat slowly and meticulously washing its paws beside the fireplace. I bent down to stroke it, reminded of the cats we had kept long ago in our Hampshire home. The animal paused briefly, inspected me with unwinking yellow eyes, and then continued to clean itself with deliberate disdain.

"I'm afraid that Topaz doesn't care for strangers."

I looked up startled by the voice that came from behind me. She was standing, half-hidden, in the shadows of the room: an old woman with a mass of white hair piled in an elaborate coiffure on top of her head. Her bearing was proud and unmistakably aristocratic and her gown as stylish and elegant as the most fashionable London lady might have worn. A large diamond brooch glittered at her throat and several beautiful rings gleamed on her fingers.

She surveyed me in silence for a few moments and then moved forward into the pool of light cast by the ruby chandelier. I saw that she was even older than I had thought: her face was pale and very lined and her hands gnarled and blue-veined with age. But her eyes were piercingly bright and shrewd.

"So you're Miriam Chell's child. You're not a patch on her for looks are you!"

I was so used to this comparison that I scarcely noticed it; far more important was the fact that she had spoken of Mama.

"You knew my mother?"

She did not answer at first but walked slowly over toward the fireplace and sat down, stiff-backed, in a tapestry chair, motioning graciously with her jeweled fingers for me to sit opposite her.

"Your name is Alice, I understand. Miles told me you were coming to live at Aysgarth and I saw you arrive from my window. No, my dear, I never knew your mother but I remember seeing her several times years ago when she was the toast of London. She was a famous beauty, of course. It would be a miracle if nature had reproduced such perfection in you but no doubt you have other qualities, child, just as important. Your eyes are quite passable—a most unusual color and anything different is to be commended. There is nothing more dreary than uniformity!"

She smiled at me kindly. "I am the Contessa de Montefiore—as no doubt Frugoni has told you already. You may call me Contessa when you address me. An Italian title confuses English people I find."

"You are not Italian yourself?"

She had no trace of an accent, which had puzzled me more than ever.

"Certainly not!" she replied, looking rather annoyed. "I am as English as you. I am a kinswoman of the Metcalfes—aunt to your godfather, to be precise, since my sister married *his* father."

The cat, Topaz, its toilet completed, leaped lightly up onto the contessa's lap and settled itself comfortably on her knees, staring at me with its sphinxlike yellow eyes. She stroked its soft fur absently for a while before continuing to speak.

"I was married to the Conte de Montefiore when I was only seventeen—at the end of my first London season. There wasn't a girl who didn't envy me. He was twenty years older than me—rich, handsome, distinguished, and the head of a noble Italian family. I thought he was the most wonderful man in the world!"

I heard her sigh and watched the wink and gleam of her rings as her fingers moved gently over the cat's gray fur.

"It wasn't many months before I discovered that my husband was cruel, selfish, and incapable of giving any love or kindness. We lived in a magnificent palazzo outside Rome—a fairy-tale palace of marble and mosaic with fountains and terraces and gardens that seemed to go on forever. . . . I had everything a young bride could wish for—except my husband's love. I was a very pretty child but after a while he grew tired of me and went back to his mistresses. I had been a new, amusing toy which had ceased to divert him."

"He must have been a monster!"

The contessa smiled. "Not really, my dear. Just a typical Italian aristocrat. I was very young and very English and much too romantic! I soon adjusted to the situation and quite enjoyed being the Contessa de Montefiore. We lived a very busy, gay life with lots of parties and dancing to make me forget how miserable I really was. I had one child—a daughter called Lucia—but she died when she was six years old. Her loss is the one real regret of my life."

"And you came back to England in the end?"

"Yes, I came back. Not until after the count died about fifteen years ago. I stayed on at the palazzo for a while but a very dull cousin had inherited the title and everything else and I decided to leave before he bored me to death! I came back to London with a few meager possessions, including faithful old Frugoni. She has looked after me since I was first married; I couldn't possibly manage without her now."

"Aysgarth must have seemed very different from Italy," I said, fascinated by her story.

"Oh, I didn't come here to live straightaway. Nothing would have induced me to bury myself in the wilds of the North— besides my sister was already dead by then. I lived in London for several years—very extravagantly, I'm sorry to say. I had developed a taste for gambling at cards in Italy and my luck seemed to run out in England. I lost everything the count had left me. There was nothing but these few sticks of furniture and a jewel or two and I couldn't bear to sell any of those. It was a choice between the dull cousin in the palazzo or my nephew here in the North. As things are, I suppose I made the wrong decision but still what does it matter at my time of life . . . ?"

She closed her eyes, apparently lost in reminiscence, and was silent for so long that I began to think she must have fallen asleep. However, she suddenly opened them again and looked at me with renewed interest.

"And what do you think of Miles?"

"I'm afraid I haven't met him yet."

"Wasn't he there to welcome you when you arrived? How very remiss of him and how very typical of him too."

I hastened to explain. "Mr. Metcalfe had no idea that I was arriving this evening. There was no time for a letter to reach him before I did so myself."

"Well, you'll meet him soon enough, I suppose, depending on his mood."

I said awkwardly: "I've heard he was badly crippled in a riding accident."

The contessa darted me a penetrating glance. "Not afraid of that are you?"

"I don't think so."

"I hope not. A nimby-pimby, milk-and-water miss wouldn't last long in *this* household. You've no need to be nervous of him, my dear, even though he's the moodiest and worst-tempered man I've ever met. You'll soon get used to him and you must make allowances; he suffers a lot of pain still all the time. He was a helpless cripple at first, you know—bedridden for two years after the accident. But he never gave up. He taught himself to walk again—with sticks, mind you, but he manages well enough. He even rides now and once he's on a horse he's as good as any man and better than many."

"I am grateful to Mr. Metcalfe for inviting me here," I said politely, feeling the need for some remark but inwardly dismayed by the contessa's words. The picture she had painted of my godfather was alarming, to say the least. The jovial, bearded man of my memory might have made life in this bleak house supportable, but it would seem that his accident had changed him completely into a tortured, irascible creature who shunned all company. I shivered with apprehension at the joyless future that must lie before me.

The contessa was watching me. "Beggars can't be choosers, can they, my dear? We have something in common, you and I. Both of us have been blown here by the winds of misfortune: we should be of some comfort to each other."

She put the gray cat gently down onto the carpet and rose to her feet, indicating that the interview was at an end. Then, to my surprise, she suddenly moved toward me and kissed my cheek.

"I am pleased that you have come to live at Aysgarth, Alice, and I shall do what little I can to help you. You remind me of my daughter, Lucia—she was a plain little thing like you. . . ."

She touched my arm lightly. "Signorina Frugoni will give you a candle to light your way back to your room. We shall meet again tomorrow."

The Italian woman had appeared from the shadows, silently, as if by magic, and she held out the little brass candlestick she had been carrying before. The candle was already lit and its small flame glowed in the depths of her dark and beady eyes as she looked up at me.

"The signorina can find her way?"

I swallowed and nodded, thinking unhappily of the long, black passages, the confusing twists and turns, the bare stone walls that all looked so alike. . . . But I had no wish to confess my fears, nor to put her to the trouble of guiding me all the way back. With luck I should be able to remember my way.

The candle's flame fluttered feebly in the drafty passageway as I hurried along it in the direction I hoped would eventually lead me to my room. I passed a small, stone-embrasured window set high up in the wall that seemed familiar, and descended a short flight of uneven stone steps that I was sure I remembered clearly. After that I became less certain. Had Signorina Frugoni turned left or right here? I chose the left and pressed on hopefully. Presently the passage veered sharply to the right and finished abruptly in a dead end. I tried to open a door, thinking it might lead me back on the right course, but it was locked. I tried another door, and then another and another, rattling their heavy iron handles with growing exasperation, but all of them were fast locked. And then I noticed the dark mouth of another passageway, which beckoned me invitingly, and entering it, I found myself in a long, rambling tunnel which seemed to go on forever. My footsteps echoed loudly on the wooden boards as I walked down it and my heart began to thump with fear as I plunged deeper and deeper into the unknown darkness ahead. The only light to be seen anywhere came from my candle, which trembled in my hand, its flame leaping and dancing in the cold draft that seemed to blow toward me up the passageway. Black, formless shadows floated around me and a sudden soft, pattering noise at my feet made me cry out in alarm as a huge rat scampered past my skirts and vanished into a black recess in the wall. I groped blindly for the stonework to steady my shaking knees and it felt chill and slimy beneath my fingers. Panic began to threaten my reason. I might be lost for hours in this nightmarish maze, wandering helplessly about until the candle burned down and I was left in total darkness. . . . And all around me I sensed a weird and potent atmosphere, as though the old stone walls were breathing their ancient secrets into the air. I could feel the presence of the past pressing in on me—the ghostly beings who had once belonged to this place long ago.

The candle guttered wildly as though it might go out at any minute, and gasping with fear, I began to run, stumbling and tripping along the uneven surface in blind, frenzied panic. Thick, trailing cobwebs brushed caressingly across my face as I fled through the blackness—full tilt up a flight of stone steps and round a corner. For a brief second I glimpsed the dark silhouette that loomed in front of me before I cannoned violently against it. There was a loud, hissing gasp, a thud, a clattering sound, and then I screamed once—a high-pitched shriek of terror.

As the sound died away, echoing eerily through the depths of the house, I opened my eyes slowly and stared into the shadows. Miraculously the candle had not gone out and its trembling flame showed me the crumpled figure of a man leaning against the passage wall—half-lying, half-sitting, with his face turned away from me. He was groaning faintly, and as I advanced cautiously toward him, he turned his head and glared at me ferociously.

"Perhaps you would be good enough to make some amends for your clumsiness by picking up my stick for me. You'll find it somewhere over there I think."

His voice was deep and had a pleasant timbre but its expression was one of icy fury. He waved his hand impatiently. "My stick, girl! For pity's sake be quick about it. I won't eat you!"

This was certainly no specter from the past but a flesh and blood man in a towering rage and, small wonder, since I had knocked him flying in my headlong dash round the corner. I groped hurriedly around me on the floor and found the stick lying near the wall. It was silver-topped and made of heavy ebony.

"Bring it here!" The command was rapped out curtly as though he spoke to a servant.

I went warily toward him and held out the stick in silence. It was snatched rudely from my grasp.

"Give me your arm. The least you can do is to help me to my feet," he said savagely.

I proffered my arm, somewhat unwillingly, and he seized it a strong and painful grip, so that, with my help and that of the stick which he used as a lever, he managed to haul himself upright and stood, swaying slightly, before me. He had released my arm and I retreated away from him and raised the candle high so that I could see him more clearly.

He was a tall man with broad, powerful shoulders, and except for a white neckcloth, was dressed in dark, sober clothes. His black hair was rather long and curled in a disorderly way on his collar. His eyes, which were surveying me with grim displeasure, were very dark with hooded lids and heavy lashes and his nose was long and aristocratic. His face reminded me instantly of an invalid's for it was deadly pale and etched with deep lines of pain and suffering around the eyes and mouth. Despite these I also saw that he could not be more than ten years or so older than myself. His youth was, at this moment, masked by the twisted pain in his face but I recognized it in his eyes as he stood, leaning on his stick and staring at me, his brow beaded with perspiration and his breath rasping in his throat. At last the breathing eased and he gave a sigh and said coldly:

"Of course, it must be Alice Chell! I can think of no other strange young lady likely to be running like a lunatic around the corridors of my house. Is that who you are?"

"Yes, sir."

He looked at me with a gleam of amusement in his eyes. "And I suppose you lost your way. This is the east wing—nobody uses this part of the house except me. Your room is at the western end."

He pointed behind me with the ebony stick and his dark, hooded eyes swept over me casually. "I thought you might be a beauty like your mother—the contessa tells me she was the toast of London—but you're as plain as a pikestaff. Not that it matters one way or the other."

I said nothing. His boorish, ill-mannered remarks should not provoke or hurt me, I was determined of that. Whoever he was he had no right to be so rude.

He leaned back against the wall behind him and contemplated me in complete silence for such a long time that, at last, I felt obliged to speak.

"You have the advantage of me, sir. You know *my* name but I haven't the least idea who *you* are."

At that a slow, and decidedly wolf-like, smile spread across his face. "My name, my dear Miss Chell," he said with a good deal of enjoyment in his voice, "is Miles Metcalfe. Who else could I be?"

"But you can't be!"

He raised his eyebrows, feigning astonishment. "Can't be? What's this, Miss Chell? Insolence in my own house! Pray why can't I be?"

I flushed with dismay and embarrassment. "There must be some misunderstanding. Miles Metcalfe is my godfather, I know, but he must be a much older man than you."

He gave me a mocking bow. "I'm flattered that you should find me not entirely decrepit, even in my unsatisfactory state of health. You are perfectly correct in your deduction, Miss Chell. I am not your godfather but my name *is* Miles Metcalfe."

I looked at him, bewildered. "I don't understand. Mr. Pendleton must have made a mistake in writing to you, of course, but why did you answer him as you did and why did the contessa speak of my godfather if he does not live here?"

"Ah! So you have met the contessa already. I should have welcomed you myself but I had no idea that you were going to arrive so soon. The coach service from London must be better than I thought."

He shifted his weight away from the wall onto the ebony stick and moved a little nearer to me, covering the ground with an awkward, stiff-legged gait that I tried to ignore. Then he paused and looked down at me, his face white and inscrutable in the candlelight.

"Your godfather is dead, Alice Chell. He died more than five years ago. I answered that letter because it was addressed to me: Miles is a traditional name in our family and I was christened after my father. I am your godfather's son and the present Master of Aysgarth."

I stared up at him. "But why pretend to be my godfather? There was no need."

He said irritably: "My dear Miss Chell, I am not pretending anything at all, nor did I in that letter if you read it again carefully. I simply offered you a home at Aysgarth—no more, no less. I understood you had been left alone in the world—an orphan without relatives of any kind—so I felt a sort of inherited responsibility for you, if you like. My father would certainly have done the same."

I struggled desperately for composure. The situation was impossible. It had been one thing to accept shelter from my proper godfather; but it was quite another to accept it from his son. *He* had no obligation to me whatever, and judging from what I had seen of Aysgarth, he could scarcely welcome the prospect of another mouth to feed.

"I can see from your face, Miss Chell, that you are about to tell me that you cannot possibly stay here now. Isn't that so?"

"It wouldn't be right."

"Not right!" he mocked. "I fail to see why! You really are a most ungrateful girl. When my father died I took over all his responsibilities as my own, heaven help me! You are one of them. It's as simple as that. As to the propriety of the situation—my great-aunt, the Contessa de Montefiore, will make an excellent chaperone and there is my sister Eweretta for additional female company—if you can stand her vain, foolish prattle. You need have no fears for your reputation I can assure you. And however monstrous I might seem I do not eat young girls!"

My cheeks flamed scarlet. "I wasn't thinking of that . . ."

"No? But I can see you are still in some doubt about the matter. Tell me, if you don't stay here where precisely would you go and what would you do? You have very little money left, or so I understand, and the world tends to treat impoverished, defenseless women somewhat harshly."

His highhanded, patronizing manner riled me greatly. I said

stiffly: "I shall return to York and find a post as a governess there. It should be perfectly possible; I am well educated."

His eyes traveled over me once more, in a casual and impertinent manner. "I'll grant you're plain enough to pass as an ideal governess and I don't doubt you can read and write, but I think, Miss Chell, that you would do very much better to stay here. I suggest that you respect what would undoubtedly have been your late godfather's wishes and remain under my roof and under my protection."

I hesitated, not knowing what to answer, and he sighed and added in a cold, indifferent voice.

"It's nothing to me whether you go or stay but we may as well decide one way or the other. You are too sensible a girl, I am certain, to take too much account of my poor manners and too wise to go rushing off into the wide world without giving the matter at least a little serious consideration. Don't you think you should think things over for a few days before making any rash decisions?"

"I suppose I should."

"So you will stay at least for the time being?"

I nodded and he looked down at me for a moment and then shrugged his shoulders carelessly. "Then that's settled. Perhaps you will bring us some good fortune at last, Miss Chell. Who knows? And now, if you will turn back the way you came and walk ahead of me I will guide you back to your room."

He motioned brusquely with his stick for me to precede him and thus we progressed back through the house—myself walking slowly ahead, holding the dwindling candle high to light the narrow passageways, while he followed behind me. And all the way I listened apprehensively to the echoing tap-tap of his stick and the painful dragging of his feet, without daring once to look over my shoulder. Such a man, I knew, would be enraged by any sign of pity or curiosity from a stranger.

At last we reached a corridor which I recognized as the one leading to my room. I stopped.

"I know my way back now, thank you, sir."

He leaned against the wall, his face very pale. I thought he was still in great pain.

"Do you like your room?" he asked unexpectedly.

"Very much, thank you. It's very pretty."

He smiled faintly. "We still have a few pieces of furniture left. I told Mrs. Silver to arrange the best possible for you. I am sorry about the state of the house but there's nothing I can do about it at the moment. One day things may be different but until then you'll have to make the best of it. Good-by, Miss Chell, for the present."

"Won't you need a light?" I hesitated to leave him there in the dark.

He looked at me impatiently. "My dear girl, I know this house like the back of my hand. Leave me now, I beg of you. I've had enough of your company!"

I turned away and hurried back to my room feeling confused, mortified, and indignant. The contessa had not exaggerated his boorishness one bit; he was insufferably arrogant, rude, and overbearing and I had no desire whatever to stay in this grim place and be beholden to such an unpleasant creature.

The bedchamber seemed like a blessed sanctuary when I opened the door. It looked warm and comforting. The lamp glowed softly beside the fourposter and somebody—Thurza, I supposed—had drawn the curtains across the windows and lit a fire in the grate. A jug of hot water steamed beside the marble washstand and a tray of cold supper had been set on a low table in front of the fireplace.

Later, I lay for a while in the dark depths of the fourposter bed, listening to the creak and groan of the old house, the hoot and screech of owls outside, and the sighing of the night wind in the trees. And then I fell into a deep and dreamless sleep.

CHAPTER III

I was awakened the next morning by the harsh cawing of the rooks. The noise permeated my dreams insistently, dragging me unwillingly back to consciousness.

I had been dreaming and in my dream I was happy. I had been riding across the fields of Hampshire, once again, with the three brown and white spaniels gamboling faithfully along beside me and the sun shining warm and bright on my face. It was a shock to wake and find myself lying instead in a strange bed with the cold, gray light of the North seeping dimly through the curtained windows. I listened for a while to the endless calling of the rooks as they circled the roof tops overhead and then I became aware of the sound of a horse's hoofs outside—the crunch and clop of the gravel and a sudden burst of laughter: shrill, feminine giggling which floated up from below my window. I slid out of the fourposter bed and pattered quickly across the room, drawing aside the curtains an inch or so in time to see a young girl dismount from a gray horse, devotedly assisted by a tall, fair-haired groom. Peering curiously through the crack in the curtains, I watched as she laid her small, gloved hand on his arm, laughing coquettishly up into his face, which had blushed a deep, fiery red. And then she turned away from him, tossing her head playfully, and ran lightly up the steps toward the front door. As she did so, she glanced up upward so that I saw her face clearly for the first time.

She was ravishingly pretty and not more than sixteen years old at the most. Golden curls bobbed from beneath her veiled riding hat, her complexion was like pink porcelain, and her eyes large and blue in a delicate, heart-shaped face. She was as tall and graceful as I had sometimes, in my weaker moments, yearned to be, and the green riding habit she wore set off her slender figure to perfection. I watched her vanish indoors and sighed wistfully.

"That's Miss Eweretta, miss."

The small voice made me jump and I turned to see Thurza, the little maid, standing quietly behind me, a heavy brass jug clutched in her skinny arms.

"Good morning, Thurza. I guessed it might be. She's very pretty, isn't she?"

"Yes, miss." Thurza's thin, childish face was blank. "I've brought your hot water, miss."

She looked less timid than at our first meeting and I should have welcomed her company for a while, but she set down the brass jug with a rush and hurried to the door.

"I have to go now, miss. Mrs. Silver's given me ever so much work to do and it's half-past nine already. She said to tell you there's breakfast downstairs for you if you want it."

She bobbed a quick curtsy and was gone. I dressed slowly and despondently, reluctant to face what lay beyond the bedroom door. In the end, of course, I had to emerge from my sanctuary and fortunately I was more successful, this time, in finding my way through the house. By daylight it looked no less grim and foreboding but at least I could see my way more clearly and I reached the top of the wide stone staircase without mishap.

The great hall lay below me, dramatic and desolate in its vast emptiness. That same smell of damp and decay that I had noticed on my arrival hung in the air and I shivered in the cold that seemed to rise from the flagstone floor. The massive roof beams crisscrossed in arches above my head, festooned with thick cobwebs and dust and pitted with age. I looked down at the scene in dismayed silence for a moment before descending the stone stairs slowly. Before I had reached the lowest step, Mrs. Silver, her ugly face as gaunt and unsmiling as before, appeared in the hall and glided toward me.

"Breakfast is waiting for you, Miss Chell," she told me, and showed me into a small parlor which was very plainly but adequately furnished. A dish of broiled fish had been left on the sideboard, together with some coffee, toast, and butter, but the table was set for one person only. There was no sign of any other member of the family.

"You have everything you need?"

"Yes, thank you." I hesitated, reluctant to appear the least bit foolish in her critical eyes. "Perhaps Thurza, or someone, could show me my way round the house later on. . . . It is rather confusing with so many rooms."

"A great many of them are locked and empty," she responded in wintry tones. "They need not concern you. As to the few that are in use, I shall show you them myself when you have breakfasted."

I should have much preferred Thurza's mouselike little presence to this grim, taciturn woman but there was nothing to be done about it. The housekeeper swept from the room leaving me to chew dispiritedly at the fish, which was cold and dry, and to sip bravely at the coffee, which was equally unpalatable.

I had expected that the housekeeper would take me on a grand tour of the whole house later, but I was wrong. She showed me only three rooms—the library, the dining room, and the drawing room, all of which led off the great hall. And she did so with ill-concealed impatience.

"All other rooms on the ground floor have been shut up," she told me, "except, of course, the master's study, which is private, and the kitchen wing, which naturally is not your concern. There is nothing else for you to see."

Her tone implied that it was idle curiosity on my part, rather than a real desire to learn the geography of the house, and, in part, she was right. I *was* curious, anxious even, to see more of the place that was intended to be my new home.

The library proved to be another pleasant surprise: its walls were lined with rows of beautiful old leather volumes, all neatly arranged in their shelves. I looked at them with a more hopeful heart—life would not be so grim here if I could come and browse sometimes among these books. I moved closer to the shelves and was surprised to see that every one was carefully dusted.

"The master doesn't allow anyone but himself to touch the books," said Mrs. Silver in a frigid voice as I put out my hand toward them, and I snatched it back hastily.

The dining room was equally attractive, with dark, oak-paneled walls and a magnificent, long table that could have seated at least twenty people or more. But my attention was caught most of all by two portraits that hung on each side of the stone fireplace. Ignoring the impatient jangle of the housekeeper's keys, I walked over to look at the pictures more closely.

They were very fine portraits in oils of a man and woman. Both were young, the man dark and very good-looking in a rather florid, fleshy way, with a hint of dissipation in the smiling eyes and around the slack, full-lipped mouth, while the woman was pretty but sad-looking, with a thin, pale face and wistful, round blue eyes.

"Who are they?" I asked Mrs. Silver.

"The late master and mistress," she replied reluctantly, making it clear by her expression that she considered family affairs to be no business of mine. My godfather and his wife, in fact, and painted, presumably, soon after their marriage. I stared up at the man and wished desperately that he were still alive and master of this place instead of his son. He did not look the sort of man, for instance, who would support a housekeeper as vinegary as Mrs. Silver and my single, dim remembrance of him was as a jolly character—a recollection borne out by his portrait.

The housekeeper coughed irritably. "I will show you the drawing room now, Miss Chell. I have other work to do . . ."

I followed her across the echoing flagstones of the great hall toward a big, double door of carved oak on the opposite side. As she turned the heavy brass handle the sound of a spinet playing could be heard—a pretty, lilting waltz tune that floated gaily on the air. The room itself was furnished with extravagance and style, although its original splendor had become somewhat worn and dimmed. The buff and gilt fleur-de-lis wallpaper was faded and the curtains and chair coverings of striped damask and velvet were all worn and shabby. The furniture, on the other hand, gleamed with the richness of age and quality and the entire floor, from the ornate marble fireplace to the opposite walls was covered by a beautiful Chinese rug of blue, pink, and gold. I guessed that this room had been left exactly as it had been in my godfather's lifetime. It savored a panache and elegance that belonged to the smiling man in the portrait and never for a moment to the brooding, bitter creature I had met in the dark passageway.

The spinet was at the furthest end of the room, beneath the windows, and at my entrance, the playing had stopped abruptly in mid-phrase. Eweretta Metcalfe sat staring at me, her fingers frozen over the keyboard. She had changed from her green riding habit into a cornflower-blue silk dress that matched her eyes, and her golden curls had been brushed charmingly into ringlets. I saw at once the strong resemblance she bore to her mother, except that there was nothing faded or weak about this prettiness: it was backed by an obviously strong and willful character, and her round, blue eyes—so like her dead mother's—were glaring at me with a look of undisguised hatred. Before I could say a word she had rushed past me with a wild flurry of skirts, thrusting me aside from her path as she rushed from the room with the petulant, uncontrolled fury of a small child. I watched her go, shocked and bewildered by a display of hostility which exceeded even her brother's, and as I turned, I caught the expression which flitted, unguarded, across Mrs. Silver's face: it was one of triumphant, gloating glee.

The contessa sent for me later that day, and when Signorina Frugoni came in search of me, I found that I welcomed the idea of her company. The cold enmity of the housekeeper and the inexplicable rejection by Eweretta had unnerved me more than I cared to admit to myself, and I sat alone and dejected in the little breakfast parlor for a long while before the Italian's currant-bun face peeped round the door to summon me to her mistress.

The contessa was in good spirits. Elegantly attired in emerald-green bombazine, her snowy hair piled dramatically high on her head, she eyed me beadily from her chair. The gray cat was curled on her lap, asleep, and to my surprise, it opened its yellow eyes at my entrance and jumped down to stalk toward me and circle my skirts with the gracious condescension of its kind.

The old lady chuckled. "At least someone else in this household, besides myself, is glad of your company," she remarked, as Topaz twisted to and fro at my feet, allowing himself to be stroked.

"I'm afraid Mr. Metcalfe's sister can't even bear to speak to me. She ran away as though I were some sort of demon!"

"Eweretta? I'm not surprised to hear that," the contessa said acidly. "The girl's a vain, silly little fool with the manners of a trollop! I'll tell you why she doesn't want you at Aysgarth: she's frightened you might try to curb her precious freedom. Her father spoiled her ridiculously and she's been allowed to run wild ever since her mother died."

"But why should she think that?"

"Miles told her so, that's why. He said it was high time she had a sensible companion near her own age who could keep an eye on her and see that she behaved. He felt you might answer the problem admirably, judging by the letter he received about you—your lawyer was very complimentary, you know. Miles tells me, incidentally, that you are just what he hoped you'd be."

Plain enough to pass as an ideal governess, I thought bitterly. No wonder he had prevailed on me to stay!

"I wish he had not told her that. No wonder she resents me!"

The contessa shrugged indifferently. "She would resent any intruder, whoever they were, foolish girl! And especially another woman. Eweretta doesn't like competition of any kind."

I had to smile at that remark. "Surely she can scarcely view me as a rival beauty!"

"You underrate yourself my dear," the contessa admonished me. "It's true, as I so tactlessly pointed out when we first met, that you cannot touch your mother for looks. However, your violet eyes are most striking and unusual and if only you would learn to dress less drearily you would really be quite presentable. Never pretty, I fear, but certainly pleasing. Now, why on earth do you wear such terrible gowns? The one you are wearing now makes you look like some downtrodden governess—no wonder Eweretta fled in horror. You have plenty of spirit, I'm thankful to say, and you should show it in the way you dress. Fly the flag, my dear Alice, fly the flag!"

"I thought it suited me," I protested, looking down at what appeared to me to be a perfectly respectable dress of dark blue tarlatan.

The contessa clicked her tongue impatiently and waved her hands in horror. "It's appalling, my child. No flair! No style! And positively no elegance at all! Never mind. We shall do something about it. I brought a whole trunkload of lovely silks from Italy with me which that old harridan of a housekeeper has hidden away somewhere. I shall see that she finds it and has it brought to me. Frugoni shall get to work and make you something worth wearing. She's a wonder with her needle, you know. Without her I should not be able to dress as well as I do."

I looked at the contessa's beautifully made green gown and acknowledged that beside it my own dress looked very ordinary.

"Mrs. Silver is a strange person," I said, hoping to divert the contessa, who was beginning to rake through a huge pile of French fashion journals on a table near her—a very purposeful expression in her eye.

The contessa stopped and snorted with distaste. "The woman's mad! She prowls about the house at all hours of the day and night, poking that ugly nose of hers into everything and behaving as though she were mistress and not housekeeper."

"If she is so unsatisfactory why does Mr. Metcalfe keep her?"

"She has only been here for two months and it seems that she was the best that could be found. Our old housekeeper died, after years with the family, and nobody wanted to come in her place. Who can blame them, my dear? A half-empty house, which is practically falling down, and a mere handful of servants to run it—it could scarcely be termed a desirable post! And then, of course, people are afraid of Miles. Since his accident he seems to have acquired the reputation of an ogre locally. Odd how things change . . . when his father was still alive, and before the accident, everything was very different."

"What was my godfather like, Contessa? I can't remember him at all clearly and I should like to know the sort of person he was."

She considered the question for a moment, a finger held to her lips. "Charming but irresponsible, my dear, is the answer to your question. He was attractive and amusing but he lived only for himself and the fun he could get out of life. Life, for him, should be an endless round of parties and hunting and shooting and gambling—he could never bear to be quiet for a second. A very selfish man, in many ways, I'm afraid, and Eweretta has inherited his worst points."

"And his wife?"

"Poor Anna!" the contessa sighed. "She was a pretty creature, I suppose, but with no spirit at all. She hated the sort of life her husband loved. They were very ill-matched. At first she used to pretend to be ill to avoid having to go out hunting, which terrified her, and then, later on, it became such a habit that she grew into a permanent invalid and spent all her time lying on a couch in her room. It was the only way she could cope with life, I think. I felt sorry for her sometimes, though I could have shaken her for being so feeble. She was always complaining—not an attractive trait in my opinion. In the end she really did become ill, whining and bleating to the very last, I regret to say."

"I should like to have seen Aysgarth in those days," I said.

The contessa's face softened and her blue eyes sparkled. "It was worth seeing, child, I can tell you. It was magnificent: every room full of beautiful things. You should have seen all the furniture, the paintings, the silver, the glass . . . and the great hall was superb! The walls were hung with huge Flemish tapestries and there was a wonderful collection of armor, all of it used by the Metcalfes in battles through the years. There have been Metcalfes at Aysgarth for over seven hundred years, you know. It's a long time."

"But what happened, Contessa? Why has it come to this?"

"I told you that your godfather was only concerned with amusing himself. He took no interest whatever in running the Aysgarth estate—all the farms and land that belong to the family. And gradually, over the years, everything ran down so badly that there was no more income from the land—the stock was diseased, the timber rotting, the land useless, and to make matters worse, the bailiff was idle and dishonest. He cheated and falsified the accounts. The day of reckoning had to come in the end, as with most things in life."

"But what about his son? Surely he should have helped?"

"Young Miles? He was away abroad and knew nothing about it, my dear. He and his father never really got on well with each other. He didn't care for the life his father led and for a house always full of guests, all eating and drinking their heads off, and gossiping like a pack of wolves. Some of them were not very pleasant people."

"I can imagine that," I said, with feeling, remembering Mama's society friends.

"Your godfather ignored all the warnings and carried on in the most extravagant style imaginable until the day he died.

When his son, Miles, returned to Aysgarth after his death, he found nothing but a pile of debts and disaster and everything in the most dreadful mess."

"And what happened then?" I asked, curious to learn the whole story and feeling, for the first time, a faint hint of sympathy for the new master. I too knew what it was like to be faced with ruin.

"We went from bad to worse, my dear," the contessa replied cheerfully. "Miles had to sell nearly everything in the house but it was nowhere near enough to pay the debts his father owed. Most of the estate had been mortgaged and neglected farm land takes years to put right, even with money to help. Without money it's a herculean task. He worked from morning till night, doing everything that could be done, and things were just beginning to improve a little when he fell out hunting. The horse rolled on him and crushed his spine. At first it was simply a battle to live at all. Then it was a battle to walk. It will be a long time before he can fight again for Aysgarth."

Topaz, the cat, deserted me and returned to the comfort of the contessa's lap, purring loudly and blinking his golden eyes.

"I wish you had known Miles before his accident, Alice. He was quite a different person—quiet and introspective still, of course, but very charming and so handsome. He was engaged to be married, you know, to Catherine Benton. They had known each other since children—Castle Benton is only a few miles from Aysgarth. The wedding was two weeks away when he was thrown from his horse. After that, of course, the engagement was broken."

"Was that necessary?"

"You have not met Miss Benton," the contessa remarked dryly, "or you would not ask me that. She is not the sort of girl to harness herself to a helpless, twisted cripple for the rest of her life. And, not only that, Miles was far too proud to let her. She visited him only once after the accident and that was enough for her. Not long after she wrote him a letter and it was all over between them. So perhaps you can understand why he is a little bitter with life. He has lost everything and for these past two years he has lived like a recluse. Nobody comes here and we see no one. It is not a happy house, as you can tell for yourself."

She smiled at me suddenly, with great warmth. "But now there is you, my dear. *You* have come to visit us and perhaps you may bring us better fortune."

Her great-nephew had used very similar words to me, but less pleasantly. For the contessa's sake I hoped it might be so; I was less sure that I cared much about her great-nephew.

I said: "Why didn't you tell me that my godfather was dead, Contessa?"

She looked surprised. "I thought you already knew, child."

I shook my head and she laughed, greatly amused. "I imagine that Miles didn't trouble to inform you, and no wonder! If you had known you might never have come to Aysgarth."

To take over the role of governess and mentor to his sister, I thought angrily.

The contessa watched me, serious once more. "I hope you have no thoughts of leaving us, Alice. We all need you, you know, in our different ways, so don't run away from us just yet!"

In the days that followed, I put the decision of whether to go or stay from my mind. There would be time enough to reach some conclusion when I had learned more of Aysgarth. Eweretta continued to be as cold and distant as possible and refused to speak more than was absolutely necessary. She spent a great deal of her time out riding over the moors, accompanied by the fair-haired young groom who looked after the few horses left in the stables. She avoided me pointedly whenever our paths crossed in the house and I grew used to her flouncing past me on the stairs with a toss of her curls, or deliberately turning away in the opposite direction whenever she caught sight of me in the distance. Eventually I managed to persuade myself that her behavior was more amusing than insulting: it was so exactly that of a naughty, spoiled child that it should not be taken too seriously.

"Excuse *me*, Miss Chell," she would say with exaggerated formality, her pretty blue eyes snapping with malice.

I longed sometimes to ask her if I could ride out with her too but the thought of inviting a certain snub prevented me. I had not ridden since our horses had been sold after Papa's death and I could not help watching with secret envy from the window as Eweretta trotted past on her gray mare.

The contessa only appeared downstairs for dinner. It depressed her, she told me, to see the parlous state of the house and so she kept to her rooms for most of the time, emerging in dazzling finery for the evening. Her dinner gowns were invariably brilliant in color and extravagant in style, lavishly trimmed, and adorned with exquisite old lace. Her old fingers sparkled with even more rings than usual and she was bedecked with a variety of brooches, necklaces, and bracelets—all beautiful pieces of jewelry that winked and gleamed richly in the candlelight. She would sit at the long table, straight-backed and imperious as a queen, dispensing cutting criticism to Eweretta, who sat in sulky silence, and sharp orders to old Unwin, the butler, who shuffled round the table with shaking hands and nodding head, hopelessly confused and incompetent.

As for the master of the house: he was never to be seen. A place was laid every evening for him at dinner but during those first days he failed to appear. Neither the contessa nor Eweretta seemed surprised or remarked on his absence and Unwin made no comment as he cleared away the untouched knives and forks. Puzzled, I asked Thurza one day why this should be so.

"He's bad at the moment, miss," was her response. "Like I told you, we don't see much of him at the best of times but when he's going through one of his bad times nobody's allowed near him. He stays in the west wing and cook says he drinks to kill the pain. You can't blame him really, can you, miss?"

No, I thought, I could not blame him. And I was miserably aware that his fall in that dark passage might well have caused the present bout of suffering.

The cool, rainy weather changed at last and the gray skies cleared to make way for the sun. Everything began to look a little more cheerful and even the great hall took on a less gloomy aspect with the late summer sun slanting down through the mullioned windows. Stifled by the indoors, I took to walking outside and breathing in the fresh, northern air that blew down from the moors above Aysgarth. There was a clean, heathery tang about it that made me long more than ever to be able to ride out over the moorland and to gallop across the open, wind-swept spaces with only the wild birds and the sheep for company.

The contessa had told me that there had once been beautiful

gardens surrounding the house: smooth, green lawns, symmetrical flower beds, and clipped yew hedges. But now everything was a tangled wilderness of rank weeds and long grass and the rambling rose briers had entwined inextricably with the overgrown yews to form an impenetrable jungle. One day, struggling to find some way through the chaos, I caught sight of Daniel Duck. He was chopping wildly away at some of the dense undergrowth, grasping a shining sickle in his huge fist and laying about him in a frenzy of uncontrolled strength that only created a worse shambles. I was afraid of him and nothing could alter that fear no matter how hard I tried to control it and to remind myself that little Thurza was quite untroubled by him. I hid behind an overhanging branch and shuddered with horror at the crazy mumblings that slobbered from his lips as he slashed away with that sharp blade. As soon as his back was turned I hurried away in the opposite direction and walked as quickly as I could from that spot.

I stumbled on the path by accident. At its beginning it meandered unpromisingly through a thorn thicket, so sharp and prickly that I almost abandoned the idea of exploring it. But something about it inspired me to carry on and I plunged deeper and deeper into the scrub, pulling my skirts free of the thorns that snatched at me as I passed. Soon the winding track led me into a tunnel of thick bushes whose highest branches were interlaced above my head to form a ceiling, shutting out the sunlight so that I walked in a green and gloomy shade.

The path was a long one and once or twice I nearly turned back, thinking that there seemed little point in pursuing such an overgrown route. There was a dark mystery about the green tunnel that gave me the same alarming feeling I had sensed when I wandered lost in the old passages at Aysgarth. I knew, instinctively, as I groped my way cautiously through the overhanging foliage that this path had been trodden by many others before me, for hundreds, perhaps thousands, of years, far back into the forgotten past. A glimpse of sunlight ahead encouraged me, however, and I battled on to emerge at last into the sun and open air where I stood, blinking a little at the unaccustomed glare and also at the totally unexpected sight that met my eyes.

The path had led me to a gentle, sheltered sward of grass, well protected from wind and weather by tall trees on the one side and a rise in the land on the other, so that the place had a sealed-off, secret appearance. There was a shallow, stony stream running by the foot of the slope and beside the water straggled the ruins of what must once have been an ancient abbey. Most of the old, gray walls had long since crumbled and fallen and broken stones and fragments of masonry lay scattered everywhere in the grass. But, in just a few places, a complete portion of the abbey still stood, with empty, high-arched windows pointing to the sky and carved doorways that led nowhere any more. And over all these walls had grown a thick curtain of ivy, smothering the stones with dark, glossy leaves. It was a peaceful scene: birds sang undisturbed, bees buzzed among the wild flowers, and the stream splashed and gurgled its way past the old stones as it must have done for hundreds of years.

Almost unable to believe my eyes, I wandered happily among the ruins, picking my way carefully across the mossy stones and passing through the few, skeletonlike archways that remained. Here and there I saw clues to the old building: a crumbling flight of steps that led upward to the sky, a line of broken pillars, a niche in the wall, a carved gargoyle grinning down at me from a high corner, an altar stone with five crosses incised on it, and rising above the altar, a huge east window which soared impressively into the blue sky. No one at Aysgarth had mentioned the existence of an abbey to me and yet this must have been one of considerable size and importance.

I strolled into the cloisters—a large square of grass bounded by the stumps of columns that had once supported the roofed arcade round the edge where the monks had read and walked and meditated. Now, only a few black-faced sheep grazed indifferently among the stones. Beyond the cloisters I found an octagonal-shaped room where traces of a long stone bench could be seen along the base of the wall. I sat down on a smooth section, and leaning back against the ivy-clad wall, I began to dream idly of the monks of long ago. A dragonfly droned nearby, and high above me, a skylark trilled its exultant song. I dozed a little, eyes shut, my face lifted to the sun.

"What are you doing here?"

I started violently at the harsh voice that came from somewhere in front of me. The sun was shining directly into my eyes, blurring my vision, and it was a moment or two before I adjusted to its brightness and saw the large bay horse that stood so quietly a little way off. It's rider, dark and grim-visaged, was staring down at me with cold disapproval.

As I gazed up at him, shielding my eyes with my hand, he added with a sneer: "What's the matter, Miss Chell? Why don't you answer me? Don't you recognize me? Surely you have not forgotten me already—but perhaps I look different on a horse: almost like any other man, in fact, instead of a misshapen freak!"

He is an impossible person, I thought to myself, determined that I would not let him intimidate or embarrass me as he so clearly wished to do. And he *does* look quite different sitting there on that fine horse. One would not know there was anything wrong with him and his face looks less haggard than before. The lines about the eyes and mouth are not so deep and I can begin to imagine what he looked like before the accident . . .

Aloud I said calmly: "I did not see you clearly at first, Mr. Metcalfe, because the sun was in my eyes. Nor did I expect to see you at all. After all, I have not set eyes on you since the first day I arrived. I understood you had not been well."

He said nothing to this but continued to glare down at me, chewing his lip broodingly.

"You haven't answered my question yet, Miss Chell."

"I'm sorry, sir. I've forgotten what it was."

He shifted impatiently in the saddle. "What are you doing here—that is what I want to know?"

"Am I trespassing?" I asked innocently. "If so, I am sorry. I thought this was still part of your estate."

"So it is. So it is," he replied irritably. "But you should not wander so far from the house on your own, and in any case, these ruins are unsafe. The walls are dangerous and you might come to harm."

I could not see that it could matter to him if I did but I bit back the retort and said instead: "I should very much like to know exactly what ruins I am sitting on. Perhaps you would tell me, sir."

"You are sitting, Miss Chell," he said in measured tones, "in the chapter house of Aysgarth Abbey. You are on the bench which the monks used when they met daily to discuss the affairs of the abbey and you are facing the spot where the abbot sat in his chair presiding over the meeting. You can see, if you are observant enough, the gap in between the benches at the center of the eastern end which held the abbot's chair."

"And those huge stones?" I asked, indicating several heavy slabs of limestone that lay in a semicircle, half-embedded in the earth.

"The tombs of the abbots," he replied shortly. "It was customary to bury them in the chapter house. There are thirteen of them altogether."

I looked about me at the silent stones that guarded their secrets so well. What, I wondered, had happened within these walls throughout the centuries? What drama had unfolded here in the chapter house and what sort of men had lived and died here? As for the thirteen abbots, had they been good, devout men or greedy and grasping as so many of their kind?

Mr. Metcalfe had let the bay's reins slip loose so that the animal could crop at the grass, and he was watching me speculatively.

"I can see that this place interests you."

"I had no idea it was here at all!"

"Why should you? Nobody ever comes here. As far as most people are concerned, it's simply an overgrown ruin, best forgotten and left alone for nature to finish off in her own good time."

"But *you* come here," I pointed out.

He frowned. "For precisely that reason: for solitude. No one disturbs me here. You are the first person to do so."

He turned his head away from me to look across the walls toward the stream that meandered quietly beside the ruins. "It's a peaceful place and I feel at home here. My family has been involved with the abbey since it was founded in the twelfth century. A monk, called Hugh de Quincy, came here from Normandy seven hundred years ago and leased the land from my ancestors who lived at Aysgarth even then. He had heard that the local population were in need of Christian teaching and no doubt he was right. They were a pagan lot from all accounts. He and a handful of other monks built the abbey here and lived and worked in this place for four hundred years until it was destroyed by Henry VIII. The buildings were smashed to the ground, the monastery looted of everything of any value, and the rest left to rot away."

"It must have been a very beautiful place."

He looked at me again. "It was once upon a time. But now it is all gone. Look at it! Nothing remains forever, Miss Chell, and before long Aysgarth will be nothing but a pile of rubble like this too!"

"You talk like a defeatist," I said, not stopping to consider the effect my words might have on him. "You have given up the fight!"

He went white with anger and jerked at the horse's reins so that the animal pranced uneasily beneath him.

"Nothing gives you the right to say that, Miss Chell, so far as I am aware," he said in tones as chill as the wind that blew from the moors. "Perhaps, after all, you were right in thinking that you should not stay long at Aysgarth. . . ."

I stood up to face him, equally angered myself by *his* words.

"I should be delighted to leave as soon as possible, but then, sir, you would not have a suitable companion for your ill-mannered sister!"

He glowered down at me. "What do you mean?"

"The contessa told me how you decided that I might be useful to teach Eweretta some better manners. *That,* I understand, is the reason you invited me to Aysgarth and not your noble, inherited sense of responsibility!"

He muttered a string of oaths beneath his breath, and bringing the horse beside me, leaned down toward me. I had a brief, frightening glimpse of his dark face, eyes glittering with devilment, before I felt his arm, strong as iron, grip my waist and I was scooped roughly from the ground and dumped, like a sack of potatoes, onto the saddle in front of him.

"Nobody is permitted to speak to me like that, Miss Chell," he hissed close to my ear. "As I told you, you should not wander so far from the house alone. I shall now escort you safely home."

I had neither the time nor the breath to protest before he had urged the bay forward, away from the abbey, and set off through the trees homeward at a headlong gallop. As we traversed woodland and fields I sat rigid and helpless, crushed against him by an arm that held me like a vise, while I seethed with resentment and fury and the tears of mortification slid down my cheeks.

As we reached Aysgarth and clattered into the stable yard my mood was not improved one bit to see that Garrick, the young groom, was observing us with astonishment over a loose-box door. His astonishment gradually turned to ill-concealed amusement as he hurried forward to help me dismount.

As I struggled to free myself the arm remained tight about my waist. "One moment, Miss Chell, before you fly off in a high dudgeon. Tell me, can you ride?"

But I refused to answer him, and choked with tears and anger, kept my head turned resolutely away.

He seemed to have recovered his good humor for he laughed and said pleasantly, "No matter. But if you do ride, as I suspect you do judging by the way you sat on this horse, then you are welcome to go out any time you please. Garrick will escort you and there is an old, quiet horse called Melody who should suit you well."

At last he released me and as the groom helped me to the ground, he said to him: "See that Miss Chell rides out on Melody whenever she wishes. But keep a close eye on her. She is somewhat inclined to wander too far afield!"

I heard him laugh again as I stalked away from the stables and burned with fury at his highhanded, patronizing manners. Old, quiet Melody indeed! As though I were some nervous, incompetent beginner who could not be trusted to handle a decent horse!

"One moment, Miss Chell," he called again. He had followed me a little way on the bay horse and as I turned, unwillingly, he looked down at me and said soberly: "I *do* feel a responsibility for you, Alice Chell, whether you like it or not. The fact that you might do my sister some good is beside the point, I promise you. This is your home for better or worse."

There was the ghost of a smile about his dark eyes. "Whether you will do *me* any good is much more doubtful. I rather fear, on present record, that you may be the breaking of me!"

And he swung the horse away from me without another word.

I turned and walked slowly back toward the house.

CHAPTER IV

Some days later a visitor arrived at Aysgarth. I heard the sound of a carriage in the driveway, and peering from my bedroom window, caught a glimpse of a stranger hurrying up the steps to the front door. I distinguished nothing more than a slight, shadowy figure dressed in brown and I could not help being curious. The contessa had said that no one called any longer at the house, and indeed, the man I had just seen was the first visitor since myself. I wondered who he could be and hoped that he was receiving a warmer welcome than I had experienced. Old Unwin was so muddleheaded and confused that he might easily send him away whatever his business.

Later on, when I went downstairs to the drawing room to join the contessa and Eweretta as usual, I found to my surprise and dismay that Miles Metcalfe was also present. Since the incident at the abbey ruins I had cordially welcomed his absence and should have been very thankful never to have seen him again. But now, there he was, leaning with arrogant languor against the marble chimney piece and twirling the ebony stick idly in one hand, his long fingers curled loosely round its silver knob. For once his dark clothing was relieved by an elaborate and colorful waistcoat, which, with his long, carelessly dressed black locks and lined face, gave him a very dissolute air. He glanced toward me and I could tell by that gleam in his eyes that he was about to make some derogatory, teasing remark at my expense. The contessa intervened, however, calling across the room in her authoritative manner.

"We have a visitor, Alice, my dear. Just fancy that! You must come and meet this rare bird at once before he decides to fly away to more agreeable surroundings!"

The "rare bird" rose a little nervously and awkwardly from the high-backed chair where he had been sitting, concealed from me. He was a young man, only a year or two older than myself, of medium height, slender build, and curly, mouse-brown hair. His face was ordinary and unremarkable, but nonetheless pleasant, and the clothes he wore were very plain and unpretentious and a little shabby. A pair of round, wire-framed spectacles perched on his nose, and as he bent politely over my hand, his gray eyes blinked at me from behind the thick lenses. I felt an instant sympathy for him: here, besides myself, was someone uncertain of his reception and who felt at a loss in this unnerving household.

Miles Metcalfe spoke in cool, detached tones from beside the fireplace. "Allow me, Miss Chell, to present the son of a friend of my late father—Mr. Philip Paige. Mr. Paige is studying archaeology and is writing a thesis on the monasteries of Yorkshire. He has expressed great interest in the ruins of Aysgarth Abbey and is to stay with us for a short while in order to explore them."

He turned to the young man. "Miss Chell also has an insatiable interest in the abbey. No doubt she will be asking you endless questions!"

Mr. Paige smiled at me shyly. "My father visited Aysgarth often in the past and he always spoke of the abbey ruins. I am so grateful to Mr. Metcalfe for allowing me to come and make a special study of them."

The contessa, resplendent as always in a dazzling gown and jewels, raised her lorgnette to study the visitor more closely. She seemed unable to make up her mind about him.

"You surprise me sometimes, Miles," she commented at last. "First Alice and now Mr. Paige. We shall soon have the whole house swarming with people if you continue at this rate!"

He raised an eyebrow and regarded his great-aunt quizzically.

"Hardly that, Contessa. Both Mr. Paige and Miss Chell are the children of old friends of my father and are therefore special cases, don't you agree? Besides, Miss Chell has already expressed the gravest doubts about staying long with us. As she knows, it would be very inconvenient for me if she left, so I am hoping that Mr. Paige will enliven the scene for her and encourage her to find the prospect of Aysgarth more attractive. It seems to me that they have a great deal in common . . ."

He was looking at the contessa as he spoke and did not once

glance in my direction, although I knew that he was perfectly aware of how much he infuriated me by his words. I did not mind being bracketed with the shy Mr. Paige but the implication that his presence would persuade me to stay was outrageous—as though I were some desperate spinster with no aim in life but to trap some unsuspecting man into marriage. I racked my brains to think of a riposte but could think of nothing to say that would not also offend Mr. Paige and so I remained silent, while longing to snatch up that ebony stick and hit its arrogant, ill-mannered owner over the head with it!

At that moment, the door opened and Eweretta walked in. Floated in might better describe the manner of her entrance, in a cloud of gauzy yellow muslin, which I knew Signorina Frugoni had recently made for her. The dress suited her superbly. It had a close-fitting bodice and tight, elbow-length sleeves trimmed with deep bands of blond lace. The collar was prettily frilled with a yellow satin bow tied in the center, and the full skirt that swayed about her feet was edged with a wide flounce and decorated with tiny blue forget-me-nots. Blond ringlets were clustered about her ears and tied with blue ribbons that matched her eyes. It was clear that Eweretta had made a special effort to impress the newcomer.

Philip Paige had risen hastily to his feet again at her appearance and had gone quite pale at the captivating picture Eweretta made as she glided toward him. He gulped audibly and blundered clumsily into a small table, knocking a porcelain shepherdess to the floor. The figurine rolled across the carpet and stopped at Eweretta's feet. She paused to stare at him as he shuffled and mumbled miserably, his face now flushed a painful red, and I saw her blue eyes cloud with disappointment, mingled with contempt, as she summed up the young man and dismissed him as a dull, clumsy nobody. Without a word, she stooped to pick up the shepherdess and replaced it carefully on the table before turning away with a disdainful shrug of the shoulders.

"Do tell me more about the abbey ruins, Mr. Paige," I said hurriedly. "I should be very interested to hear what you know of them."

There was hurt and bewilderment in his gray eyes and he fumbled nervously with the little round wire spectacles.

"As yet very little, I'm afraid, Miss Chell," he said. "They have not been touched for over three hundred years so who knows what priceless relics of the past might be buried there."

"Such as the Cross of Aysgarth, I suppose," said Eweretta with cold sarcasm. "Perhaps you think you will succeed where everyone else has failed."

Philip Paige looked even more bewildered. "The Cross of Aysgarth," he repeated, shaking his head. "I'm afraid I've never heard of it."

Eweretta gave a cruel little smile. "You seem to be afraid of everything, Mr. Paige. Surely you have heard of our legendary cross."

He shook his head again and appealed to his host, who had moved from his post against the chimney piece to slump broodingly in a wing-backed chair beside me.

"Mr. Metcalfe, what is this cross? I feel I should have known of it."

The ebony stick rotated incessantly and maddeningly. "Your manners are appalling as usual, Eweretta," the stick's owner observed coolly. "Why should Mr. Paige have heard of the cross? It is scarcely world-wide news but simply one of the more colorful stories about Aysgarth. The sort of tale Miss Chell would doubtless find interesting since she has a very romantic nature."

Again, he did not look at me at all but continued smoothly. "Since you are going to study the abbey ruins, Mr. Paige, it should be of some interest to you as well. When Hugh de Quincy came here from Normandy to found the abbey in the twelfth century, he brought with him a magnificent cross of solid gold encrusted with many hundreds of precious jewels. It was a priceless work of art as well as being of great intrinsic value, and when the abbey church was finally completed he placed the cross on the high altar where it remained for nearly four hundred years—the most valuable treasure that the monks possessed."

Philip Paige's eyes blinked rapidly behind the wire-framed spectacles. "Where is the cross now?"

"Ah, that is the mystery, Mr. Paige. Nobody knows. It vanished in the sixteenth century at the time of the dissolution of the small Monasteries when Aysgarth suffered the same fate as so many other abbeys in Yorkshire. It was looted of everything of any value by Thomas Cromwell's men and maybe the cross was stolen by them. It may have been broken up, the jewels extracted, and the gold melted down, for it has never come to light anywhere since that time. There is, however, another possibility: the last abbot—Abbot Haby was a muddleheaded sort of man who got the abbey into such serious financial difficulties that he had to sell off most of the church plate to raise money. I think it very likely that he sold the cross too."

"He would never have done such a thing!" Eweretta protested with surprising vehemence.

Her brother smiled sardonically. "Like my late father, Mr. Paige, my sister passionately believes that the abbot hid the cross somewhere safe from the King's men. She surmises this, I should explain, because the first abbot—Hugh de Quincy—pledged the cross as a symbol of good faith and gratitude to the Metcalfe family, who had leased him the land for the abbey and helped him all they could. Before his death he willed that it should be given to us if ever the abbey failed or was abandoned. That was in the twelfth century and the promise was never forgotten by the monks through the years: the Cross of Aysgarth became a sort of talisman for the Metcalfes—a symbol of their state of grace, if you like. Eweretta is superstitious enough to believe the legend that its power could save our family in time of trouble. She is afraid that unless it can be found we are doomed."

There was a small silence.

"And what do you believe?" I asked before I could stop myself.

He barely glanced at me. "I think that it will never be seen again. If it were found, Eweretta is right, our fortunes would certainly be restored since we could follow the good Abbot Haby's example and sell it."

"Have you looked for it?"

"My dear Miss Chell," he replied impatiently. "Generations of Metcalfes have searched high and low for the cross. My father was convinced that it was hidden somewhere in this house—because of the close family tie with the abbey. But he was no more successful than the rest, even though he ransacked the place."

"That fool of an abbot sold it, I've no doubt of that," remarked the contessa. With reverent fingers, she touched the exquisite ruby necklace that she was wearing. "One should never sell jewels unless there is no possible alternative. And if he did so then he broke the sacred vow to the Metcalfes. A wicked man as well as a foolish one!"

"You're rather hard on him, Contessa," her great-nephew protested mildly. "He was a popular abbot by all accounts, despite his inefficiency. The Miles Metcalfe who lived here in 1536 liked him very much. They were excellent friends, according to the documents we still have. He can't have been all that bad."

"What happened to him anyway?" the contessa demanded.

"Alas, the poor man came to an unfortunate end. He was unwise enough to take part in the Pilgrimage of Grace as a protest against the dissolution. He was arrested and imprisoned in the Tower of London."

"And then?"

"And then he was hanged, drawn, and quartered at Tyburn."

"I told you the man was a fool!" said the contessa.

Eweretta had gone to sit at the spinet and was plucking carelessly at the keyboard. I recognized the lilting refrain of the waltz I had heard her play before.

"Well, Mr. Paige, what do *you* think of the story?" she asked mockingly.

He cleared his throat and hesitated before answering her. "In my experience, Miss Metcalfe," he said at last, "such tales are usually only legends that may once have had some basis in fact but have become distorted and exaggerated through the years. The cross may have existed but, no doubt, it was a very simple affair, perhaps with a small jewel or two. And it's most unlikely that it still exists today."

He looked rather self-satisfied with his opinion, no doubt imagining that she had sought it seriously. But I knew Eweretta better than that: she was playing him like a fish on a hook. The pretty tune of the waltz stopped abruptly and she stared across at him with a cold, contemptuous little smile.

"How strange that you should think that, Mr. Paige! I thought you were an archaeologist who knew all about such things. You are quite wrong about the cross, you see. It did exist exactly as my brother described and we have proof of it. There is a portrait hanging on the wall in his study of the Abbot Haby with the cross beside him. It is painted in detail and you can see every jewel—every diamond, ruby, pearl, sapphire, emerald—go and look for yourself, Mr. Paige, and be careful before you dismiss our legends again so lightly."

Poor man! I felt so sorry for him as he sat pale and humbled, fingering his wire spectacles. And yet, for the first time I was on common ground with Eweretta. Not because I condoned her unkind treatment of Philip Paige, but because of her obvious obsession with the Cross of Aysgarth. As her brother had so shrewdly predicted, I too found the story and the mystery of its whereabouts very intriguing. I longed to see the portrait she had spoken of, but it hung in his study—a forbidden lair which not even the contessa dared to penetrate, and I certainly could not bring myself to ask his permission to see it. That would be laying myself open to yet more taunts and ridicule.

Tired of baiting the visitor, Eweretta had returned to the spinet keyboard and the little waltz melody. Her playing was as pretty as her appearance and I saw that Mr. Paige, despite his snubbing, was having some difficulty in keeping his eyes away from her direction as the contessa engaged him in an imperious conversation about Italy.

Beside me, Miles Metcalfe seemed to have sunk into a dark and silent mood. He sat hunched in the wing-backed chair, grim and withdrawn, revolving the black stick with the tips of his long, thin fingers. I felt ill at ease so near to him and rose quietly to move away, but as I passed by his chair his arm shot out with lightning speed and grasped my wrist so tightly that I could move no further.

"Where are you going, Miss Chell? It's exceedingly bad manners to run away from your host. Please sit down again."

I did so because I had no alternative, for his fingers still held my arm. Scarlet with embarrassment, I sat rigidly in my chair, my head turned away.

He tugged a little at my wrist. "You seem rather annoyed with me, Miss Chell. Tell me, am I forgiven for carrying you off in that cavalier fashion the other day? It was a trifle wild of me, I admit, but you had made me very angry. You have a knack of doing that, you know. I wonder why. Now, say you have for-given me or I shall continue to hold onto your arm until you do so."

But still I refused to answer him, sensing that he was laughing at me.

"Very well, Miss Chell. But the others will soon notice and think it very odd that we are sitting like this."

I looked and saw to my discomfort that Eweretta was staring at us across the room.

I shrugged my shoulders, feigning indifference. "I had forgot-ten the incident already, I assure you."

"So you forgive me?"

"Of course."

"And don't forget you may ride out on Melody whenever you wish."

"I had not forgotten. Thank you."

At that moment Unwin appeared at the door to announce din-ner and Miles Metcalfe released my wrist abruptly so that at last I was able to move away from him.

I fully expected that Eweretta would make some waspish com-ments to me as soon as the opportunity arose. But to my surprise, when I passed her the following day in the great hall she smiled at me for the first time, and laying her hand lightly on my arm, said: "Miles tells me that you would like to go riding one day. You may come out tomorrow if you wish. I will take you with me up on the moors."

I stared at her in astonishment.

"Well, would you like to?"

"Yes, of course. I should be delighted."

She gave me an odd, sidelong look. "Good. That's settled then. I take it you have ridden before? I shall tell Garrick to saddle up a suitable mount for you."

"Your brother told me I was to ride Melody."

"Pooh! Not that dull old armchair," she said, pulling a face. "I'm sure you can ride better than that—you always look so com-petent. There is no need to take account of what my brother says. He has gone to York today and won't be back to see which horse you ride."

Warning bells should have rung in my mind but they did not.

I was entirely deceived by her apparent friendliness and her innocent blue eyes. Perhaps I wanted to be deceived for I remember that I was pathetically grateful for her offer.

"We shall ride out in the afternoon, if that suits you?"

"Perfectly."

She gave me a little nod and was about to move on when she paused, as though suddenly remembering something.

"Perhaps you could do me a favor in return?"

"If I can."

"I'm supposed to visit Mrs. Cropper today. She is the widow of one of the laborers. She lives in a cottage on the estate and Miles insists that I take some provisions there once a week. You can't imagine how I dread going—it's so dark and dirty and the children are like little savages. . . ."

"I don't mind going instead of you," I told her, anticipating what was coming. "In fact, I'd be glad of the chance to do something useful for a change."

She sighed and smiled at me prettily. "I only wish I could feel like that about it too—but then I'm just not as virtuous as you, Alice. Mrs. Silver will provide you with the basket to take and I will show you the way. It's not far across the fields and I know you like walking."

And so, later that day, I found myself clumping along a winding, grassy path that led to Mrs. Cropper's cottage, and carrying the large and heavily laden basket that Mrs. Silver had reluctantly given to me earlier on.

"Miss Eweretta is supposed to take this," she said sharply. "Those are the master's orders."

I was tired of her unpleasantness.

"Then I shall be answerable to him myself," I told her and walked away, leaving her staring after me with a tight, resentful expression on her face. I wondered whether she was a little mad: as the contessa had warned, I had discovered that she prowled endlessly about the house and had often startled me by materializing suddenly from dark corners, emerging from the shadows like some phantom figure, to stand silently watching as I passed by, hands tightly clasped at her waist, her ugly face pale and impassive.

As I walked along in the sunshine I felt pleased to be free

once more of the oppressive gloom of the house. There was a fresh breeze and the fields were yellow with buttercups. I climbed over a stile, hauling the heavy basket after me, and followed the narrow track downhill toward a cluster of trees. The Croppers' cottage lay in a dip of land just beyond the trees, and from a distance, it looked a pretty place. Wild honeysuckle rambled over the old stone walls and the sun was shining down on the slate roof. I began to wonder at Eweretta's fierce distaste for visiting the family.

The path led me on beneath a line of horse chestnut trees; their wide, overlapping branches cast a green and pleasant shade and as I walked along I hummed a little to myself. Suddenly, something hit the brim of my straw bonnet and bounced onto the path in front of me, bowling along merrily until it rolled to a stop. I saw what it was a spiky, green fruit from the tree above and that the casing had split open to reveal a gleam of coppery brown. I bent to pick it up, prizing open its prickly cover to hold the conker in my hand and admire its glossy sheen and satin smoothness, and as I did so, another struck me on the arm. And after that, two or three more hit me in rapid succession and all with such force and accuracy that it was clear that nature could not be held responsible. I peered upward into the thick, fanlike leaves above me and caught a glimpse of bare, brown feet dangling from a high branch and heard the sound of muffled laughter.

"Who's there? Come down at once and stop that nonsense this minute!"

I spoke far more crossly and sternly than I really felt as I realized that this was merely some childish prank, but at the same time, I had no desire for the next aim to hit me in the eye. There was a moment or two of silence as the leaves quivered above my head and then, very slowly and cautiously, they parted and an impish little face with a snub, freckled nose and tilted green eyes peeped down at me, grinning as entrancingly and mischievously as a woodland elf.

"Well," I demanded with assumed severity, "are you coming down or shall I come up and fetch you?"

"You couldn't!"

"Don't you believe it! I could climb trees just as well as you once upon a time and I haven't forgotten how to I promise you."

"Ladies don't climb trees," was the scoffing response.

"And I shall show you that they do," I said, putting down the basket and marching toward the trunk of the horse chestnut.

There was a scrabbling, rustling in the branches and two legs, thin as broomsticks, swung into view. I saw a flash of ragged, blue cotton trousers, there was a soft thud, and he landed easily on the path and stood looking at me, half-smiling, half-apprehensive, his small body crouched like an animal's for instant flight. He was not more than six or seven years old and yet his pinched face had a curiously knowing, adult air about it and the green eyes were alert and aware. Apart from the tattered trousers, he wore a torn check shirt, many sizes too big for him, and an old cloth cap on his tangled, dark hair. His feet were scratched and black with dirt, and indeed, I saw all too clearly that the child was filthy from head to toe.

"Are you one of Mrs. Cropper's children?" I asked in pleasanter tones.

Now that he saw I was not angry, he stood up and folded his skinny arms defiantly across his chest.

"I might be."

"Because if you are," I continued smoothly, "you can help me carry this basket of provisions to your mother. There's a plump chicken, some butter and bacon, oatmeal, potatoes, and a seed-cake. . . ."

He swallowed convulsively, and putting out his grubby hand, seized the handle of the basket.

"Course I'll help you, miss," he said eagerly.

But I delayed matters a little, resisting the little tugs he was making at the basket.

"Before we go, you must tell me your name," I told him. For some reason I felt that it was important to know this.

He pulled at the handle impatiently.

"It's Dobbin, miss."

"Dobbin! That's a strange name."

He shrugged his shoulders indifferently. "That's what I'm called anyway."

"Is your mother at home?"

"She's always at home. She can't go anywhere 'cos of the baby."

"How old is the baby?"

"Six months, I think. He was born just before me dad died. I don't like him very much, if you want to know. He's always crying and now he's got a fever and he's been screaming for days. Can't you hear him?"

I listened as we walked together down the path carrying the basket between us and I could hear piercing, fretful wails coming from inside the cottage. Now that I was close to it, I could see that the place was in a sadly dilapidated state. Black holes gaped where tiles had fallen and the rotting and broken windows were clumsily blocked with pieces of sacking. The honeysuckle, which had looked so pretty from a distance, rampaged voraciously over the walls, clawing and creeping its way under the slate tiles, choking the gutters and penetrating the window frames. The door, dingy and paint peeling, hung open drunkenly by one hinge, and on the threshold, watching our approach with round, speculative eyes, were three small children. They made a pathetically ragged trio, thin, pale, and listless. The largest scratched his head continually while his brother, beside him, coughed loudly and repeatedly and with such violence that his small frame shook. The third child, a girl, had stringy, fair hair and large blue eyes; she might have been pretty except for her filthy condition and the weeping sores all round her mouth. Like Dobbin, all three had bare feet; a few chickens scratched in the dust about them, strutting freely in and out of the doorway.

Dobbin thrust the children aside and gave me an odd, jerky little bow as he stood aside for me to go inside. He might have been ushering me proudly into some immaculate, comfortable villa instead of the dank, dark, and fetid little hole in which I found myself. The strips of sacking nailed across the windows shut out a good deal of the light but I could still see enough to recoil in horror at the dirt and disorder. The floor had obviously not been swept for many weeks and the hens pecked hopefully among the refuse. A rickety wooden table was piled with greasy, unwashed plates and pans and the single chair had a broken leg and was propped up by an old box. Despite the warm sunshine outside, the air inside the cottage felt damp and chill and was thick with an unmistakable reek of filth and squalor. I was no longer surprised at Eweretta's reluctance to visit the place.

The baby had stopped crying and its feeble little hiccuping noises guided me through the gloom to a far corner of the room where a woman stood in the shadows, clasping the child close to her and rocking it silently to and fro in her arms.

"Mrs. Cropper?"

She had not heard me come in and started, turning toward me to stare apprehensively. Her face was pale and lined and her eyes—the same green as Dobbin's—looked dull and exhausted. She seemed an old woman but was probably less than ten years older than myself, and now she gazed at me, not speaking or moving as I held out the laden basket in front of her.

"I've come in Miss Metcalfe's place," I said gently. "This is for you."

"There's room on the table," she replied in a lifeless voice, and began to croon to the baby, bending her head down to the ragged bundle and swaying her thin body from side to side.

Behind me Dobbin made an impatient movement and seized the basket from me. He staggered with it to the wobbly table, and sweeping aside a hen that was stalking round among the dirty utensils, he dumped his burden in the only clear space and began to unload its contents. The three other children gathered round him and watched avidly as the food appeared, item by item, before their eyes.

I saw that at last the baby had fallen asleep, its face flushed and swollen unhealthily. The woman laid it gently in a rough wooden cradle on the floor and tucked the tattered shawl about it anxiously. When she had finished she stood looking down at the child, twisting her work-worn hands together in mute despair.

"I just don't know what to do with him," she said, after a while. "He's never been right, not since the day he was born. And now he's got this fever and he cries all the time. . . ."

"Shouldn't you send for the doctor?"

She turned her head to stare at me and her face twisted into a derisive, toothless grin. "Doctor! Did you say to send for the doctor, miss? And tell me how I could pay him? We can't afford no doctors in the Cropper family."

I felt deeply ashamed of my stupid and thoughtless remark and appalled by the poverty that confronted me. Once I might have considered myself to have fallen on hard times, but no longer. Compared with these cottage folk I was fortunate beyond measure.

I said awkwardly: "I hope the provisions will be a help."

She glanced at the table and nodded wearily. "It'll be the saving of us, thank you. Miss Eweretta didn't come last week and we've been living off tea-kettle broth for days."

"Tea-kettle broth?"

"Yes, miss. I put crusts in a bowl with a mite of salt and pour boiling water over them. We eat them when they're soft enough."

I looked at her and the children in consternation. The meals served at Aysgarth were far from luxurious, and indeed, sometimes highly unpalatable, and Mama and I had been reduced to the simplest diet when we lived in the Clapham lodgings, but I had never had to experience a fraction of the privation this firmly seemed to endure daily. And yet Eweretta had neglected to call on them at all last week. The contessa and her brother had both called her vain and foolish; she was also, in my opinion, wickedly selfish as well.

I surveyed the ragged little group clustered round the table and listened to the middle boy's continual, racking cough.

"Have you any other children, Mrs. Cropper?" I asked, terrified that there might be yet more hungry mouths to feed somewhere outside.

"Only my eldest, Sarah. She's away at the mill."

"The mill?"

"The cotton mill, miss, at Grimton. She's nine now and old enough to earn so I sent her to live with my brother near the mill. She gets three shillings a week and after she's paid her keep she brings the rest home when she visits us. Not that she can come very often—the coach costs too much. She helps my brother's wife in the house too, so she's not got much time to spare anyways."

I was appalled. "Does she have to go away? Nine years old seems so young to leave home and work all day in a mill."

Mrs. Cropper was puzzled by my concern. "There's plenty younger than her there, miss. Besides the work's not hard—all she has to do is pick up the cotton threads off the floor. My brother says she's always complaining she's tired and wants to come home but she's a sight better off there. At least she eats decent most of the time. She's luckier than us."

I did not know what to say to this, and at that moment, the two smaller boys began to squabble and fight among themselves over the division of the seedcake from the basket. Dobbin sprang forward to intervene, gripping each one fiercely by a lock of hair and dragging them apart with surprising strength, considering his puny size. The noise woke the baby, who began to wail miserably once again and its mother rushed over to the makeshift wooden cradle. I stole quietly out of the cottage, taking the empty basket with me, and walked away up the path in a thoughtful and sober mood. I was determined that in human charity a doctor should somehow be sent to see the sick baby but how could I arrange this? I was fully prepared to pay him myself if only I knew a doctor in the neighborhood. To send for one meant consulting Mr. Metcalfe, or at least the contessa. And would they approve and agree to the idea? I was not sure and *he* was away in York and might not be back for several days.

I plodded on across the fields toward Aysgarth, feeling depressed but very determined to do something to help the wretched family I had seen. I was certain that the baby would die without attention, and I knew that in some strange and magical way the little elf-like boy, Dobbin, had taken a place in my heart and would remain there forever.

I was so deeply absorbed in my thoughts that I failed to notice the figure ahead of me on the path, waiting for my approach. It was Philip Paige. He stood there, shuffling a little awkwardly, and smiled at me timidly as I drew near, his gray eyes blinking behind his spectacles.

"I saw you in the distance, Miss Chell, and wondered if I might escort you back to the house."

I found him charmingly well mannered and eager to please—in marked contrast to his host. His diffidence was rather endearing and touching and I welcomed his company for the rest of the way.

As we walked along he talked about the abbey ruins, which he had already begun to reconnoiter. He had just come from there, and as he spoke, his face glowed with enthusiasm.

"It's the most wonderful chance for me, Miss Chell. Imagine, the ruins have been virtually unknown and untouched for three hundred years—it's a great honor to be the first to make a serious study of them."

"I must admit," I told him, "that I am surprised that Mr. Metcalfe gave you permission. I should have thought him the sort of man who would prefer to keep everything belonging to Aysgarth to himself."

He nodded. "I had heard that he had a reputation for being somewhat difficult and unfriendly—since his accident, of course. I was not very hopeful about my chances when I wrote to him. But then, I suppose one might say that his family have a debt of honor to mine. Perhaps that has something to do with it."

"A debt of honor?"

He smiled slightly. "My father lent the late Mr. Metcalfe a very large sum of money, when he was in financial difficulties you know. Unfortunately he failed to repay it. As a consequence, my father was virtually ruined himself. He might have recovered, of course, but for a decline in health which brought him to such a low pitch that he was never able to recover his position. He died almost penniless a few years ago."

"How dreadful! But you have the right to claim the money from the present Mr. Metcalfe surely?"

"He has already repaid a small part of the sum and has promised to repay the remainder when he is able, but you can see for yourself that this is not likely to be so for some time. I can assure you, Miss Chell, that this chance that Mr. Metcalfe has given me is more than adequate recompense. There is only myself left in the family, you see. My mother is dead and I have no brothers or sisters to look after. Money alone holds no interest for me—my work is all that matters. You should come and see the abbey. I could explain it all to you and I'm certain that you would find it of great interest."

"I have already seen the ruins and found them fascinating," I told him. "But I should be delighted to look at them again through your eyes. There was so much I wanted to know about the old abbey and I found the story of the legendary cross intriguing. I suppose there's no possibility that you may find it there?"

He smiled at me again and shook his head. "I'm afraid not. As I said before, it is most unlikely that any trace of it exists and even if it did, by some miracle, *I* could not hope to find it. I am merely making a preliminary study of the ruins on my own with very little digging involved. It would need a large team of men to excavate the abbey properly in order to uncover any of its treasures. I hope I may be able to persuade Mr. Metcalfe to allow this to be carried out in the future and then we are sure to find some priceless archaeological relics. But as for the Cross of Aysgarth—I'm afraid *that* will never come to light."

"I wonder if it couldn't be hidden somewhere in the house," I said thoughtfully. "There was a close bond between the monks and the Metcalfe family, and according to the legend, the cross was always promised to them if the abbey disbanded for any reason. It could have been so well concealed that nobody has been able to find it for hundreds of years. The walls are six feet thick in the oldest part of the house, you know. There must be secret places or even a secret room!"

I thought of the meandering confusion of old passages at Aysgarth, the huge chimneys, the odd-shaped rooms, and the multitude of queer little nooks and crannies.

"You have a vivid imagination, Miss Chell," Philip Paige teased gently. "The late Mr. Metcalfe believed the same, of course, didn't he? I wonder if he had any good reason for that?"

"Not as far as I know. But it seems a logical idea to me. The abbot would surely have done everything he could to avoid the King's men seizing the cross."

"If he had not already sold it! Miss Metcalfe evidently thinks he would never have done that though. I'm afraid she holds a very low opinion of me. I'm not quite sure why."

I touched his arm. "Don't take any notice of Eweretta. She takes a great pleasure in taunting people sometimes—especially those who show they mind. Don't let her hurt you."

He looked at me gratefully with his gentle, gray eyes.

"I'm so glad that you are staying at Aysgarth, Miss Chell. I find Mr. Metcalfe a somewhat alarming person and the Contessa de Montefiore is rather overwhelming. At least we may find a little comfort in each other's company perhaps sometimes?"

It was absurd how he reminded me so vividly of my three

brown and white spaniels; he had exactly the same trusting and anxious-to-please expression. I smiled up at him reassuringly and we walked on together toward the house.

Later, I found the contessa in her rooms, seated in the tapestry chair with the cat, Topaz, curled in a semicircle on her lap. A pile of French fashion journals lay on a small table by her elbow.

She raised her lorgnette and looked at me critically. "Wherever have you been, child. You look a hideous mess! Your hair is coming down at the back and there's mud all over your skirt!"

She was exaggerating although I certainly fell short of her high standards of grooming. But then the contessa would never dream of walking across muddy fields and climbing over stiles.

I told her about my visit to the Croppers and all my feelings of horror and pity at the miserable poverty I had found at the cottage—the ragged children, the exhausted mother, the child of nine away working in a mill, the horrible dirt and squalor of the place, and the sick baby who was in vital need of a doctor. She listened in silence and then said:

"I know, my dear. Miles has told me about the Croppers. The husband died two years ago and he does what little he can for them. It's only thanks to him that they have a home at all. Most landlords would have turned them out and they'd have been sent to the workhouse."

"But have you seen the state of the cottage? It's not fit for pigs to live in. The roof leaks and the windows are all broken."

"And what about Aysgarth?" the contessa said mildly. "If Miles cannot afford to repair this house he certainly cannot afford to mend all the cottages on the estate."

"But something must be done for them!"

She looked up at me, her blue eyes sharp. "Alice, my dear child, there are thousands and thousands of families like the Croppers all over the country. Of course it is wrong but what can we do about it? You mustn't allow it to distress you so much."

"Surely a doctor could be sent to the baby at least. If not I'm sure it will die."

"It may be possible to arrange. You must ask Miles when he

returns from York. I dare say he will agree to help—he does what he can for his tenants."

"When does he return?"

"I'm not sure. Late tomorrow or the day after, I believe. Approach him by all means, my dear, but be careful not to make him angry as you seem to have a talent for doing. And now, come and tell me what you think of these latest fashions from Paris. The journals arrived for me today and Frugoni cannot wait to copy several of them . . ."

I sat dutifully beside her while she leafed eagerly through the pages. The illustrations were all charming, I suppose, but I scarcely noticed them. Paris modes did not seem very important to me at that moment. My mind was too full of the Croppers and all those other thousands of families like them.

CHAPTER V

"Are you sure you wouldn't like to change your mind?" inquired Eweretta the next day. Her voice and manner were unmistakably challenging.

"No, of course not. Why should I?"

She gave a little shrug of her shoulders. "No reason. I just thought you might be feeling a little nervous. Some people are terrified of horses but try to pretend that they are not."

"Well I am not," I told her coolly. I had not forgotten her heartless neglect of the Croppers and was in no mood to be overpleasant to Eweretta, despite her apparent overtures of friendship.

"So much the better. I've asked Garrick to saddle up Seraphim for you, by the way. Old Melody is no fun at all and besides she's lame and can't be ridden. You'll find Seraphim an exciting ride I promise you."

She spoke casually as we were walking down the wide, stone staircase to the great hall. Eweretta looked pert and stylish in her green riding habit with its velvet collar and tiny, silver buttons down the front. The severe lines of the top hat she wore contrasted strikingly with her fragile, porcelain prettiness and its gauzy veil drifted gracefully behind her as she moved. Her small hands were buttoned into gauntlet gloves and she carried a leather riding whip with a silver fox-head handle. My own costume was far less attractive: a plain black affair with no trimmings and little to commend it. The contessa, needless to say, had been appalled by its complete lack of elegance and fashion. It had belonged to one of Eweretta's governesses who had hated horses and left it thankfully behind her on her departure. Not having one of my own I had been only too pleased to borrow it and cared little what it looked like.

Garrick, the groom, was waiting patiently outside with three horses—Eweretta's little gray mare, a big-boned chestnut, and a beautiful black thoroughbred. Garrick was holding the first two while, to my dismay, I saw the giant figure of Daniel Duck standing beside the third horse. He was stroking the animal's neck and crooning to it in his weird gibberish. I could not yet master my irrational fear of him, despite Thurza's insistence that he was harmless.

"That's Seraphim," said Eweretta, pointing her riding whip at the black horse. I looked at the thoroughbred with delight. He was a perfect creature with long, delicate legs, a fine, proud head, and a gleaming coat. He tossed his black mane and pawed the ground restlessly, and every inch of him lived up to the meaning of his name—a six-winged angel. One glance had also told me that he would be a very difficult, if not dangerous, ride but I had no fear for myself. It would give me great satisfaction to show Eweretta that I could handle the horse perfectly well, despite her obvious certainty that I could not. I knew that she had deliberately and maliciously plotted for me to ride the most uncontrollable mount in the stables.

I felt sorry for poor Garrick, who eyed me apprehensively, his good-looking face clouded with worry. I guessed that he had been against the whole idea but his blind infatuation for Eweretta had made him easily persuadable.

"I hope you can manage him, miss," he said. "The master's the only one who can handle him proper. He's a real demon if you don't take hold of him right firm from the start." He was looking thoroughly alarmed now. "The master said you were to have Melody but Miss Eweretta insisted you didn't want such an easy ride. I hope you won't tell him, miss, or there'll be the devil to pay and I'll lose my job."

So much for Melody's "lameness," I thought wryly. I managed to reassure the wretched man that I would be able to hold the thoroughbred and promised that the ride would remain a secret. As I spoke I looked across at Eweretta and had the satisfaction of seeing her color deeply and turn away. My growing dislike of her had now turned to a cold anger and I swept past her without a word and went over to Seraphim. Daniel Duck stood at his head, nodding and grinning dementedly at me and mouthing a stream of nonsense. He made frantic gestures and I saw that his usually vacant blue eyes held a gleam of alarm. But it was hopeless to try and understand or communicate with him. I could only smile and steel myself not to shudder and hurt his feelings when he cupped his huge hands to hold my foot as I sprang into the saddle. The black horse danced and pranced a little with quick, sideways steps as I settled myself on his back. His pointed ears twitched back and forth as I spoke to him quietly and stroked his neck. With great reluctance Daniel Duck let go of the bridle and we moved off with a clatter of hoofs. I glanced back once to see him standing there still, hands hanging loose and heavy at his sides, mouth open in dumb dismay. Something moved at one of the windows in the house behind him and caught my eye: the gaunt, black figure of Mrs. Silver floated behind the glass, her face white and ghostly as the moon as she stared downward.

We made our way uphill toward the moors and I felt exhilaration and excitement growing within me. Seraphim moved like a coiled spring, picking his way delicately across the ground so that it felt like riding on air. Eweretta went ahead on her gray mare, the long veiling on her hat streaming out behind her, while Garrick hovered close on my heels as though he expected me to fall off at any moment. I could sense the pent-up power of the animal beneath me, but I felt no fear, only delight at riding once again.

Soon we had left the sheltered slopes behind and reached the open moors. They lay before us, wide and wild, purple with heather and black with strange outcrops of rock that rose desolate and forbidding against the skyline. The wind blew keen and fierce and overhead the lapwings wheeled and circled lazily while curlews mewed their plaintive, mournful cry and a few sheep grazed on the coarse grass. Seraphim began to jig and paw at the turf impatiently, snorting with anticipation at the intoxicating space in front of him.

"Can you hold him, miss?" Garrick leaned across and put his hand on the thoroughbred's bridle. "I doubt you'll be able to stop him if he gets away with you so hang on tight for pity's sake!"

"Don't worry, I'll manage," I shouted back to him against the wind.

Away went Eweretta, cantering fast across the turf; I urged Seraphim forward and he leaped away like some fairy-tale, winged horse, flying over the heather as swift as Pegasus. Garrick on the clumsy chestnut had no chance to keep up with us and we soon overtook Eweretta's little mare. I was out on my own with Seraphim and we traveled together as one. I kept a light hand on the reins and he responded to the slightest touch so that, after a while, I was able to pull him up easily and sat waiting for the other two. Eweretta's face was unusually pale and strained.

"You certainly know how to ride, Alice," she called out with grudging admiration. "I didn't think you'd manage him so well."

I looked at her steadily. "I realize that. You must be rather disappointed that I haven't yet fallen off and broken a few bones."

She said nothing but turned away as Garrick lumbered up on his horse, looking vastly relieved.

"You handle him almost as well as the master," he said. "Carry on like that, miss, and we won't have any trouble."

We rode on at a gentler pace, up along the wild crags, zigzagging our way among the rocks, and splashing across shallow streams where miniature falls of water trickled downhill in little silvery cascades. In winter, I guessed, the streams would turn to torrents and the falls become cataracts, and cold, white snow would drift over the moors and cover the purple of the heather. The skies had become dark and menacing; heavy drops of rain began to fall, sploshing down so wetly that we were all soaked within a few minutes. We turned quickly for home, cantering steadily downhill in the direction of Aysgarth. Pride comes before a fall. I had grown too confident and casual with Seraphim and held him only on a loose rein. Perhaps all might have been well but for the fat red grouse that rose suddenly from the ground in front, flapping clumsily into the air with raucous cries of indignation. Seraphim reared up on his hind legs, twisting and plunging around in terror, and then with a wild lunge he set off at a mad, headlong gallop. I struggled to control him, pulling as hard as I could on wet reins which slipped through my fingers, but it was hopeless to keep on battling with him—all I could do was to cling on to his black mane for dear life and pray I could manage to stay in the saddle. The rain was pouring down, blinding me so that I could scarcely see ahead. Beyond the fact that Seraphim was racing downhill at a terrifying, breakneck speed, I could tell nothing. Had he stumbled and fallen I know I should have been killed.

And then, suddenly, I became conscious of the sound of thudding hoofs behind me. For a moment I thought that it must be Garrick, who had somehow whipped up enough speed from his chestnut horse to catch us, and then, out of the corner of my eye, I caught a glimpse of a dark brown horse—a huge and powerful bay—thundering down on our heels. In a dreamlike daze I saw a dark figure crouched low in the saddle, black cloak streaming out behind like some devil's mantle. A long-fingered hand stretched forward to grasp at Seraphim's bridle, but the black horse was the faster. He drew away from his pursuer and we galloped on as though all the hounds of hell were after us. I was not actually frightened but seemed almost paralyzed in mind and body, able only to sit helpless and exhausted in the saddle, wet and disheveled from wind and rain and very near to tears. My chief thought was of Eweretta's undoubted pleasure at my humiliation and this idea so absorbed me that I had not yet realized the identity of the rider of the big bay horse.

As we reached the bottom of the slopes and began to near the house, I sensed that Seraphim was tiring. He began to slacken his crazy pace a little and it was just enough for the bay horse to draw level once more. Again its rider's hand reached out and the long fingers brushed against the reins but failed to take hold. Alarmed and indignant, Seraphim plunged sideways and then, finding himself directly in the path of a large oak tree, veered sharply to avoid it. The two unexpected movements finally proved my undoing: the first partly dislodged me and the second finished the job. I flew from his back in a graceful arc and landed painfully and heavily on the grass beneath the oak tree. And there I lay in a stunned, ungainly heap, gazing up at the pattern of leaves above my head.

"You stupid, disobedient, half-witted little fool!"

The words floated to me through a vague haze, and plenty more, equally uncomplimentary, followed. I turned my head a little in their direction and a white and furious face swam mistily into view, a black hat and cloak swirling about it. It looked like the devil himself, and very prudently, I chose that moment to faint clean away.

"The master's still in a terrible mood," Thurza confided to me breathlessly a day or two later. Her thin, childlike little face peered at me from the end of the fourposter bed where I lay recovering painfully from concussion and bruising. She looked at me with a mixture of awe and pity, her hands clasped tightly to her chest.

"I've never seen him so angry," she went on, round-eyed with the recollection of it. "He was storming round the house, shouting and yelling so loud we could hear him in the kitchen. And Miss Eweretta was weeping and wailing that it wasn't *her* fault you'd ridden that horse, but he didn't believe her. We all thought he'd strike her to the ground, we did. Garrick's been dismissed and he's right upset about it all, I can tell you. . . ." She paused and stared at me admiringly. "I must say, miss, I think you were ever so brave and clever to ride that great brute of an animal. Nobody but the master can manage him. You being so small and all, miss, it just doesn't seem possible."

"I'm afraid it *wasn't* possible in the end, Thurza," I said dryly. I had listened unhappily to her prattle with an ever-increasing feeling of guilt. I did not wish Eweretta to take the blame. After all, I could have refused to ride Seraphim, but I had chosen, with open eyes, to accept her challenge. As for poor Garrick, it was essential to put things right for him. He must not be dismissed for something that was not his fault.

I threw back the bedcovers. "Will you help me dress, Thurza? I must get up at once."

She looked shocked. "The doctor said you were to lie quiet for at least a week, miss."

"I know, but that's too long to wait I'm afraid, Thurza. I've some very urgent business to attend to. Where is the master now?"

Her eyes widened even more and she moved her hands round and round nervously. "You're not thinking of seeing him now, miss? I shouldn't do that, really I shouldn't. . . ."

"Nonsense, Thurza, he can't eat me, can he? I shall be perfectly all right. Now, where is he? Tell me quickly."

"In his study, I think. But nobody's allowed in there—except Mrs. Silver to dust sometimes. I've never even seen inside the room."

"Then I shall soon be able to describe it to you," I told her calmly, and with far more bravado than I was actually feeling.

Dressing was a slow and tiresome affair; my body was still badly bruised from the fall and my head ached violently. I felt sick and dizzy and unexpectedly weak as Thurza struggled clumsily with fastenings, pulling and tugging this way and that and giving little clucks of disapproval all the while. She made a brave attempt to dress my hair but somehow the pins seemed to fall out almost as fast as she put them in and the finished effect would not have impressed the contessa one bit. I looked pale and hollow-eyed and, to my mind, an exceedingly unattractive and depressing spectacle. Not that I minded particularly for myself but I should have preferred not to be at any disadvantage for the coming confrontation. It would have been nice to be able to sweep into that forbidden study looking tall, elegant, and supremely assured instead of short, dowdy, and terrified.

I walked slowly and unsteadily along the passageway to the head of the staircase, and with shaking knees, descended to the great hall. The rusty pieces of armor hanging crookedly on the walls seemed to mock me as I passed; perhaps I should protect myself from the master's wrath with one of the crossed swords or, better still, the poleax? I managed to smile at the thought and told myself firmly to keep matters in proportion.

The study door, as usual, was firmly shut and it took me some time to find the courage to knock loudly and firmly. I listened carefully, straining my ear against the thick oak, but could hear no response whatever. I knocked again and there was still no sound from within. I grasped the handle and turned it slowly so that the heavy door swung open and I found myself in the master's study.

It was a dull room, somberly furnished in browns and greens. The walls were paneled in dark oak and the windows were small and leaded. But for the amber glass lamp on the desk in the far corner of the room it would have been a very gloomy scene. Its orange glow cast a pleasant, mellow light which, for a moment, beguiled me into thinking that everything might be well, and then I saw him, seated at the desk, behind the lamp, and one glance proved to me the truth of Thurza's words.

He was apparently engrossed in a pile of papers in front of him and though he must have heard me knock and enter, he did not trouble to glance up but studiously and coldly ignored me, continuing to read down the pages as I stood uneasily waiting for him to speak. I dared not interrupt his work and it was almost a relief when, finally, he spoke in icy tones.

"No one is allowed in this room, Miss Chell, I thought you knew that. It seems you are impudent as well as disobedient! However, now that you're here you can oblige me with an explanation of how you came to be riding the most dangerous horse in the stables—against my orders and, deceitfully, in my presumed absence."

He looked up at last and stared at me, his dark eyes almost black with anger. As usual, I began to feel indignant at his overbearing, despotic manner. But I was also beginning to feel giddy from standing too long with an aching head. I moved forward a little.

"Do you mind if I sit down?"

He waved his hand impatiently toward a chair and then drummed his long fingers on the leather surface of the desk as I purposely took some time to settle myself.

"Well?"

"I felt sure I would be able to manage Seraphim," I began . . .

He interrupted sharply. "Seraphim is far too difficult for any woman to handle. You could easily have been killed. It was all too obvious that you could *not* manage him at all."

"I had controlled him perfectly well until a grouse flew up in front of us and startled him, and even then I should never have fallen off if you had not grabbed at his reins and made him swerve. He was getting tired and I know he would have pulled up soon."

I stopped speaking, dismayed. This was not at all how I had planned the conversation to go: I had intended to be all meekness and repentance and now he was looking as black as a thundercloud and glaring at me across the desk.

"Are you suggesting then, Miss Chell, that the whole affair was *my* fault?" he asked with heavy sarcasm.

"No, of course not, sir. And I'm extremely sorry about it. I wanted to explain that it was entirely my idea and wish to ride Seraphim. I have ridden a great deal in the past and was quite accustomed to handling difficult horses. I felt that Melody would be too quiet for me. The blame is mine alone. Eweretta had nothing whatever to do with it and Garrick did everything he could to dissuade me, but I insisted on riding the horse."

He stared at me and I met his gaze steadily. I did not mind about Eweretta but it was imperative for Garrick's sake that he believed me. I was prepared to tell all manner of lies to keep the blame from *him*.

"Are you sure of this?" he asked at last. "I suspected Eweretta of one of her more unpleasant notions of a joke—she was always fond of playing similar tricks on her many governesses. As for Garrick, I have dismissed him. The final responsibility was his. He is in charge of the stables and should never have permitted you near Seraphim."

I moved forward onto the edge of my chair. "Then I must beg you to reconsider your action, sir. I repeat that the blame was entirely mine and my conscience will trouble me to the end of my days unless you have the fairness to reinstate him. After all, no real harm was done. . . ."

"That's only due to good fortune," he replied quietly. "I was riding Lucifer, half brother to Seraphim, when I had my accident. He was an even wilder animal but, like you, I thought I could control him. I was proved wrong, as you can see for yourself. Just reflect on that, Miss Chell. You might have been crippled like me and left a helpless, twisted, repulsive being. *That* is why I am so angry: you are my responsibility and in my care."

He had spoken in a matter-of-fact way that sought no pity; nevertheless I sensed the deep and unending bitterness and regret within him at the accident that had marred his whole life. I felt a compassion that I knew he would have instantly spurned had I dared to express it. Instead I challenged his last remark.

"With respect, sir, I am *not* your responsibility at all and nor am I in your care. You were generous enough to offer me a home with your family, but there your commitment ends. I am responsible for myself."

He gave a faint smile, and twirling a quill pen in his fingers, he remarked:

"When you are not driving me to violent anger, Miss Chell, you amuse me very much. Tell me something. Why do you dislike the thought of being in my care so much? Do you find me completely loathsome?"

I flushed with embarrassment, and was unable to meet his eyes. "Not at all, sir. It's simply that I prefer to feel that I still have a measure of independence."

"Ah yes! Your independence. I had quite forgotten that. You may feel as independent as you like in spirit, Miss Chell, but what about the financial facts of the matter? Have you forgotten those?"

"Not for a moment. But as I told you when we first met, I have been well educated and am fully prepared to find work as a governess and look after myself in the world. No doubt you would welcome my departure, in any case, after the episode with Seraphim. If I could only have your assurance that you will not dismiss Garrick, after all, I should be able to leave with a clear conscience."

He passed a hand over his mouth and looked down at the papers before him for a moment before replying.

"There are times," he said at last, "when you leave me breathless, Miss Chell. No, I should *not* welcome your departure, as you put it; in fact, I should infinitely prefer you to stay. There is no need whatever for you to go rushing off in search of employment, however worthy and commendable your motives. As far as Garrick is concerned, since you speak so persuasively on his behalf, I have decided that he should stay and shall inform him so immediately. Does that satisfy you?"

I sighed with relief. "It does indeed, and thank you, sir. May I ask you one more favor?"

He groaned in mock despair. "Really, Alice Chell, you presume too much on our short and somewhat tempestuous acquaintance. What is it now?"

And so I told him as rapidly and briefly as possible about Mrs.

Cropper and her sick baby, almost afraid to watch his face in
case he rejected my second request out of hand. "The child
needs a doctor desperately and of course there is no hope that
they could afford payment. . . ."

"And you are proposing that I should send a doctor to them?"
he said, his pale face quite impassive. I had no idea what he was
thinking.

"Well, yes. I felt sure you would wish to help save the baby
since its father worked for you. The contessa says you always do
your best for your tenants."

He said wryly: "Is that so? I'm afraid my best, at the moment,
is pitifully inadequate in most cases. I cannot afford to help all
and sundry, Miss Chell, much as I might wish to. However, you
may rest easy so far as the Cropper baby is concerned. The
contessa told me of the child's sickness soon after your accident
—she said you were very worried about it and thought the baby
was dying. I sent the doctor to attend to it and he has reported a
rapid improvement. I don't think you need worry any more."

I suppressed a wild and ridiculous impulse to rush over and
seize his hands in gratitude. It was the first sign that any human
warmth lay beneath his cold and forbidding exterior. But I sat
primly on my chair, hands folded in my lap, and thanked him respectfully.

"I hope you won't mind if I say something else," I went on.

He waved his hand wearily. "Speak on, Miss Chell. What more
is to come, I wonder."

"I can't help worrying about the whole family," I said hurriedly. "Even if the baby is better it won't be long before it falls
ill again, I'm sure. The cottage is in a dreadful state of repair—
the roof leaks badly and all the windows are broken. If something is not done before winter comes I don't see how the
Croppers can survive in such a place. And, not only that—they're
half-starving. Sometimes they live off bread crusts and water for
days on end. . . ."

I stopped, afraid that this time I had gone too far. He was
watching me without expression and I thought it perfectly possible that he was about to launch into savage abuse of me for my
impertinence. After all, his tenants were none of my business. I
waited apprehensively.

"You surprise me more and more, Miss Chell," he said after a moment or two. "Young ladies of eighteen, with your birth and breeding, do not usually bother themselves overmuch with the needs and living conditions of the poor. It is normally below their attention. From what you say I can see that Eweretta has been neglecting her responsibilities once again. A basket of provisions is sent from Aysgarth to the Croppers once a week and I instructed Eweretta to take it personally in the vain hope that it might teach her some sense and to be less discontented with her lot. There is nothing like seeing the far greater misfortunes of others to realize one's own good fortune in life—don't you agree?"

I nodded and he continued. "Perhaps you would take over that duty in my sister's place, Miss Chell. I feel you would be a more reliable go-between. As for the cottage repairs—I had no idea things were so bad. I will send Daniel Duck to do what he can. He is amazingly skillful and will at least carry out the most essential work. And now, is that all?"

"Yes."

"There is nothing else that you are about to demand I attend to?"

"No."

"Good. Then I shall not detain you further." He rose awkwardly from his chair and grasped the ebony stick, which had been propped beside him. "By the way, Miss Chell, what on earth have you done to your hair?"

I put my hand up to my head in astonishment. "My hair?"

"Yes. It looks very strange, you know—rather as if a monkey had tried to arrange it for you. It's all coming down at the back."

"Not a monkey, I'm afraid, but Thurza," I said, trying hurriedly to restore order. Most of the pins she had jabbed so painfully into my head seemed to have fallen out and the more I struggled blindly the more chaotic the situation became until most of my hair was falling about my shoulders. To my vexation I saw that he was laughing.

"That explains it," he said. "Thurza is the clumsiest creature imaginable. I take it you didn't feel well enough to attend to it yourself—you would scarcely have permitted her efforts otherwise, although I must admit that the result is refreshingly informal!"

"I have a slight headache still," I conceded cautiously, not wishing to remind him of the incident that had brought me to his study in the first place. Also I was very piqued by his growing amusement at my expense.

"Then I suggest you return to your room until you are completely recovered. I believe the doctor stipulated at least a week's rest. I admire your stoic sortie on another's behalf, Miss Chell, but it will not help any of us if you delay your return to full health—and it certainly won't help the Croppers."

I saw the sense of his remark and stood up to leave. As I walked toward the door I passed a small painting which hung against the paneled wall and I stopped to look at it closer. It was a portrait in oils, gilt-framed and very old—a picture of a fat, middle-aged monk, dressed in white robes and seated at an oak table. In the background was a high-arched stone window and from it a shaft of light streamed down from above the monk onto the table in front of him. One podgy, dimpled hand lay on the arm of his chair and I noticed that he wore a gold and ruby ring on his little finger—the gold smooth and gleaming, the jewel blood-red and egg-shaped. The other hand was stretched out toward the glittering object that stood on the table, bathed in the light from the window: a magnificent golden cross. This was the portrait of Abbot Haby that Eweretta had spoken of. I had almost forgotten its existence and now, for the first time, I was looking at the legendary Cross of Aysgarth. It was far larger than I had imagined—fully two feet high and wonderfully worked in an elaborate tracery of gold, delicate and light in its form and yet heavy with its priceless burden of jewels. I had never seen so many clustered together—diamonds, emeralds, rubies, sapphires, and huge milk-white pearls blazed in a dazzling spectrum in their golden setting. Eweretta had not exaggerated in her description.

"What do you think of him?" His voice spoke near my shoulder and with a jolt I realized that he had moved over from his desk to stand close behind me. I had been so absorbed in the painting that I had not noticed. He was uncomfortably close and his height and broad shoulders were disconcertingly overpowering. I moved a little to one side away from him. He did not appear to notice.

"How does the good Abbot Haby strike you?" he asked again.

I looked once more at the portly monk in the picture. His pale, gooseberry-green eyes stared down directly into my own, his face was round and ruddy with good eating and good living, and treble-chinned, so that the fat folds of flesh melted into the collar of his robe. There was a hint of a smile about the corners of his mouth that softened the strict piety of his pose.

"He looks a rather greedy and self-indulgent man," I said thoughtfully, "but a very human and sympathetic sort of person. I feel I should have liked him very much had I known him."

"My own sentiments exactly, Miss Chell. I have often thought that it would be nice to meet him."

I was silent for a while, contemplating the portrait of the monk who had been dead for three hundred years and yet whose presence seemed somehow to linger on in the minds of the living at Aysgarth. Did he also perhaps walk the long, empty passageways of the house or haunt the crumbling remains of his abbey? My imagination was beginning to run riot and I moved firmly away from the painting.

"It's a beautiful cross," I said politely.

"The fabulous Cross of Aysgarth? Yes, it is magnificent isn't it. I wish I shared my sister's conviction that it still exists—hidden somewhere by the abbot. I used to believe so once but I have grown too cynical I'm afraid for such fairy tales. Now, you are a romantic, Miss Chell, tell me your opinion in the matter. Do you share Eweretta's view or do you think, like me, that the cross has long since vanished—broken into little bits by thieves and disposed of jewel by jewel . . . ?"

"I'm not sure what I think. I hope for your family's sake that one day it will be found, but it seems unlikely. Mr. Paige doesn't think so."

"Ah, Mr. Paige. I had almost forgotten him. Of course, he might be expected to know best on the subject. Tell me, Miss Chell, what do you think of Philip Paige?"

"Think of him?"

He moved away a little and leaned against the paneling in a weary manner. His face looked very white against the dark wood behind him and the lines were etched deep around his eyes and mouth.

"Yes. How do you view him as a person? Do you like him or

dislike him? I have seen you walking outside with him so I assume you find him at least amenable?"

Maddeningly I blushed again, but this time it was from pique rather than embarrassment. It was annoying and unnerving to find that I was spied upon. I had not reckoned on him watching me from some window; it was bad enough that Mrs. Silver peered and pried in every corner but to think that *he* was observing me was intolerable.

"He is pleasant company certainly and takes pains to make himself agreeable," I replied stiffly.

"Which I do not, of course."

"I did not say that."

"It doesn't matter whether you did or did not. It's what you meant. I was simply interested in your opinion of him, Miss Chell, and if you find him acceptable then so much the better. There is little enough to amuse and entertain at Aysgarth these days."

He turned away from me abruptly, as cold and distant as ever. "That is all then, Miss Chell. We have nothing more to discuss, I think, and I trust this is the last time you will invade this room."

I left the study feeling oddly disturbed. Past and present mingled together mysteriously in this house and it seemed to me that its master belonged more easily to the past. It was not difficult to imagine him ruling the roost at Aysgarth in medieval times. I thought of the Miles Metcalfe who had lived here three hundred years ago—the Abbot Haby's friend and benefactor—and I wondered if he had resembled in any way his dark and arrogant descendant.

◎◎◎

The doctor's advice had been wise as I soon found later on that day. I had tried to stay up and dressed in my room but my head ached so badly that in the end I was forced to return to bed. The altercation in the study had taken its toll and it was several more days before I felt well enough to get up again. In the meantime I lay downcast and depressed in my fourposter, listening to the never-ending cawing of the rooks and remembering everything that had once been happy and cheerful in my life —all of it vanished, seemingly forever. Sometimes I half-slept, dozing confusedly so that reality and dreams merged and I was no longer sure which was which. Sometimes I fancied I heard footsteps outside my room at night and other strange sounds coming from somewhere within the house—ghostly creakings and tappings that made me burrow more deeply beneath the bedclothes and cover my ears with my hands.

And then, one night when at last I was feeling better and lay wakeful and clearheaded in the darkness listening to the hooting of the owls and the moan of the wind in the elm trees, I heard again the footsteps that I had supposed existed only in my fevered imagination. I listened in terror to the stealthy creak of boards in the passage outside my room and knew that someone was prowling in the darkness of the house. It took me a while to find the courage to leave the warmth and safety of the fourposter to investigate, but I knew that I must. It was better to do that than speculate for long nights to come on the nature and identity of the owner of the footsteps. I slid quickly from the bed and crept barefoot across to the door. The old hinges squeaked as I turned the handle and pulled the door open toward me.

At first the passage looked deserted. Moonlight streamed in through the narrow, stone-mullioned windows and cast a pale, white light along its length. And then, something moved suddenly in the shadows and a figure flitted swiftly and silently away and was lost in the inky blackness at the far end of the corridor. I had only a brief glimpse of it before it vanished and could not have said whether it was man, woman, or some formless spirit from the past . . .

"Surely you should be in bed, Miss Chell."

The voice startled me so badly that I nearly screamed with fright. Mrs. Silver stood close behind me, a guttering candle held in her hand, her night robes trailing gray and witchlike about her. Above the flame her face was without expression. She spoke again.

"You should be in bed, Miss Chell. You have not been well."

"Something disturbed me. I thought I heard footsteps outside my room and just now I'm sure I saw someone at the end of the passage."

Her dark eyes glittered in the candle's flame. "You were mistaken, Miss Chell. There was no one or I should have seen them myself—I know everything that goes on in this house. You have been feverish and your imagination has played you tricks."

I was about to protest but then realized that it was pointless: whatever, or whoever, had been outside my room had now vanished completely. There was nothing to be done but bid the housekeeper good night and return meekly to my bed. It was only later that I asked myself why Mrs. Silver should have been wandering about the house in the middle of the night. Had she too heard something sinister or did she prowl and pry during the dark hours as well as by day?

It was near dawn when at last I fell into a restless sleep. When Thurza came into the room soon after daybreak I knew instinctively that something dreadful had happened. She stood beside my bed, white-faced and agitated.

I sat up at once. "What is it, Thurza? Tell me quickly what's the matter?"

She stared at me, her childlike eyes wide with shock and horror. "It's Mrs. Silver, miss . . ."

"What about her?"

"She's *dead*, miss."

"Dead? That's impossible! I saw her only a few hours ago outside my room. How could she be dead?"

Thurza swallowed and with an effort said: "She fell down the stairs, miss. I found her lying at the bottom of the stone steps in the great hall, first thing this morning. She was still in her night robe, miss, and her eyes were open and staring up at me. . . . It was such a shock, you see, miss, I don't think I'll ever be able to forget it. . . ."

She broke down at last into a pitiful fit of weeping and her thin shoulders shook violently under her lilac print dress. I put my arms round her and tried my best to comfort her, and all the while, as I murmured soothing words, I thought of the gray, witchlike figure of the dead housekeeper as she glided through the dark corridors of the house, the flickering candle in her hand probing the unknown shadows ahead of her. And I asked myself whether she had fallen accidentally down that long, cold stone staircase or whether in fact she had been pushed by someone or something. . . .

CHAPTER VI

The contessa made no secret whatever of her satisfaction at being free of Mrs. Silver. She was outspoken on the subject as always.

"Not that I actually wished the woman *dead*, or even ill for that matter," she said to me as I sat in her room a day or two after the tragedy. "But I feel a great deal happier now that she's gone from this house. It will be a relief not to have her sour, ugly face glaring at me round every corner. Of course, I'd sooner she'd left quietly in the normal manner than have all this fuss with doctors and inquests and so on. . . . It's very inconsiderate of her to have done anything so careless and stupid. Poor Miles has been most upset."

It was true that her great-nephew had been looking even grimmer than usual. His temper had been appalling and I had kept out of the way as much as possible while he dealt with the necessary formalities that followed the housekeeper's death. The doctor had been summoned immediately and in his opinion Mrs. Silver had died of a severe skull injury incurred in her terrible fall down that long stone staircase. Later, the coroner's court had returned a verdict of accidental death. Mrs. Silver had, apparently, no living relatives left in the world, or none that came forward or could be discovered, so she was buried in a windswept and lonely corner of the churchyard up the hill from Aysgarth. It seemed to me, as I watched her coffin being carried from the house, a pathetic and sad end to a bitter, unhappy life.

For many days after that my thoughts were full of the dead housekeeper. I felt as though somehow and in some way she was still present at Aysgarth. As I walked down the gloomy passages of the house I half-expected to see her gaunt figure materialize out of the shadows in ghostly fashion, and as I descended the sweep of the staircase to the great hall I saw, in my mind's eye, her thin, gray form tumbling hideously over and over down the cold, stone steps to her lonely death. . . .

It had seemed obvious to everyone that she had missed her footing in the dark that night and toppled dramatically from the top to the bottom of the stairway—an unlucky and unfortunate accident. Despite my uneasy misgivings, I persuaded myself at last that this must be the simple explanation. I had imagined both the footsteps and the shadowy figure at the end of the passageway. After all, Mrs. Silver herself had insisted that I was mistaken and surely nothing would have escaped those sharp eyes and ears. It had been nothing more than an overfanciful imagination from a mind still suffering from the effects of concussion.

Thurza, once she had recovered from the shock, seemed quite as relieved as the contessa that Mrs. Silver no longer ruled the roost in the servants' hall.

"It's that much nicer without her, miss," she said, echoing the contessa's feelings one morning a week later. "She had a cruel tongue and she was always on at me and Mrs. Bizzy and poor Ann too—Ann used to cry all day long. She never could seem to please Mrs. Silver somehow."

I had never seen the little scullery maid who was apparently even younger than Thurza, and had only caught brief glimpses of the cook, Mrs. Bizzy. I had never penetrated the dark labyrinth of the kitchen wing at Aysgarth. I knew that the passage to it led from the lower end of the great hall, but whenever I had been tempted to explore and make the acquaintance of the other servants, Mrs. Silver had seemed to appear from nowhere to stand and stare at me, an expression of cold scorn on her face. I knew very well that she would disapprove of any such venture and lacked the courage to run the gauntlet of her increased contempt. From the moment of my arrival I was well aware that she had categorized me instantly as a penniless nobody, unworthy of consideration or respect. I was not one bit surprised to learn that the wretched little scullery maid had feared her. And the endless work involved in keeping a house the size of Aysgarth even partly clean must be a nightmare struggle for the small handful of servants. In better times there must have been a staff of fifteen at least.

"I do so hope that the master finds a decent housekeeper," Thurza said suddenly. "Cook says that Mrs. Silver was only employed because nobody else answered the advertisement. But she didn't care anything at all for the place—I think she hated it. She was always telling us that it was a waste of time to bother much with it, that it would soon fall down altogether and the sooner the better. I didn't like to hear that, seeing how long the family's been living here. . . . Now, if someone came who really *cared*, if you know what I mean, miss, I'm sure everything could be managed ever so much better. I'd like to see that happen here at Aysgarth. . . ."

I was deeply impressed by her loyalty and simple goodheartedness, and I felt ashamed of the fact that I had, at times, shared some of Mrs. Silver's feelings about the old house. It had not occurred to me until then that Thurza, born and bred in the locality, might be very fond of Aysgarth and hope for its salvation. But now, as I listened to her and watched the wistfulness on her face, an idea was suddenly born in my mind which began to grow and grow of its own accord. Almost before I realized it, I had decided to act—quickly and before I lost the courage.

I found him outside the stables, standing talking to Garrick in the cobbled yard and leaning heavily on the ebony stick. As I approached, he half-turned toward me and his black locks blew wildly about his face in the wind, giving him an even more satanic look. He said nothing as I walked toward him but regarded me coolly.

"May I speak with you a moment, sir?"

He lifted his shoulders impatiently. "What about, Miss Chell? You can see that I'm busy."

I stood my ground, but unfortunately the wind gusting down from the moors and the loud, incessant cawing of the rooks overhead in the elm trees compelled me to shout to make myself heard.

"Can we go indoors for a moment? It's difficult to speak to you here."

He looked annoyed. "It's too far for me to drag myself back to

the house, Miss Chell, even for you. If you insist on this interview I suppose we could go into the stables."

I followed him into the warmth and peace of the stables where
the only sounds were of horses munching contentedly and the
rustle of clean straw as they moved quietly round in their stalls.
Seraphim's noble head nudged over the half door near us to
whinny a gentle greeting.

"Well, come on, Miss Chell. Tell me what is on your mind."

I told him plainly and without deviation. He listened in silence, frowning deeply, and when I had finished speaking he
stared down at me for a moment and said harshly:

"Out of the question, Miss Chell. The role of housekeeper
would be quite unsuitable to someone of your breeding. It's a ridiculous suggestion and a waste of my time proposing it."

"I don't see why." I could feel myself provoked, as usual, into
indignation and anger by his cold arrogance. I struggled for control and continued calmly: "It may take you some time to find a
replacement for Mrs. Silver. At least let me do what I can to help
run the household smoothly in the meantime. There is such a lot
that could be done, you know, to improve matters. . . ."

"I am well aware of that. I cannot imagine, however, that you
could care enough about Aysgarth to attempt the impossible."

"It's not impossible to clean things up a little and improve the
quality of the meals served . . . and it would give me the chance
to be useful for a change instead of being a mere burden."

His expression softened a fraction. "I don't think I could ac-
cuse you of being that, Miss Chell . . . a thorn in my side sometimes, perhaps, but not a burden. Very well. You may amuse
yourself by taking charge of the housekeeper's duties for a while
if you wish, but I think you will find it a far harder task than you
so innocently imagine. It will not be long, in any case, before I
find a proper replacement. . . . Yes, play at housekeeper by all
means, Miss Chell. . . . Now that I have considered the matter
further I can see its advantages since it will occupy you
sufficiently to keep you out of my way."

And with that brutal remark he turned away and moved painfully across toward Seraphim's stall where he stood, back to me,
stroking the animal's sleek black neck and speaking to him in
low and gentle tones.

I left the stables quickly before he could change his mind and also before I lost control of my tongue and said things I might later regret. I did not want him to have the satisfaction of seeing how much he had annoyed me with his churlish manner, and he had done so so successfully that I was trembling with indignation. A horse, it seemed, rated more politeness and consideration. Why bother with the wretched, tumbledown place, I asked myself angrily as I hurried across the cobbled yard? Why should I care what became of it? I was a fool to concern myself with its fate when its owner was apparently indifferent and preoccupied only with his own bitterness. And yet, some deep, inner compulsion seemed to urge me to continue my plan: it was almost as though the old house had cast its spell on me. I stopped and stared up at the gray stone walls and suddenly, in my imagination, I could picture it restored to its former glory—roofs mended, gutters replaced, chimneys straightened, masonry cleaned and repaired, new glass in the broken windows . . . The front steps were rebuilt and whitened, the gravel drive weeded and swept, and, beyond the house, were close-clipped green lawns and neat flower beds and a rose garden sheltered from the wind that blew down from the moors. And then I shivered in that wind as it whistled round me, blowing my skirts and tugging at the fringes of my shawl. The image faded and the house stood silent before me, as gray and desolate as ever.

In the days that followed I set about my self-appointed task with a determination to do everything possible to improve the household affairs. I forgot my indignation and thought only of the challenge.

As a first step I made the acquaintance, at last, of Mrs. Bizzy, the cook. She was enormously fat and blowzy with a coarse, red face and toothless grin, and Ann, the little scullery maid, was so shrinking and shy that she was almost invisible, scuttling into corners like some frightened animal. The kitchen quarters were as dank and depressing as I had feared: flagstone floors echoed hollowly to the click-clack of the cook's wooden pattens as she waddled ahead of me down a maze of damp-smelling passages. I inspected pantry, stillroom, scullery, larder, laundry room, and empty storerooms—all dirty, dusty, and unswept, and my heart sank as I looked at the neglect of years. The kitchen itself was a large, gloomy room with a greasy range set in the old, open fireplace, a cracked stone sink, and an enormous brown-painted dresser covering most of one wall and festooned with a chaotic jumble of plates, cups, pots, pans, lids, spoons, knives, mops, and jugs. There was a large wooden table in the center of the room, covered with odds and ends of food—stale bread, moldering cheese, a pitcher of sour milk—and, beside the range, a high-backed wooden chair where the cook evidently spent most of her time. I looked around me and up at the beamed ceiling where thick, black cobwebs hung undisturbed, like battle banners, and I no longer wondered at the congealed, unappetizing meals served in the dining room: the miracle was that they were even edible.

I called a meeting of all the servants—Mrs. Bizzy, old Unwin, Thurza, and Ann, explained carefully to them that I was to act as housekeeper for the time being, outlined my plans, and asked them for their help. "If we could all work together, I'm sure we could improve things so much," I said, hoping I looked even more confident than I really felt. As I surveyed the little group I began to realize that I might indeed find it all far more difficult than I had imagined. The cook was obviously slatternly and lazy, Unwin, the butler, looked so frail and old as he stood gaping at me with trembling hands and watery eyes, and the scullery maid was scarcely strong enough to be of much use. Only Thurza and I would be capable of any real hard work. . . . I sighed inwardly and wondered if there was any point in continuing. . . .

There was a violent crash as the door flew open. Cups and plates jangled on the dresser as Daniel Duck strode into the kitchen and stood before me grinning widely and nodding in a desperate, pleading way.

"He wants to help you, miss," whispered Thurza beside me. "He's that strong he could really be useful and he wouldn't do no harm, I promise."

Oddly, I found that I could now face this strange creature without fear. I saw the eagerness in his brilliant blue eyes and realized that, despite his crazy mind, he shared with Thurza a deep love of Aysgarth, and with his help so much might be possible. . . .

I moved toward him and held out my hand. He grabbed it eagerly, crushing my fingers between his huge palms; I struggled to control a *frisson* of revulsion and to leave my hand calmly in his but his grip was so fierce that tears of pain came into my eyes.

Thurza moved forward. "Let go, Daniel," she said quietly. "You're hurting Miss." She stretched forward, and prizing open his first firmly, released my bruised fingers. The big man dropped his arms to his sides and backed away, hanging his head miserably and wagging it from side to side, eyes downcast and ashamed. With an effort, I smiled at him reassuringly and he cheered up instantly, nodding and winking at me like some mechanical toy.

Old Unwin spoke: "I shall be of little use to you, miss, I'm afraid." He held out his hands which were twisted and bent with rheumatism. "I'm no good for work any more and that's the truth."

"On the contrary, Unwin, you will be the greatest help," I told him. "You can tell me where everything is kept and what is to be done. I know very little about household affairs and shall need your advice."

He shook his head anxiously. "My memory's not what it was but I'll do my best. . . ."

"What he can't tell you, I can," said Mrs. Bizzy with surprising enthusiasm. She had looked exceedingly doubtful about the whole prospect at first but had now evidently decided to give it her support. I realized, with relief, that she was basically a well-meaning, cheerful soul. It was just as well: a great deal needed to be done in the kitchen quarters and I should achieve little without her co-operation.

I went over to the little scullery maid, who had retreated to a dark corner beyond the dresser and was watching the proceedings with rounded eyes. I bent down toward her.

"Will you help us too, Ann?"

"She'll do as she's told, miss," said Mrs. Bizzy firmly, and settled the matter.

Looking back, I can see that my life began to change from that point in time. It took on a meaning and an objective instead of being a mere idle passing of the hours. I now had something worth while to do. I rose from my bed very early and looked forward to the busy day ahead. There was so much to be done: rooms to be swept and cleaned properly for the first time for years, furniture to be polished, windows and curtains to be washed, carpets to be taken up and beaten and countless cobwebs brushed away. Our strangely assorted little team moved steadily through the house with mops and dusters and brooms, while Daniel Duck shifted and lifted the heaviest furniture to and fro, carrying solid oak as though it weighed only a matter of ounces, and grinning and jabbering happily all the time.

Mrs. Bizzy accepted the onslaught on the kitchen quarters good-naturedly and waddled about the place, giving friendly encouragement in her deep, fruity voice while Thurza scrubbed and tidied the dresser and scoured the sink and table, and Ann cleaned and blackened the old range, her thin arms working away in frenzy. I left Daniel to sweep away the black cobwebs from the beams and went into the storerooms. Mice squeaked and scampered for cover as I sorted through the sacks of flour, oats, and sugar, examined salt and spices, coffee and tea, dried fruits and preserved—ejecting the rancid, moldy, or contaminated items and noting the necessary replacements. I had little knowledge of cookery or household requirements—I had had no need to for even in the rented lodgings in Clapham the landlady had always prepared meals for my mother and me—but common sense and Mrs. Bizzy both came to my rescue and a comprehensive list of urgently needed goods was drawn up.

"Of course," said the cook, seeking exoneration, "the master won't allow more than a pittance to be spent in the kitchen these days. Now, if I could spend what I liked you'd be eating the best dishes you've ever tasted; but why should I bother myself, miss, I says to myself, when all I can make is the same old things all the time. It ain't worth making the effort, if you understand me. . . . Things was very different in the old days, I can tell you. When the late master was alive, and had company, there'd be twenty dishes or more at dinner, soups, fish, oyster patties, four entrées, two or three roasts, sweets, desserts, ices. . . ."

I cut short her reminiscences hastily: "All the items on this list are absolutely essential, Mrs. Bizzy, and I shall see that you get them."

She eyed me with some amusement. "I doubt you'll have the master's approval for all that lot, but still, you never know."

In fact I had to take on myself the responsibility of ordering everything needed since there was no opportunity of seeking his approval or otherwise. He had not been seen for several days, failing, as before, to appear even for meals.

"He's bad again, miss," Unwin confided unhappily. "The pain's terrible at the moment and there's nothing to be done but wait for it to pass."

I saw from the sadness in his eyes that he was deeply upset.

"Is there nothing that can be done to help him, Unwin? Surely the doctor could prescribe some drug at least?"

He shook his head wearily. "He won't have the doctors near him any more, miss. He says he had too much of them and none of them ever did him any good at all. The only remedy for him is brandy, I regret to say, miss. It dulls the pain enough to make it bearable, he says, and, for the rest, all he asks is to be left alone. . . . It never seems right to me—shut up in his room all by himself with not a soul to comfort him."

"Knowing your master," I said dryly, "I should think anyone who did try would probably get their head bitten off."

He smiled a little. "You may be right, miss. He's not the easiest of men, I'll admit that, and he hates pity more than anything. But just the same, it doesn't seem right. . . ."

Privately I agreed with him, but what could *I* do about it. I knew it would be hopeless to try to interfere in any way, and even if I found the courage to seek him out in the east wing of the house, I could only meet with anger and rejection. He had shown all too clearly how much I irritated and wearied him, so how could I possibly be of any help or comfort. And yet, as I went about my work, I could not prevent myself from thinking of that lonely and tormented figure who had shut himself away from the world.

I had not been in the eastern end of the house since the first evening of my arrival when I had been lost in its frightening maze of old passageways. Only Unwin was permitted there and, occasionally, Thurza to sweep and clean as best she could.

"And real gloomy it is too," she told me once, with a shiver. "It gives me gooseflesh just to be there for a little while—the rooms are so dark and creepy. I'd swear there are ghosts: I've *felt* them, miss, all around about me. I've never seen anything, mind, but I know they're there."

I believed her, remembering my own experience when I was lost in the darkness there. "But not *evil* ghosts, Thurza," I suggested.

"Not exactly, I suppose," she admitted. "But just the same it frightens me. I don't like that part of the house."

Apart from the east wing, there was still a great deal of the house that I had never seen. Many of the rooms, both upstairs and downstairs, had been locked for several years and although I was now in possession of Mrs. Silver's heavy bunch of keys, I left these undisturbed. I did not like to pry merely for the sake of curiosity and since there was no question of the rooms being opened up and used, there was no point in investigating them.

We could do little to improve the great hall beyond clearing away as much of the cobwebs and dust as could be reached, and washing the grimy windows so that they let in a little more light. With Daniel's help the rusty armor was fetched down from the walls, cleaned and polished and replaced straight and shining once more. The threadbare banners that hung above the minstrel gallery were too fragile to be moved lest they fall to pieces. I looked round at the bare stone flags and cold emptiness despondently.

"Is there no other furniture at all in any of the locked rooms?" I asked Unwin.

"None that I can remember, miss. It all had to be sold."

A voice spoke sharply behind us: "My brother forbids those rooms to be opened. Really, Alice, you are taking too much on yourself!"

Eweretta stood on the staircase. Dressed in pale green muslin, she looked as enchantingly pretty as always but there was the usual sulky, petulant look about her eyes and mouth, and this time, a good deal of spiteful ill-temper. Since the accident with Seraphim she had avoided me completely; I watched uneasily as she drifted on down the stone steps, the green gown trailing behind her, one small, white hand touching the banister. Unwin had shuffled away and the great hall was empty but for ourselves. She reached the bottom of the stairs and came toward me, staring at me with wide, blue eyes.

"I don't understand, Alice, why you should concern yourself

with Aysgarth. After all, it belongs to the Metcalfes and has nothing whatever to do with you . . . there have been Metcalfes here for over seven hundred years. You have only been here for a few weeks and it is not your real home."

"I am aware of that."

"So why do you care about it when it is not your affair? Why have you taken it upon yourself to do all this dreary work about the place?"

"I might as well be useful as not."

"Exactly! Except that *I* think there is more to your motives than that. Do you know what I think?"

"I'm afraid I have no idea."

She gave a little pirouette round on the stone floor, the green muslin skirts of her dress floating prettily out around her feet, and then she tapped a finger thoughtfully to her lips. She seemed almost playful but I knew Eweretta better than to be deceived.

"I believe, my dear Alice, that you picture yourself as mistress of Aysgarth one day. You think that if you work hard enough and make yourself useful enough then, with a little good fortune and subtle persuasion, my brother might, just possibly, be mad enough to marry you. But let me tell you, Alice Chell, that you are quite, quite wrong. My brother may be a cripple but he is still a Metcalfe and Master of Aysgarth and he would never marry a plain, penniless nobody like you. If ever he marries, it will be to someone rich and beautiful like Catherine Benton and *then* Aysgarth will really be just as it always was when my father was alive. . . ."

I gazed at her in horror, speechless with shock and indignation.

"Have you nothing to say in reply then? I see that I have guessed correctly. I shall warn Miles to be on his guard against you."

At last I found my voice and it trembled with fury. I caught at her arm as she made to pass by me. "You'll do no such thing, Eweretta! What you have suggested is monstrous and utterly untrue!"

"You mean you do not hope to marry my brother?"

I took a deep breath. "I wouldn't marry him if he were the last man on this earth. Not because he is a cripple but because he's the rudest, most arrogant, and most unpleasant man I've ever had the misfortune to meet. . . ."

From somewhere above us, in the shadows of the minstrel gallery, there was a faint sound, the creaking of wood or the sigh of the wind—I was too preoccupied to be more than half-aware of it. Eweretta drew her arm from my grasp disdainfully. To my surprise she seemed almost relieved, when I had expected her to defend her brother.

"I am glad to hear you say that, Alice," she said, and for once she looked surprisingly sincere. "Not that what you say is true, of course, but I would prefer you to think that it is so."

And without another word she left me. I sank down on the cold, stone steps of the stairway and the tears which had threatened began to fall, silent and unchecked, down my cheeks as I sat and stared blankly at the empty cavern before me. The clean windows, the shining armor, the swept floor—all had lost their pleasure and purpose and I began to wish with all my heart that I had never taken on the role of housekeeper, and most of all, that I had never come to Aysgarth in the first place. . . .

It was the contessa who came to my rescue with her practical common sense. She had watched my efforts with a mixture of approval and amusement.

"We shall go out for a drive," she announced firmly one morning. "You have done quite enough for the time being and I am beginning to feel extremely neglected. You will accompany me on a short tour of the countryside. There is no one worth calling on but we can amuse ourselves nonetheless and, for once, the weather is clement."

It was indeed: the gray clouds and cold wind of the past few days had given way to warm sunshine and blue skies.

"I very seldom drive out these days," the contessa remarked as we descended, with care, the dilapidated steps outside the front door. "I find the Yorkshire weather most unpleasant—it's nearly always too cold and windy for me to set foot out of doors. Now, in Italy it was a pleasure to go out instead of a penance."

"Except perhaps when it was too hot. . . ."

The contessa sniffed. "The heat was occasionally somewhat op-

pressive but that is infinitely preferable to being forever too cold,
in my opinion. I do not, as you know, child, live up in this barbaric county from choice but from necessity—any more than I
drive out in a ramshackle old carriage, such as we have now before us, other than because there is none other available."

The carriage was, it was true, old and very shabby, but I recognized at a glance that it had been beautifully built and must
once have looked extremely fine. The dark green paint was dull
and scratched, the metal rusty, and the red cushions torn and
faded, but there was still an unmistakable air of quality and elegance about it and the pair of bays that stood patiently in the
shafts were immaculately groomed, while Garrick himself looked
impressively handsome in his green and gold livery.

"We look very passable," I said as we set off, bumping and
jolting over the potholes and ruts in the driveway.

"We'd look a good deal better if you had not worn that dreadful bonnet," was the tart response. "Or that dress either. Both of
them are impossibly out of fashion and lemon yellow is *not* your
color, my dear—you should know that by now. It makes you
look positively consumptive and does nothing at all for your
complexion. You should wear shades of blue to bring out the
color of your eyes: violet eyes are, after all, somewhat unusual
and you can ill afford to overlook your good points."

I smiled to myself, not the least offended by her. I was used to
the contessa's blunt comments and I found her briskness the perfect antidote to the mood of dejection and self-pity engendered
by Eweretta. She herself was faultlessly attired in black and
white silk and wore a fine straw bonnet trimmed with black satin
and adorned with glossy black plumes, which ruffled gently in
the light breeze as we drove along. In one gloved hand she held
a white parasol, its wooden handle exquisitely carved with
flowers, the frilled silk and lace shielding her from the hot sun.
Altogether she was an imposing sight and a tribute to Signorina
Frugoni's skill. As we passed through the gateway at the top of
the drive, Garrick reigned in the horses and inquired politely
where he should take us.

"Wherever you like," replied the contessa. "It all looks much
the same to me; pretty enough I'll grant, but not a patch on
Italy."

To me she was wrong. I had never seen Italy in my life but nothing could have looked more beautiful than the dales of Yorkshire that day. The lane wound its way peacefully along the shady valley and all around us were the gentle green slopes, crisscrossed by dry-stone walls and dotted with grazing sheep. There were a few old cottages, thick-walled and slate-roofed, and a lonely farmhouse or two huddled at the foot of the fells. We clattered across an ancient, single-arched bridge beside an old mill and the stream cascaded downhill beneath us, plunging on over its steep and rocky bed in a sparkling froth of white foam. I watched it as we passed and felt a strange and unaccountable affinity with it all that made me wish that things might have been different—my godfather still alive and Aysgarth not a sad, neglected ruin.

The harvest was in progress and the August sun shone down on fields of ripe corn. The reapers toiled away with their scythes, swinging the long blades in wide rhythmical strokes through the golden sea before them, their faces ruddy above their white smocks. The women and girls walked behind them, binding the cut corn into fat sheaves to be stooked together. They looked hot and exhausted, hair escaping from their bonnets to cling damply to foreheads, cotton dresses limp and dusty. When the field was finished a sign would be put by the gate for the gleaners to come and gather what little was left; widows, old women, and little children would scavenge eagerly among the stubble to pick up the few ears of corn they might find. I thought of the Croppers and determined to visit them again as soon as I possibly could.

The horses jogged on in perfect unison, ears pricked, harnesses jingling pleasantly. The lane began to wind upward, climbing the hillside until the view was clear around us for several miles. In the distance I saw a castle, a magnificent, fairy-tale place of castellated walls and pinnacled turrets, clinging dizzily to a huge outcrop of rock high above the dale.

"What is that place, Contessa?"

She followed my glance and snorted disparagingly. "That, my dear, is Castle Benton, ancestral home of Lord Benton and his thoroughly selfish daughter, Catherine. He is a widower and a very slobbery, fat little man—you would not care for him at all, I assure you. She, as you may remember me saying, was once engaged to my great-nephew—before his accident, of course—

when she saw that he would be crippled for life she changed her mind about marrying him. Mind you, I've heard she still has a hankering after him . . . that's her misfortune. After what she made him suffer she deserves a little discomfort herself."

I felt it was not for me to comment and said mildly: "It's a wonderful castle—almost like something out of a fairy story."

"That depends on whether you like vulgarity and ostentation —not to mention desecration. *I* don't. It *was* once a very fine old place before the present Lord Benton inherited and made all those perfectly hideous alterations and additions—all those turrets and curlicues and bits and bobs stuck on all over it are his work, and inside the furnishings are a nightmare of bad taste. He has too much money and no idea how to use it. Sometimes I thank God that Catherine has never got her hands on Aysgarth; heaven knows what horrors would have been perpetrated by now. I'd sooner the old house fell down—which it probably will soon if something doesn't happen to save it." She sighed and patted my hand absently. "What a pity *you* are not a little heiress, my dear."

"Me?"

She smiled. "Yes. Then you could marry Miles and restore Aysgarth together to its former glories. It would all be most satisfactory. It used to be a lovely house once, you know, and could be again and I can see from all your efforts that it has begun to mean something to you. It's all such a pity. . . . If you were rich and beautiful and Miles a less bitter and difficult man, it might have been possible. Now, no girl in her right mind, rich or poor, would put up with him."

She had turned her head away and was speaking half to herself, and to my great relief, did not seem to expect an answer. I could think of nothing to say to such strange and alarming speculations—except to agree wholeheartedly about her great-nephew. However, I did not wish to offend her and remained silent. For the rest of the drive we talked only of trivialities and I carefully avoided mention of the Bentons or their castle again.

I did not forget the Cropper family and that afternoon I went to visit them again, taking with me a basket piled high with provisions, including a large joint of smoked bacon and a meat pie which I had persuaded Mrs. Bizzy to cook for me. She had shaken her head in disapproval.

"You'll spoil them, miss, and no mistake. They ain't used to all this food and it'll do them no kindness in the end."

I could see that she was quite undisturbed by the thought of people going hungry; she was a kindly soul but the poor and destitute did not trouble her conscience. She accepted them as an inevitable fact of life and forgot about them. But I could not do so. I could and should help the Croppers.

The basket was very heavy and the long walk across the fields in the hot sunshine was tiring. I was glad when the cottage came into sight and grateful for the cool of the horse chestnut trees as I walked the last part of the way beneath their shady branches. I half-expected to be shied at again and to see the boy Dobbin's elfin face grinning down at me through the leaves, but there was no sign of him. Two of the children played in the dust near the door, absorbed in a game with smooth pebbles. I saw at once that several improvements had been made to the cottage: tiles had been replaced, broken windowpanes and door hinges mended, and the honeysuckle cut back tidily. I knocked and went indoors.

Mrs. Cropper was sitting in the broken chair, holding the baby in her arms and singing softly to him. I saw immediately that the child was better: his color was healthy and he slept contentedly. His mother, seeing me, put a finger to her lips and carried him over to the wooden cradle on the floor in a corner of the room. I put the basket on the wobbly table and looked about me: the walls had been whitewashed and some attempt had been made to sweep the floor. Mrs. Cropper's eyes were on the basket and I began to unpack the contents and spread them on the table.

She passed a tongue over her thin lips. "We'll be right glad of that lot," she said, jerking her head at the table. "Thank you for bringing it."

"I'm glad your baby is better, Mrs. Cropper."

"Doctor came, that's why. The master sent him it seems. He sent Daniel to put a few things right with the cottage too." She nodded at the mended windows. "I'm that grateful to him. He's been good to us when most folks wouldn't have bothered and we'd have been in the workhouse long ago." She crossed her thin arms over her chest and shuddered slightly.

The two children who had been playing outside appeared in the doorway and stood, thumbs in mouths, staring avidly at the food on the table. Presently they were joined by their sister, the little girl with fair hair and blue eyes. There was no sign of their elder brother.

"Where's Dobbin, Mrs. Cropper?" I asked.

Her green eyes, so like her son's, grew cold. She shrugged her shoulders and turned away from me. "I don't know. I haven't seen him since yesterday. He's hiding out there somewhere—sulking, I suppose. He's nothing but trouble that lad, I can tell you. He's always into mischief and now he's just defying me, and his uncle too. I shan't be sorry to be rid of him."

"Rid of him?"

She looked at me defiantly. "Yes—rid of him! I told you that my brother has my oldest, Sarah, to live with him and his wife so she can work at the mill. Well, he came to see us t'other day. He says it's high time Dobbin started work too and he's found him a job in the mines. They'll keep him for me, same as Sarah, so long as he hands over enough of his wages for food and keep. It's an easy job, my brother says. He'll get sixpence a day and he can work his way up to be a proper miner."

I stared at her, a cold, sick feeling inside me. I could not believe her words. "You're going to send Dobbin to work down a coal mine? You can't really mean that, Mrs. Cropper. You couldn't do such a thing to him—why he's only a child!"

Her face was white and closed. "He's seven years old and there's plenty younger than him working in mines. He's lucky to get the chance to work at all. My brother had trouble finding him this job—there's many others anxious for the money."

"But what work could a child of seven possibly do down a mine?"

She laughed shortly and there was scorn in her voice. "Lord, miss, you don't know much about the way poor folk live, do you? Women and children work down the mines, same as the men. I'd go myself if I hadn't the little 'uns to look after somehow. And go Dobbin must, however much he tries to get out of it."

"But surely with the master sending you food it won't be necessary. I promise I'll bring you enough provisions every week. Please don't let him go. You mustn't. . . ."

She looked at me with something like hatred in her green eyes.

"Coming here with the master's charity doesn't give you the right to interfere. How do I know how long the master will go on sending us food? He might change his mind or just forget all about us. We've no right to be in this cottage, you know. He could turn us out any day."

"I'm certain he would never do such a thing."

"*You* may be, miss. *I'm* not. I've learned to expect nothing from life. Nothing good lasts for long and I know it. Dobbin goes to work next week when his uncle comes to fetch him."

I saw that it was useless to try to persuade her. She had moved away to see to the baby, who had awaked and begun to wave its small fists about.

"You've no idea where he might be, Mrs. Cropper?"

She didn't turn her head from the cradle. "No. He'll turn up soon enough—when he's hungry. And he'll get a beating when he does."

I left the cottage and walked out into the bright sunlight. A scraggy hen was pecking hopefully at the pebbles left scattered about by the children. I looked around me at the fields and trees that surrounded the place but knew it was hopeless to search for Dobbin. He would know every inch of the countryside and could be hiding anywhere, as difficult to find as if he really were some elf of the woods. I walked back up the hill, beneath the chestnut trees, carrying the empty basket over my arm.

"Miss! Miss!" The faint hiss came from above me and I stopped and stared upward through the leaves. At first I could not see him and then I saw a small patch of blue cotton trouser among the green.

"Dobbin—is that you? Come down here. I want to talk to you."

I spoke gently, anxious not to frighten him but to give him reassurance. At first there was no answer and then, slowly, the branches separated above me and the freckled and tear-stained face of Dobbin peered down at me.

"Come on down," I repeated quietly.

He shook his head. "I can't, miss. I daren't or *she* might catch me."

I put down the basket. "Very well. Then I shall come up to

you. We can talk quite as well up there as down here. Wait a moment."

It was a more difficult climb than I had imagined and I had lost the knack; it was many years since I had scrambled up and down trees on our country estate in Hampshire as a little girl. With my skirt hitched over my arm I hauled myself painfully up onto a lower branch, scraping knees and elbows in the process. Dobbin slithered swiftly down from his higher perch and sat beside me, brown legs dangling, green eyes fixed on me tragically. I put my arm round his shoulders.

"Your mother is looking for you, Dobbin. She's anxious about you. You haven't been home for a day."

He shook his head fiercely. "She's not worried about me. She knows I'll be all right. All she wants is to send me away. My uncle's coming to fetch me."

"I know, she told me about it."

He looked at me, his eyes brimming with tears. "Did she tell you where they're going to send me?"

I nodded and held him tighter.

"They're going to make me work down a coal mine," he said bitterly. "Down in the dark all day and never seeing the sun and the trees and fields no more. . . ."

"Perhaps it won't be quite as bad as you think, Dobbin," I said. I did not know what else to say and a deep and agonizing pity for the child was growing in my heart.

"Oh yes, miss, it will be bad all right. I know that. My uncle told me what I'll be doing. I'm to be a trapper."

"A trapper?"

"Yes. I sit by myself in the dark all day opening and shutting a door for the coal carts. My uncle's told me all about it. He says it's an important job to do—something to do with keeping the air all right in the mine. I don't care how important it is; I'll die if I have to go down in the dark underground. . . . I'd sooner die anyway, miss, really I would. . . ."

His voice was strangled by the heavy sobs that began to convulse his small frame. He turned away from me, and rubbing his eyes with clenched fists, struggled for control. I said nothing but stretched my hand out and gently stroked his tangled locks.

When the sobs ceased I said calmly and despite the horror and turmoil within me:

"Try not to worry, Dobbin. Perhaps you may not have to go after all. Your mother may change her mind, or I might find some way to prevent it."

He turned to me, his face streaked with dirt and tears, and the misery I saw there was unbearable. "*She* won't change her mind, I know that. She wants to be rid of me—she told me so. I'm a nuisance and get into trouble all the time. And anyway, what could *you* possibly do about it, miss?"

I sighed heavily and took his hand in mine. "I don't know, Dobbin. I just don't know. But if there's a way to stop you going I promise you that I shall try to find it."

I left him huddled in his hiding place in the horse chestnut tree and made my way back across the fields toward Aysgarth. I had torn my skirt climbing down and my face was scratched and dirty but I did not care about either of those things: my only thoughts were of the little boy I could not help.

I was so distracted that, at first, I did not notice the carriage waiting outside the front door, and when I finally did so, it was with astonishment and curiosity. Visitors had clearly called at Aysgarth. The carriage was a sumptuous and gleaming affair of maroon and gold paintwork and crested doors, the horses were two perfectly matched grays, and the groom who stood beside their heads, an impressive complement to the equipage in his spotless red and gold livery. He stood stiff, straight, and contemptuous as he eyed the crumbling house in front of him and as I passed him to hurry up the front steps, his thin eyebrows rose almost to the brim of his hat as he took in my sadly bedraggled appearance.

Who could have called? "*Nobody comes here and we see no one,*" the contessa had said. But whoever had come in that carriage was obviously someone of importance.

The great hall was as bare and empty as usual but sounds of talk and laughter came from within the drawing room. Acutely aware of my disheveled state, I ran toward the kitchen wing, intending to return the basket and then escape to my room. At that moment the drawing room door opened and Miles Metcalfe emerged.

"One moment, Miss Chell!"

He leaned on his stick and surveyed me for a while in silence. I had stopped dead and the shock of encountering him so unexpectedly when I had assumed him to be still shut away in his rooms, left me also bereft of speech. We stared at each other and while my eyes noted, unconsciously, the deathly pallor and new lines of pain and suffering on his face, his eyes roved casually over me, taking in my straggling hair, my scratched, muddy face, and the dusty and torn gown. At last he said:

"I was looking for you, Miss Chell. I had intended asking you to join our distinguished visitors but now that I see you I'm not certain it's such a good idea. Tell me, are your new duties as my housekeeper really so arduous that you are reduced to looking like a scarecrow? If so, then you must cease them immediately."

"It's nothing to do with that, sir. I have been walking across the fields," I replied coldly.

His glance rested on the empty basket in my hand. "Visiting the Croppers, no doubt. I admire your industry, Miss Chell, but find its effect on your appearance somewhat alarming."

"I am about to remedy that," I said, and tried to walk past him, but he seized hold of my wrist and gripped it firmly.

"There is no time for it, I'm afraid. Lord Benton and Miss Benton have expressed a great desire to meet you. They are consumed with curiosity to see what my ward is like."

"I am not your ward!"

"I always forget that. I must try to remember in future. It's a pity that you will hardly do yourself justice in your present state, but it can't be helped. We can do nothing about the tear in your skirt but at least we can clean your face a little. Stand still a moment."

He released my arm, and producing a silk handkerchief from his pocket, wiped my forehead and cheeks with it and then, as I began to back away in protest, grasped my hand and drew me relentlessly toward the drawing room. There was no escape. I was propelled through the doorway, flushed and furious like some recalcitrant schoolgirl.

The contessa, seated on the couch, raised her lorgnette and gazed at me, dismayed. As usual, she was perfectly groomed—not a wisp of hair was out of place and she had put on a great many jewels for the occasion. Besides the large diamond brooch I had seen before, she wore a magnificent pair of diamond and pearl pendant earrings, and her hands glittered with heavy rings.

But this time even the contessa's elegance was outshone by the girl who sat beside her. She was very beautiful in a cool, aristocratic way, and her emerald-green gown was one of the most exquisite I had ever seen. The bodice was close-fitting to her slim figure and the deeply frilled bertha collar accentuated and showed off her long, slender neck. The sleeves were tight to below the ebow and edged with bands of finest cream lace, and the full skirt swept the floor around her in a rich shimmer of heavy silk. Her bonnet was in the very latest style, according to the contessa's Paris journals, and trimmed with green satin and small yellow flowers. Beneath it her complexion was flawless with clear, delicate features and large, gray eyes. Her only imperfection was her nose, which was a little too pronounced and long, but this merely emphasized her air of well-bred superiority. From the crown of her bonnet to the tip of the kid slipper that protruded daintily from under her skirts, she was faultlessly elegant and assured. And her expression, as she turned at my entrance, was a mixture of hauteur and curiosity.

"Good Lord, it's Alice! I don't believe it! What on earth are you doing here?"

The voice, high-pitched and nervous, had spoken from across the room. It was followed by a loud, braying laugh, and even before I looked in its direction, I had recognized its owner. Two men stood over by the fireplace—one short, old, and so fat that he seemed almost spherical; the other tall and very fair and dressed in fashionable dandy's clothes. He had grown a little fatter since I had last seen him and his blue satin waistcoat bulged noticeably from under his tight-fitting coat, while the points of his exaggeratedly high collar pressed into plump pink cheeks. Above the collar his pale blue eyes popped at me in baffled astonishment.

"Great heavens, Alice, I didn't recognize you!"

I could not blame him. Before me stood Lord Alfred Witherspoon, the man to whom I had once been engaged when my parents were alive—in the days when we were rich and respected. At our last meeting in London I had been dressed in ex-

pensive clothes, cosseted and indulged in surroundings of wealth
and luxury. Now, in my torn dress and tangled hair and carrying
my kitchen basket, I must be very different from his mind's
image of me. I looked at him in complete dismay: I had no wish
to meet him ever again, if only because he reminded me of painful things I would sooner forget. If I could have left the room I
would have done so then, but my hand was still held in a firm
grip. It tightened still more.

"You are already acquainted with Lord Alfred, Miss Chell?"
His voice was as cold as the moorland streams.

I nodded. "We knew each other some time ago in London. . . ."

"Yes, indeed," Lord Alfred burbled, red with embarrassment
now at the situation. "But we have not met for some time. I had
no idea that Miss Chell was in Yorkshire. . . . How are you,
Alice? I've often wondered how you were getting along, you
know. . . ."

Catherine Benton coughed delicately to attract our attention.
"Do please introduce me to Miss Chell, Miles," she said a little
plaintively. "I am *amazed* to learn that she is acquainted with
Freddie—it's quite astonishing!"

I took her limp fingers in mine and her gaze swept me in cool
appraisal, followed almost immediately by satisfaction and dis-
missal. She had summed me up as of no real consequence and
turned to Miles Metcalfe, who had at last released my hand, and
moved to stand near her.

"Lord Alfred is staying with us for the shooting," she said,
looking up at Miles with a delightful smile. "He's a first-class
shot but not as good as you, Miles. . . . You really should come
over to the castle and join the gentlemen out one day."

"I don't shoot any more, Catherine."

She frowned, vexed at her own blunder. "Of course not. I had
quite forgotten for a moment. You manage so well these days,
Miles, that really one scarcely notices . . . such courage, such
perseverance . . ." Her voice trailed away sympathetically as she
looked up into his face. He bent to say something in reply, his
dark head close to the green-trimmed bonnet. . . .

"I am so delighted to meet you, Miss Chell." The smooth,
syrupy voice was so near that I felt its owner's breath on my

cheek. Lord Benton had moved up behind me, silent as a cat. He was so short that his watery, blue eyes were on a level with mine and he stood so close that his bloated stomach almost brushed against me. There was a little frill of white, wispy hair round his bald head and his legs, beneath the globular body, were thin as matchsticks and looked too frail to bear their owner's weight.

"Your ward is enchanting, Metcalfe," he said over his shoulder. "Why have you not brought her to see us at the castle? It's very selfish of you to keep such a fascinating young lady all to yourself."

"Miss Chell is not always easy to find," was the casual response. "When she is not galloping over the moors like a hoyden she is running wild about the fields. I doubt if I could tame her sufficiently to go calling. . . ."

I could willingly have struck him for that remark. There was a general murmur of amusement and Catherine Benton laughed aloud, smiling up at him in appreciation. "I must confess, Miles, that she is not quite as I had expected your dear late father's goddaughter to be. . . ." It was a whispered aside but spoken just loud enough for everyone to hear. The contessa, however, came bristling to my defense.

"Alice takes a great interest in some cottagers on the estate," she remarked in frigid tones. "A poor widow's family, I believe. She has just come from walking several miles across the fields to visit them with provisions. I find her action most commendable."

I could have kissed her as readily as I longed to let fly at her great-nephew. I was grateful to her and childish tears pricked at my eyelids. My self-esteem had suffered severely in front of the Bentons and Lord Alfred. I had forgotten the luster and glamor that great wealth can bestow; the assurance and condescension possessed by the very rich. And Catherine Benton was so very poised and very beautiful. . . .

"I do so agree with you, Contessa," she said at once, turning from her whisperings. "One should always remember those less fortunate than oneself. I myself call frequently on our needy tenants—they are always so grateful, poor things."

"And a damned nuisance they are too," exploded Lord Benton suddenly. He had moved away from me, to my great relief, and stood, back to the fireplace, little matchstick legs planted apart, and hands behind his back. His face was pink with emotion. "They're thieving scoundrels most of 'em. I'm justice of the peace so I should know. . . . They're idle rogues who think nothing of stealing and poaching. Found my carter, Spratt, on his way home yesterday with a turnip hidden under his coat. *My* turnip! Took it from a loaded cart on his way to feed the cows with the things. I said to him 'Spratt, how are we landowners to live if you rascals steal every bit of produce?' He had no answer to that, I can tell you! I can't understand what came over the fellow. He's a wife and six children and seemed honest enough. I've given him one last chance and fair warning. Next time I'll dismiss him and prosecute him too!"

The white wisps of hair shook with indignation and he looked round for approval and sympathy.

"A shocking affair indeed, Papa," his daughter said soothingly. "Don't you agree, Miles?"

He made no reply, but Lord Alfred nodded his head so violently that his collar points all but jabbed into his protuberant eyes. "Absolutely right! You can't let 'em get away with it. It may have been only one turnip but the next time it'd be a cartload, mark my words!"

I had listened incredulously to Lord Benton's speech, and as I did so, the image of the Cropper family floated into my mind. I saw the children—thin, dirty, and hungry, the baby sick for lack of a doctor, the widowed mother without a husband even to steal for her. . . . At least the Croppers had some help and would not starve to death so long as Aysgarth remained, but what of the countless other poor families whose landlords did not care what happened to them? What of Spratt the carter who had dared to steal a single turnip? Who would help those with no one to befriend them?

"Perhaps the man was hungry, Lord Benton."

The words were out before I could stop myself and my voice was very clear in the silence. "Perhaps your carter stole to keep his wife and children fed."

His lordship's jaw dropped, lips slack and flabby as he stared at me as though unable to believe his ears. Lord Alfred's laugh brayed nervously.

"Heavens, Alice! You can't mean that. What an odd thing to say. You don't know anything about it."

"But I do, Lord Alfred. At least I know that many people go hungry because they have not enough money to buy food."

"I pay the man six shillings a week—what more does he want!" Lord Benton's eyes no longer ogled me as before. They watched me, cold and hard. "I take it you approve of theft then, Miss Chell. That you give such things your support and approbation."

"Of course not. I only suggested that the man might have been in some desperate need of the turnip he took. I hoped you might be lenient with him if you were aware of the situation."

He looked at me with distaste. "Oh, I'm aware of it all right, Miss Chell. Every landowner in the country is aware of the situation—the poaching and thieving that goes on under our very noses! They snare and steal and shoot as much as they dare and my gamekeepers can't stop them. The last one was murdered—killed in cold blood by some poacher after my pheasants. You'll be telling me next that you approve of them setting fire to haystacks and barns and stables, like happened last winter. Twenty fires or more in the district we had, Miss Chell, and never did find the culprits. What do you say to that? I suppose you'd feel sorry for them, just like my thieving carter. Well, they all behave like savages and deserve to be treated as such."

I was stunned by the virulence of his anger and fell silent. Miles Metcalfe spoke in steady, measured tones. "As the contessa said, Lord Benton, Miss Chell takes an unusually close interest in a widow and her family on my estate. Naturally she does not fully appreciate landowners' difficulties. I am certain that she did not wish to give any offense. Isn't that so, Miss Chell?" He did not even look at me as he spoke but his tone was steely enough beneath the soft words to transmit his meaning. I mumbled an apology and Lord Benton looked somewhat mollified although he still spluttered with indignant comments like a dying squib. Then, with an obvious effort, he controlled himself and addressed me with a pained smile.

"My dear Miss Chell, I accept your apology and I too must apologize for losing my temper with so charming a young lady. Let us forget the whole affair. I trust we shall have the pleasure of seeing you at the ball we are giving soon at the castle. The purpose of our visit here today was especially to invite you all to attend."

He bent over my hand once more and I shuddered inwardly at his touch.

Miss Benton had risen decisively to make her farewells. She took her leave of the contessa with fulsome phrases but swept past me with only the faintest nod of her bonnet. As she left the room, followed by her father and Lord Alfred, I heard her remark to Miles Metcalfe, who was at her side:

"What a very strange creature your ward is, Miles! Almost *farouche*, one might say, and such *odd* ideas! I feel sorry for you having to support her under your own roof; it's very noble of you. Perhaps I could be of some help in finding her a suitable post somewhere—a governess perhaps, although I confess I could hardly recommend her to any family I know. . . ." Her voice faded away as they walked down the great hall.

To my surprise the contessa broke into delighted chuckles as soon as we were left alone. She dabbed at her eyes with a lace handkerchief and regarded me with profound amusement. "My dear Alice, you really are a tonic! I've never seen that odious, puffed-up little man look more put out. Nobody ever dares to contradict or criticize him, child, not even that ice-cold daughter of his. I shan't forget his face for years—he reminded me exactly of an outraged turkey cock!"

"I was perfectly serious, Contessa," I said stiffly, unable to share her amusement. "I was simply trying to make him see reason. Obviously that poor laborer who stole from him was in great need. Why couldn't he understand that?"

The contessa wagged her head and smiled gently. "You are only eighteen, Alice, and you have such a lot to learn about people. Lord Benton is one of the biggest landowners in Yorkshire and he is well known for being ruthless where his employees are concerned. He is also well known for dealing mercilessly with those who come before him in the courts. It is quite usual, I believe, for him to sentence poachers to seven years transportation. So you can see, my dear, that it was very foolish and a waste of time for you to try and plead for the poor carter and his stolen turnip."

"But just one turnip . . ."

"One or a hundredweight—it would be all the same to a man like Lord Benton. And, to be fair to him, honesty is not measured by quantity or otherwise. Just because you have a compassionate heart, Alice, don't imagine that others see things in the same light as yourself." She took my hand in hers and patted it kindly. "And now for goodness sake go and get rid of that basket and change your dress—you look like a gypsy selling pegs. And send Frugoni to me. I must plan what to wear for this junketing at the castle to which we are so graciously invited. No doubt it will be a very vulgar affair but we must show them that we still have our pride and standards at Aysgarth. . . . Hurry, child, there's not a moment to lose."

I left the room and hurried across the great hall. Behind me a voice said in conversational tones: "I am waiting with some interest, Miss Chell, to hear your explanation for your curious behavior to my guest. You offended Lord Benton gravely, you know."

I turned with a start to see him standing in the deep shadow of the chimney piece, leaning casually against the stonework and watching me with a pale, expressionless face. The ebony stick rotated idly beneath his finger tips, round and round, round and round, its silver knob glinting hypnotically.

"Well?"

"I'm sorry. But I thought him harsh and unjust toward his employee."

"That was scarcely your affair," he remarked mildly, looking down at the stick that twirled under his hand.

"I suppose not, but I felt I had to speak."

"You are fast becoming a champion of the poor, Miss Chell. It is, as the contessa pointed out, most admirable that you interest yourself in their welfare, but I really cannot have you offending visitors. We have few enough, God knows. In future you must learn to keep your thoughts to yourself."

"I'll try to, if you wish."

"I do wish, Miss Chell. I do indeed. And since I am head of this house and you live under my roof I expect you to obey me."

"Lord Benton mentioned an invitation to the castle. Am I really invited also?"

"Certainly you are. Why not?"

"I would prefer not to go. I don't like Lord Benton, to be honest, and his daughter made her disapproval of me very plain."

"Miss Benton was somewhat taken aback by your unusual appearance and manner, it is true. You must rectify this by attending the ball and proving her to be wrong."

"Does it matter?"

"Does what matter?"

"If she doesn't like me?"

"Not particularly, but if you wish to advance yourself in Yorkshire society and make the acquaintance of suitable young men with whom you might make a match then you would be well advised to cultivate Catherine Benton's favors. And even if you don't wish it, it is my duty to see that you are given every opportunity to mix in the appropriate circles. The ball at Benton Castle will provide this opportunity, so you will be attending it, whether you like it or not. Besides it will give you the chance of renewing your long-standing friendship with Lord Alfred Witherspoon and that surely must please you. . . ."

He waited for my reply but I said nothing, refusing to be drawn on that subject. "By the way," he continued, "just how well did you know his lordship? He seemed unusually embarrassed to see you."

"That is my affair."

"*Touché!*" He shifted his weight from the chimney piece and leaned on the black stick. "In any case I insist that you attend the ball so that is an end to it."

"I have no suitable gown to wear."

"The contessa will arrange it—I shall ask her to see that you have. The matter is settled."

"If I agree to go, would you grant me a favor in return?"

His eyebrows rose. "Yet again you astonish me, Miss Chell. You are not in any position to bargain with me. I have told you that you must do as I say. What is this favor then? I suppose I may as well hear it although I would much sooner not. I can see from the militant look in your eye that it is something important to you—is it to do with the Croppers?"

"I'm afraid so. The eldest boy, Dobbin, is to be sent away to work down a coal mine. He's seven years old and will have to sit alone in darkness all day long, opening and shutting a door for the coal carts. . . . He says he'd sooner die and I believe him. I can't bear the thought of anything so terrible happening to a child. Is there something you can do to prevent it?"

Tears had come to my eyes at the recollection of Dobbin's misery, and with an effort, I swallowed them back. There was silence for a while and then at last he said in a tired voice:

"I should like to help, believe me, but I cannot. If I could offer the boy some prospect of work and a future on the estate I would do so, but there is no hope of this at the moment. . . ."

"But there must be *something* we could do! It can't be right that a little child should go and work down underground. It *must* be stopped! Women and children work in mines, Mrs. Cropper told me, and some of them are even younger than Dobbin. . . ."

"You must not distress yourself, Alice," he said, and for once his voice was unexpectedly gentle. "I cannot help your Dobbin at the moment but if I am ever in a position to do so then you have my word that I shall do everything I can for him. One day things will change and children will no longer be sent to work in mines and factories. Until then you must try to forget about it. There is nothing you can do."

Suddenly I was angry—a blind, impotent feeling of fury that welled up inside me and burst out.

"You're no better than Lord Benton," I cried out bitterly. "You're heartless and cruel. You don't care a fig for Dobbin or any others of his kind. Why, you're . . ."

"The most arrogant and unpleasant man you've ever met," he finished wryly. "I already know your opinion of me, so spare me a repetition I beg of you. Let us finish this discussion now before we both regret it. I'll detain you no longer."

He turned from me coldly and I hastened away. The tears ran down my cheeks. I should never be able to forget Dobbin or put him out of my mind. I should think of him every single day, shut away down in his black, stifling prison far from the sunlight and fresh air of his beloved fields. At the moment I hated my godfather's son for his indifferent and cold heart.

It was only later in my room that I recalled two things that I had overlooked in the turmoil of my feelings. First, Mr. Metcalfe had repeated exactly the words I had used to Eweretta that day in the great hall: *the most unpleasant and arrogant man I have ever met.* That was how I had described him to his sister and now I remembered the sound I had heard above us in the gallery and knew that he must have overheard our entire conversation. . . . *I wouldn't marry him if he were the last man on earth* . . . I felt myself burn with embarrassment and dismay at the thought of him listening to my words. And then I realized something else—something of no importance at all but remarkable and unexpected nonetheless—for the first time, just now, he had called me Alice. . . .

CHAPTER VII

"How nice to see you, Miss Chell. We don't seem to see very much of each other these days. Do you mind if I walk along with you a little way?"

Philip Paige smiled at me shyly. We had met by chance on what had once been a long terrace behind the house. Like everything else in the gardens it was overgrown with weeds, but it was pleasant to walk along the old stone flags in the sunshine and there, at least, I was safe from the contessa and Signorina Frugoni. Armed with the latest batch of journals from Paris they had made several attempts to corner me long enough to discuss the problem of my dress for the ball at Benton Castle. So far I had managed to evade them with excuses of urgent housekeeping duties, and in truth, there was a great deal that required my attention. Ann, the scullery maid, was too ill to work and had taken to her bed, which meant that the kitchen was in chaos and the cook in a temper. We had nearly run out of candles and salt, the mice had been at the flour again, and the household accounts needed checking over. Besides which, I had reasoned cunningly to myself that if I had no suitable gown to wear I could not possibly go to the ball. Not only did I hate the idea of seeing the Bentons again and enduring her snubs and his slimy blandishments, but also I remembered too well my dismal failures at the dances I had been forced to attend with Mama in London. I had spent most of my season as an unhappy wallflower and had no wish to repeat that painful experience. Smart society had held no attraction for me then, nor did it now.

Now, with a few moments to spare, I had come out into the gardens to enjoy the sun and escape the contessa's clutches. I was pleased to see Philip Paige and returned his smile.

"Do walk with me by all means, Mr. Paige, but I am not really going anywhere I'm afraid. I'm simply walking up and down the terrace but I should be very glad of your company."

I thought how pleasant and uncomplicated he was with his open, friendly face and curly brown hair. Clumsy and shy he might be, and Eweretta had continued to treat him with undisguised scorn for it, but I liked him. He was agreeable, and despite his obvious cleverness, charmingly diffident.

"How is your work progressing," I asked him after we had strolled a little way.

His face lit up with enthusiasm. "I was on my way to the abbey when I saw you here, Miss Chell. Would you care to accompany me there? I should be so pleased to show you some of the things I've been able to establish—I know most of the layout of the buildings now."

The further I was from the house the further I would be from the contessa and Signorina Frugoni, I thought, and in any case, I very much wanted to see the ruins again. I accepted his proposal at once and we walked along together, talking easily. The pathway through the thorn thicket had been cleared a good deal so that it was easier, this time, to pick my way down the long, tunnel-like track that led through to the abbey. Philip Paige went ahead, dragging aside branches so that I could walk unimpeded and unscratched.

"Daniel Duck cleared a lot of this for me," he said apologetically, holding down a particularly thorny shoot for me to step over. "But it's still very overgrown. He's been very useful, Daniel. He's extremely strong and never seems to get tired. He cut away a lot of the ivy from the abbey walls for me—it looks romantic but it's terribly bad for the stonework, you know. Not much farther now . . ."

The ruins looked very beautiful in the warm sunlight. I gazed once more at the old walls in their peaceful valley with the streams splashing and murmuring nearby.

"It's so calm and still here!"

He smiled at me. "It is not, but long ago it must have been a very different scene. Over a hundred monks lived and worked here, you know, and even more lay brothers to help them. It was a very busy place. The monks weren't only men of God, they were farmers, too, and very efficient ones. They grew all kinds of crops and kept a great many sheep up on the fells; a large part of their income was from wool and, for a long time, it made them very rich. If you could look back into the past, Miss Chell, and see it all just as it was I think you'd be surprised just how active and bustling the abbey was. There was more to being a monk here than prayer and contemplation."

He took my hand to help me across some fallen masonry. "Come with me and I'll show you what I mean."

And so began a magical tour of what had looked to me a puzzling jumble of stone walls and archways. The ruins came alive as he explained each part of them: the cloisters where the monks had read and studied, sitting on benches against the church wall, the infirmary for aged and sick monks, the warming house with its huge fireplace where they had restored the circulation to limbs frozen after hours spent in the chill of the cloister or the church.

"See this stone platform," he said, as we went into a rectangle of crumbling walls that had once been the refectory. "The prior sat up here at the high table to preside over the meals while the rest of the monks were at long tables below him. The abbot ate with the guests." He pointed upward. "If you look closely you can see the remains of the carved corbel that supported the pulpit. There was a rule of silence at meals except for one monk who read from the Bible and he stood up there."

We walked on through the kitchen, with its hatchway through to the refectory, and he showed me the long stone basin used by the monks for washing their hands before eating.

"That big recess in the wall there was a towel cupboard and those steps behind you led up to the dormitory. You can see the holes for the handrail and the way the stairs are much more worn on that side. And if we walk through this archway it will bring us to the remains of the abbot's house. . . ."

And so it went on: *cellarium*, cellarer's office, undercroft, lay brothers' refectory, sacrist's office, the chapter house where I had sat that day on the stone bench, until, finally, dizzy with it all, I followed him into the nave of the church. The hollow shell of the east window soared aloft before us as we walked through the choir. The monks would sing no more within those hallowed walls; only the pigeons cooed and fluttered in their precarious perches high above us. The altar stone stood alone in its carpet of grass, a solitary slab of limestone with the blurred outlines of five crosses cut into its surface.

"Representing the five wounds of Christ," explained Philip Paige, touching them lightly with his fingers.

I looked at the bare stone. "The Cross of Aysgarth must have stood there."

He laughed. "Your vivid imagination is at work again, Miss Chell. Yes, of course, you are quite right. The cross was kept here on the high altar and the Abbot Haby would have knelt before it just about where *you* are standing now. It's strange to think of that, isn't it? I wonder what he did with it. It's a pity we can't see back into the past or that these stones can't speak to us."

I was silent, thinking of the corpulent abbot kneeling in cumbersome homage before the glittering symbol on the altar, his plump, white hands clasped before him, the gold and ruby ring I had seen in the painting gleaming on his little finger . . . It was hard to believe that he had once lived and walked and prayed in this place.

I said aloud. "It's sad that he wasn't buried here in the chapter house with the other abbots; it doesn't seem right . . ."

"Yes, the poor man must have been thrown into some unknown grave when he was hanged at Tyburn."

"I wonder if he rests in peace. I'm sure I shouldn't if I had been him. I should want my bones to lie here in my abbey where I belonged."

He smiled at me. "You *do* have a strong imagination, Miss Chell." He moved away a little and beckoned to me. "Look, these tiles are thirteenth-century mosaic. There are only a few left so far as I can tell, unfortunately. I uncovered these myself yesterday."

I bent down to look at the reddish-brown squares, their faint sheen of glaze showing beneath the dust that still clung to them. "You must have been working very hard, Mr. Paige. You seem to have discovered so much about the abbey already."

He seemed pleased and blushed slightly, eyes blinking a little behind the wire-framed spectacles. "It's not work to me, Miss Chell, I enjoy it too much to call it that. It is *you*, I would say, who have been doing the hardest work lately—since you became housekeeper. You are always so busy. I see you even carry the keys about with you . . . you shouldn't do that—you are not a servant and shouldn't be treated as one."

I was puzzled but flattered by his concern. "Nobody treats me as one, I can promise you, and, like you, Mr. Paige, I enjoy the work. I prefer not to be idle. As for the keys"—I touched them so that they jangled on the belt round my waist—"I simply find it more convenient to have them with me. It saves time. I must sort them out one day, a great many of them belong to all the locked rooms in the house and could be put away."

"I can see that you are a very efficient housekeeper anyway," he said. "And diligence should have its reward. Here, I have something that I think will please you. . . ." He held out his hand, and taking mine, pressed a small object into my palm. I stared at it entranced. It was a bead: a tiny, oval-shaped thing of translucent amber, exquisitely carved. I held it carefully in my fingers and looked into its tawny depths, turning it this way and that so that it gleamed like gold in the sunlight. There was a hole carefully bored through its center and one side of the bead was dulled from constant fingering.

"A rosary bead?"

He nodded. "I found it in the earth when I was uncovering the floor tiles yesterday. Keep it for good luck, Miss Chell. Perhaps it even belonged to your Abbot Haby!"

My fingers·closed tightly round the carved amber. It was not impossible. The abbot could have been arrested by Cromwell's men while he was here at prayer in the church, the rosary broken in the struggle and confusion, and the beads scattered, bouncing and rolling across the mosaic tiles. . . . I would keep it as a talisman and pray that it brought us all better fortune.

The contessa ran me to earth later that day. "It's no use prevaricating any longer, Alice," she said firmly. "Miles has given me strict instructions to see that you are provided with something to wear to the ball and I intend to see that this is done. I quite agree with him that it is a great opportunity for you and must not be missed on any account, no matter how you try to wriggle out of it. I don't understand you, child, at your age I *lived* for dancing and parties." She hooked her arm through mine. "Come along, my dear, Frugoni and I are waiting."

There was no escape: I stood for hours like a stuffed dummy while they talked about and across me as though I were not there at all. Journal after journal was consulted and thrown aside unil the floor seemed carpeted with them, and lengths of material were draped around and over me—pink, yellow, white, blue, green—and, like the journals, flung down to join the growing pile of chaos. At last the contessa jabbed her finger at an illustration: "This is clearly the one for her, Frugoni. It's plain and simple enough for her looks—frills would be nothing less than a disaster—and yet it is pretty, too, with that scooped neckline and puffed sleeves. Yes, it's charming and will do very well. Which is more than can be said for all these colors—not one is right for her, Frugoni. What is to be done?"

The little Italian spread her hands deprecatingly. "If you will excuse me saying, Contessa, the signorina's eyes are noticeably her best feature—*sono bellissimi e questo colore è magnifico.* We must find a material to match them."

The contessa threw aside a piece of green silk pettishly. "I know that, Frugoni. I'm not blind, but we have none and cannot afford to buy any. Don't irritate me by suggesting the impossible."

"*Ma non è impossible,* Contessa! I remember very well a length of violet silk in the trunk we brought from *Italia*—the one that Signora Silver hid away somewhere and we have never since managed to find. It was a beautiful piece of the most delicate color and of finest quality . . ."

"But of course, Frugoni! Why didn't you say so before instead of wasting our time like this? I remember it well and it will do perfectly. Go and fetch it at once."

"But I cannot, Contessa. I don't know where the trunk is. I have searched and searched but there is no sign of it anywhere. The Signora Silver would never tell me where she had put it—she never liked me as you know, and I think it amused her to be unhelpful. . . ."

The contessa exploded with vexation. "Don't be so ridiculous, Frugoni. The trunk must be *somewhere* in the house. You must find it immediately. Go and look until you do so."

"It may be in one of the locked rooms," the Italian suggested uncomfortably. "In that case it will be difficult. . . ."

"I have the keys," I said, and shook the heavy ring on my belt so that it jingled loudly at them. They stopped and stared at me —suddenly fully aware of my presence.

The contessa, calm again, sat down in her chair with a sigh of relief. The cat, Topaz, jumped up on her lap and began to purr. She stroked his gray fur and said: "Thank goodness you are practical and sensible, Alice. It makes up a great deal for what you lack in looks. I had quite forgotten that you had charge of the housekeeper's keys. You and Frugoni will go and search for that trunk, my dear. It must be in one of those rooms, and since they are all empty now, it shouldn't be difficult to discover. Well, don't just stand there like an idiot, child. Off you go and find it!"

And so began a weird and eerie progress through all the deserted rooms in the house. Our footsteps echoed in the empty passageways and keys grated in rusty locks that had not been touched for years. The old oak doors squeaked and groaned as we turned the heavy, iron handles and peered apprehensively into the unknown . . . I don't know which of us was the more frightened, nor precisely what we feared or expected to find, but for room after room there was only cold emptiness and the sickly smell of damp. We disturbed no ghosts—only mice and spiders, and everywhere, thick shrouds of dust and cobwebs.

Signorina Frugoni looked despairing. "The contessa will be so angry if we do not find it."

"Don't worry. There are still several more rooms we haven't looked in. This one seems to have a cleaner lock than the others. Perhaps it may be in this one."

I found the key and put it in the lock. It turned easily, and with a faint creak the door swung open slowly. Behind me the Italian gave a shrill screech of terror: a man stood at the end of the room, watching us from the shadows, dark, silent, and still. . . .

Signorina Frugoni would have taken flight if I had not instantly grasped her sleeve. My heart was racing wildly and my knees shaking with shock.

"Wait! It's only a painting. It looks just like a man standing there in the corner, but it's only a picture after all. For a moment I thought . . ." I pulled at her sleeve. "Come on, there's nothing to be afraid of."

We edged our way cautiously through the doorway both ready to run if necessary; the painting had thoroughly unnerved us. A large brown mouse skittered across the floor boards near our feet and Signorina Frugoni yelped in horror. She was trembling like a jelly as she tried to drag me away. "Come, signorina, what is the use . . . ?"

But I held her arm tightly. "One moment. I want to look at that portrait." Oddly, I was no longer afraid and felt irresistibly drawn toward the watching figure in the corner.

It was a very large painting—almost life-size—and mounted in an elaborately carved golden frame. It had been left propped carelessly against the furthest wall, abandoned to the spiders who had spun their webs across it undisturbed. The subject was so lifelike in its intensity that it was not surprising that we had, for one terrifying moment, mistaken it for a real man.

Signorina Frugoni stepped forward gingerly to stare at the likeness, her head tilted a little to one side like a curious bird.

"But of course . . . it is Signor Metcalfe. . . . I remember this painting now. It used to hang in the library long ago. . . . I had forgotten all about it. I suppose it was taken down after the accident. . . . One can understand the poor man not wishing to see himself as he once was. *Che peccato! Che tragedia!*" She lifted her podgy hands in sympathy with the challenging eyes. "I had forgotten how very handsome he was—so tall and charming—*non ho mai visto un uomo più bello*. One would never recognize him now—he has suffered so much. . . ."

To my surprise I saw that her beady, currantlike eyes were moist with tears.

I had recognized him myself, but only with difficulty. The Master of Aysgarth looked out at me from his dusty canvas—but not as the man I knew and disliked so cordially. This was a young and carefree man. He had been painted standing against a background of moorland and gray skies—one booted foot set casually on a flat boulder, a riding crop held in his right hand. He was dressed in hunting clothes and carried himself with careless elegance and ease, his black locks ruffled as though blown a little by the wind, and the scarlet of his coat contrasting so effectively with the somber background that he seemed almost about to step from the frame.

But, for me, the most arresting thing was not his handsomeness, remarkable though it was, but his expression. His dark eyes were full of confidence and assurance and expectation of the future, and his mouth was not thin and twisted but curved into a half-smile. This was the man before he had suffered. No lines of pain or shadows of torment and bitterness marred the nonchalant good looks. . . .

Behind me Signorina Frugoni exclaimed suddenly: *"Grazie a Dio!* Here it is at last!"

I had been so absorbed in my contemplation of the picture that I had not noticed her poking busily about the room. The trunk was pushed into a dark corner where the ceiling sloped down steeply toward the floor. It was a very fine affair of heavy leather, tooled with elaborate patterns and studded with silver, which had tarnished to black. Between us we dragged it from its niche, choking and sneezing as the dust blew about us in clouds. Signorina Frugoni produced a silver key from a chain round her neck and fitted it carefully into the elaborate lock. Together we raised the curved lid and there inside, folded away, lay a treasure-trove of Italian silks—all of them of exquisite and beautiful colors and some shot with gold and silver threads. She took each one out with loving care and handed them, one after the other, to me. At last we came to the violet silk. It was the color of pale amethysts and shimmered as she lifted it gently from its resting place. She drew in her breath with a sigh of satisfaction and held it up against me. *"Finalmente . . .* it was made for you, signorina. Just wait until you see the gown I shall make for you. . . ."

We replaced the other materials and relocked the trunk. They would be safe there until Daniel could be sent to move it: it was far too heavy for us. I paused again to look at the portrait.

"Come, signorina." The Italian plucked at my arm. "That picture belongs to the past—that is why it has been locked away in here. It's better to forget we have seen it—like he has wished to forget. . . ."

We left the room and returned to the contessa. Signorina Frugoni trotted swiftly ahead of me, bearing her triumphant burden over her arm. I followed more slowly. I could not forget that painting. Its image stayed in my mind's eye as clearly as though it were still before me. It had been a shock to see him as he had once been. I no longer wondered at his bitterness and gall . . . at last I understood.

CHAPTER VIII

I slept restlessly for several nights. I felt strangely uneasy and unhappy but could not have said exactly why. And then, one night an incident occurred that reawoke all my fears and uncertainties concerning Mrs. Silver's death, and which confirmed my long-felt suspicions that someone at Aysgarth was dangerous. . . .

I had lain awake for some time thinking of the coming ball and of how much I dreaded it. Eweretta, I knew, was to wear a beautiful gown of white lace, frilled and beribboned to suit her golden prettiness. I knew very well that I would look dull and plain beside her, and although I had for years been reconciled to the idea of being the ugly duckling, I found to my discomfort that this time, for some reason, I cared. Perhaps it was because of Catherine Benton: I should have been happy to shine brilliantly at her ball, if only to disconcert her. It would be satisfying to shatter that cool, supercilious poise for even a second— but I knew that there was little prospect of that. She would view me as a curious insect—from a safe distance—and find every reason to make disparaging remarks in whispered asides . . . just as she had done on her visit to Aysgarth. I saw again the dark head bent down to that green-trimmed bonnet. . . .

I turned fretfully this way and that in the big fourposter. It was an unusually warm night and I had left the bed hangings drawn back so that I could see the room and the narrow sliver of moonlight that pierced between the shutters. Outside the owls hooted and called mournfully to each other; at last I fell asleep.

I was awakened later by a noise—unaccustomed and stealthy, and as I stared and listened intently in the darkness, I heard the soft click of the door latch . . . someone had either just entered the room or had just left it. I lay motionless, stiff and cold with fear. At any moment I expected unknown hands to lunge and grip at my throat or some nameless menace to attack me somehow. . . . Never, until the end of my days shall I forget the terror of those moments as I waited alone in the blackness for whatever threatened me. . . . But nothing happened. I strained my ears but no further sound came from the room about me, and at last, after long nightmarish minutes, I sat up cautiously and lit the candle beside my bed with fingers that trembled violently.

The room was empty. I lifted the brass candlestick high into the air and pointed it this way and that, lighting the room to its furthest shadowy corner. There was no one there. But I knew I had not been mistaken. Someone, or something, had been into this room. . . . With a pounding heart I slid from the bed and crept silently to the door to listen once more. Not a sound: not a single squeak or creak came from beyond the door. And yet I was not satisfied. Whoever, or whatever, had been in my room might return; perhaps I had stirred in my sleep sufficiently merely to alarm them into retreat. He or she might be waiting, unmoving and patient, just outside that door. . . . If only I could at least lock it, but the keyhole was empty and had been so since my arrival. And then I remembered the evening when Mrs. Silver had first led me up the great hall staircase and along the passageway to this room. I saw her stop at the door and set down the lamp she was carrying to take a key from the bunch at her waist. . . . That key must still be with the others that I kept with me daily. It was my custom to leave them on the dressing table at night, and with a feeling of relief, I hurried to find them. The keys were gone. I stared bewildered at the mahogany table: silver candlesticks, brushes, tortoise-shell combs, scent bottle . . . all were neatly arranged on the polished surface but the keys that I always placed on one side had vanished. Perhaps I had left them somewhere else before retiring? But I know very well that I had not; I remembered perfectly putting them down beside one of the candlesticks and the metallic clattering noise that they had made.

I was left with one conclusion: whoever had come to my room had done so to steal the keys and God knew for what purpose. The servants were well fed and would surely have no need to go to such lengths to break into the storerooms, any more than anybody else in the household. As for all those locked and empty rooms that Signorina Frugoni and I had seen, what could anyone possibly want in them . . . ? It was mysterious and somehow deeply menacing, for at least one thing was now certain. The intruder had been no ghostly being from the past roaming the corridors restlessly. Ghosts did not need keys: they had a well-known ability to pass through walls with no trouble at all. I feared no phantom now but someone very much alive and, therefore, far more dangerous. . . .

I slept no more that night but lay in my bed listening and watching for the slightest sound or movement. I thought of Mrs. Silver prying about the darkened house that night and remembered again the shadowy figure I had glimpsed at the end of the passage, and over and over again I imagined unknown hands thrusting her forward into the blackness. . . . I saw her pitch helplessly down that long staircase, bumping and rolling from step to step like a black doll. . . .

At last the dawn came, its cold light creeping feebly through the shutter cracks. I got up and searched the room carefully but the keys were not there. What should I do? Now that it was day my suspicions seemed hysterical and exaggerated and yet I longed to share them with someone. But who? Whom could I confide in? The master of the house was too grim and forbidding a man—I could not trust him: at best, he would be contemptuous, and at worst, could it have been he who had entered my room last night. . . . I could not be sure. The contessa? But, viewed dispassionately, was she not a rather strange and eccentric old lady who had certainly displayed no grief for Mrs. Silver . . . ? Signorina Frugoni? I knew so little of her. She was amiable enough but, after all, a foreigner. . . . Eweretta—who hated me so much—the thought of going to her was impossible. That left only one person who was sane and sensible. . . .

The keys were in the housekeeper's room. I found them there later on a table. So far as I could tell none was missing and nothing had been taken from the storerooms. I said nothing to the servants but went about my work puzzled and anxious.

"Can you spare me a few moments? There is something I should like to talk to you about."

He looked surprised, and then pleased. "But of course, Miss Chell. I should be delighted. . . ."

We walked along together a little way and I told him of the events of the previous night—the mysterious intruder, the missing keys, my growing fears and suspicions concerning Mrs. Silver's death. He listened courteously in silence and turned to me, an embarrassed look on his face.

"Please don't be offended, Miss Chell, if I say this. . . . I'm sure you believe what you say very sincerely, but you *do* have a very active imagination, don't you? I've seen this for myself when showing you the abbey ruins. People with inventive minds are most susceptible to surroundings and atmosphere—this is a very old house that lends itself perfectly to imagining all sorts of things. . . ."

"But on the night of Mrs. Silver's death I distinctly heard footsteps outside my room—I'm sure of that—and I'm *certain* I saw somebody at the end of that corridor. . . . And last night I heard my door open and shut very clearly—I know exactly the sound that the latch makes!"

"It was probably not properly shut and the wind blew it. I always hear all sorts of odd noises in the house at night myself—it's because it's so old," he said awkwardly. "As for the other occasion: you were badly concussed after that riding accident weren't you, Miss Chell? It's more than likely that you were wandering a little in your mind. A blow on the head can have strange effects."

"And Mrs. Silver's death?"

"Well, surely it was just an unfortunate accident. I heard the doctor telling Mr. Metcalfe that there was a tear in the hem of her nightgown that could easily have caused her to trip—let alone the slippery stone steps and the darkness. . . . The coroner had no doubts so I don't think you need to have any either, Miss Chell. You mustn't worry yourself about it any more."

"What about the keys? Why should someone take those from my room?"

He smiled at me reassuringly. "I'm sure that nobody did. I expect you left them downstairs all the time and forgot that you had done so—it's so easy to make mistakes when you are tired."

"You seem so certain about it all, Mr. Paige."

He flushed a little. "You must understand, Miss Chell, that so much of my work is concerned with sifting evidence. I cannot afford the luxury of too much imagining or I might misinterpret the facts. Archaeology relies on the truth alone, with very little speculation or guesswork, if accuracy is to be preserved in history; that is why I see your problem so clearly and can set your mind at rest. There is nothing to fear at Aysgarth; I am certain of that."

I should have been relieved and comforted but doubts still niggled at me, until I began to see the sense of what Philip Paige had said. It was true that sometimes my imagination could run riot and this house seemed a breeding ground for wild thoughts. . . . I decided to be very firm with myself and put the whole affair out of my mind. I was grateful to Philip for his quiet wisdom and valued his friendship even more. Clumsy and shy he might be but he was also kind. I knew that he had been bowled over by Eweretta's prettiness and that he still watched her covertly whenever he could. I hoped his feelings were no longer hurt by her heartless taunting and indifference.

The contessa announced that my ball gown was ready but that it was to be kept hidden from me until the evening it was to be worn.

"I want it to be a complete surprise for you, my dear," she told me. "Frugoni has excelled herself, I'm delighted to say. It will be most interesting to see you dressed in something that really suits you for a change. Frugoni herself will dress your hair—she is quite superb at that as you know. . . ." She patted her own exquisite coiffure of snow-white hair serenely. "Tell me, have you any jewelry to wear, child? Not that you should wear much at your tender age—but something, say, round your neck. . . ."

"I have only this locket, which belonged to my mother." I drew the heavy oval of silver from beneath the collar of my dress where I always wore it, hidden from inquisitive eyes and questions. Often, when alone, I opened the locket to look at the portraits of my parents, face to face inside the engraved casing. I remembered them, but I did not wish to share that memory with anyone: to do so might invite criticisms of them and remarks that I did not want to hear. . . .

The contessa moved closer and lifted her lorgnette to inspect it. "It's charming, my dear, and will do admirably with the dress. And I shall lend you my amethyst earrings and bracelet. They were given to me by my husband, the count, when I was your age exactly and whatever his shortcomings lack of taste was not among them. It will give me the greatest pleasure to see *you* wearing them, Alice."

"*You remind me of my daughter, Lucia. . . .*" I remembered the contessa's remark at our first meeting and tears came to my eyes. I felt deeply ashamed of my earlier doubts of the contessa —how could I ever have thought her capable of any evil?

When the day of the ball came I felt more nervous and reluctant about it than ever. I wished with all my heart that I could have stayed at home. I might perhaps develop a last-minute headache or sore throat? I toyed with various excuses but in the end I knew I could not disappoint Signorina Frugoni or the contessa after all their efforts. I also suspected that the master of the house would not accept any pretext for opting out, however ingenious. There was nothing to be done but make the best of it.

Thurza more than made up for my lack of enthusiasm. She scurried excitedly about the bedroom making preparations. A bath sheet was carefully laid over the carpet to take the hip bath —a very fine one japanned in brown on the outside and marbled inside—and then she filled it with warm water, dragged painstakingly bucket by bucket from the kitchen. Towels were set to warm near the fire, which she had lit since the evening was cool, and a few drops of lavender water were sprinkled into the bath.

"It's like old times, miss," she said delightedly, "when the ladies were always dressing up grandly like tonight." She hugged a towel to her chest and sighed. "If only it could be just like that again. . . ."

"Perhaps it will be one day, Thurza. Miracles do happen."

"That's true, miss. We must pray and hope for one, I suppose."

I splashed about in the scented water. "Or find the Cross of Aysgarth."

She looked at me openmouthed. "You don't really believe in that do you, miss? Mr. Unwin says it's only a story."

"I don't know what I believe, Thurza. But if we're looking for miracles it's the only kind of one I can think of at the moment."

Later Signorina Frugoni appeared. There was a mouselike scrabbling at the door and a cloud of violet silk seemed to float into the room. A pair of beady little eyes gleamed at me triumphantly over the top of the shimmering folds: "*Ecco la sorpresa, signorina!* If you are ready we will dress you now."

The gown she had carried in was more beautiful than I had ever imagined. I had not, for one moment, expected such a glorious creation: the scooped neckline, the tiny puffed sleeves frilled with cream lace, and the tight bodice fitted me as perfectly as if they had been fashioned in Paris, and the full skirt, made voluminous by layer upon layer of petticoats, each edged with deep bands of lace, billowed about me softly. The hem was gathered up into deep scallops and on each one was sewn a knot of violets tied with green ribbon.

"Sit here if you please, signorina, and I will dress your hair."

I sat patiently in the little velvet chair while she brushed my dark, straight hair and then, with deft strokes of the comb and nimble fingers, coaxed it into a deceptively simple style—parted in the center and looped softly up over my ears into a smooth crown on the top of my head.

"Nothing fussy will do for you, signorina," she mumbled through a mouthful of pins. "This way is best for you."

The contessa stood in the doorway, looking magnificent in dark blue satin, diamonds flashing at her throat and on her hands, and a glittering diamond tiara set on her beautiful white hair. She had brought the amethyst bracelet and earrings she had promised and put them on me while Signorina Frugoni fastened my silver locket round my neck. Finally, the contessa held out a pair of long white gloves and an exquisite little ivory fan. "These are for you as well, child. Now look at yourself in the glass."

I could not believe what I saw reflected in the silver mirror on the dressing table: for the first time in my life I looked almost pretty. . . . I fingered the amethysts as they glimmered in the candlelight and touched the crown of dark hair that gave me an elegant and soignée air. My shoulders looked graceful above the low-cut bodice and the color of the gown matched my eyes so perfectly that they glowed brilliantly in my face and seemed to eclipse all my less satisfactory features.

The contessa was smiling at me. "Just as I hoped, Alice, my dear. It only needed a little careful thought and planning to transform you from a plain duckling into a swan!"

I thanked her and kissed her cheek and then I took Signorina Frugoni's hands in mine and thanked her too. She blushed a deep pink. "I have done my best for you, signorina, and am well content with the result—that is my reward."

Thurza's eyes were round as saucers: "I hope I don't give offense, miss, but I've never seen you look so nice. . . . Somehow I never thought . . ."

"That will do, Thurza," interrupted the contessa briskly. "We've no time for chatter. The others will be waiting. Come along, child. Miles told Garrick to harness up the old coach tonight so we shall arrive in some style. Thank goodness it will be too dark for everyone to see how sadly moth-eaten it has become."

The petticoats rustled richly beneath the silk as we walked along the passage, and my confidence grew with every step. I felt taller and more assured than ever before and when we reached the staircase I was able to descend it with my head held high. Eweretta looked up from far below in the great hall and I saw the astonishment on her face as she caught sight of me. She was dreamily beautiful in a white lace gown, her golden hair curled into bunches of ringlets, but, for once, I did not feel plain and dowdy beside her. I was not pretty but, just for tonight, nor was I plain. . . .

As we reached the foot of the stairs, Philip Paige stepped forward. He looked nice in his evening clothes but rather uncomfortable and ill at ease. He smiled at me timidly and complimented me, stammering a little, on my appearance. The contessa eyed him kindly.

"I'm glad to see that you are a man of discernment after all. Alice certainly does us all credit and looks utterly charming—don't you agree, Miles?"

I had not noticed him before. He was standing a little way off and half-hidden in the shadows, and when I looked at him, my heart stood still. He was wearing a green velvet coat, white ruffled shirt and cravat, and a waistcoat embroidered with gold and silver threads. The black locks curled forward round his face and a heavy gold ring gleamed on his hand. . . . He looked the exact image of the man in the portrait in that locked room. . . . Once again I was seeing him as he had been before. . . .

And then he moved forward and the spell was broken: it had been a trick of shadows and imagination. I saw that he was as marred and crippled as ever. He came toward me, and taking my hand lightly in his long fingers, raised it briefly to his lips: "As usual Miss Chell astonishes me," he said. I stared up at him and for a moment we looked at each other in silence before, abruptly, he turned away.

The coach was an impressive, lumbering conveyance of vast proportions and faded splendor. It swayed and rocked like a ship along the lanes as we drove through the moonlit countryside. The stars were out and winked softly in the blackness overhead; it seemed to me an evening of magic.

Certainly, nothing could have been more magical or fairylike than Benton Castle as it rose out of the darkness, windows ablaze with light, its pointed turrets shining in the moonlight. Outside, the castle was romantic enchantment; inside, it became a glittering kaleidoscope of color, warmth, music, and light. As we mounted the long sweep of stairs to the ballroom, instead of my customary sinking of heart at such occasions, I felt an unexpected tingle of excitement and anticipation.

"See what I meant," hissed the contessa in my ear. "They've no taste at all, my dear—not a scrap. It's all so *vulgar!*"

I looked about me and understood why she considered it to be so. Everything *was* exaggeratedly opulent and grandiose. The crystal chandeliers that hung in the ballroom were the largest and most magnificent I had ever seen—even in London—and they blazed with the fire of a million diamonds. Golden curtains were drawn across the windows in long and sumptuous swags of velvet, tasseled and fringed in shining gold thread, and tall mirrors covered the walls almost from floor to ceiling, so that the room seemed to stretch away forever in a moving, brilliant pattern of countless people . . . And, over all this scene hung the sweet, heavy scent of hothouse flowers, that smothered the corners of the room in exotic banks of perfumed beauty. It may have been vulgar and ostentatious, as the contessa decreed, but it was also gratifyingly colorful and alive after the gray drabness of Aysgarth.

Lord Benton, looking as round as an orange in his tightly cut evening clothes, greeted us with slimy charm. The contessa extended her hand disdainfully and he bowed low to me. "I should not have recognized you, my dear Miss Chell. When last we met you looked quite different—charmingly informal, of course—but tonight you are a positive delight to the eye!" His watery blue eyes slid over me appreciatively, dwelling on my bare shoulders, and he continued to hold my hand for so long that I was compelled to pull it free from his grasp. He repulsed and irritated me, and in some irrational way, I feared him. . . .

As I had expected, Catherine Benton looked dazzlingly beautiful. She wore a gown made of layers of delicate white net upon satin and the wide flounces round the skirts were edged with pink ribbon. A necklace of gold and rubies encircled her slender throat and fresh, pink roses garlanded her hair. Her gray eyes were cold.

"I had scarcely expected you to favor us with your company this evening, Miss Chell," she said with a cool trill of laughter. "After what Miles told me I had thought you might prefer more rustic pleasures than we could offer."

I was spared the necessity of replying, and perhaps, despite myself, rudely, by Lord Alfred Witherspoon, who was still staying at the castle and now dashed forward gallantly to greet us. He was magnificently attired and groomed and I had no doubt that he had checked and rechecked his faultless appearance many times in every one of the mirrors in the ballroom. He was staring at Eweretta and seemed so greatly taken by her that he could hardly drag his eyes away from her to speak to the contessa. It was the first time he had seen her as she had been out riding when the Bentons had called at Aysgarth, and to judge from the expression of thunderstruck admiration on his face, it would not be the last. He claimed her instantly for the first quadrille, as the musicians began to play, and Eweretta looked up at him with demure but lively interest. The contessa surveyed them through her lorgnette.

"Well, I can think of a worse husband for her," she remarked dispassionately. "We must hope that he continues to see her through the rose-tinted spectacles he is obviously wearing at the moment. . . . After all, he is rich and amiable enough, from all accounts, even though he's a fool. He could give Eweretta the kind of life she wants. . . ." She nodded her head thoughtfully. "Yes, I shall give it all my encouragement . . . unless you want him, Alice. He's a friend of yours, isn't he?"

"An *old* friend," I said with a smile. "I assure you that is all."

She grunted. "Just as well. He's not right for you, my dear, that's certain. You'd be bored to death within six months!"

◎◎◎

I shall remember the ball at Benton Castle for a long time, if only because, for the first time in my life, I found myself no longer a dispirited wallflower but an eagerly claimed dancing partner. Perhaps it was because of my beautiful dress, or my new-found confidence, which prevented me from hiding behind the nearest pillar, or perhaps it was just because I had grown up a little since those miserable dances in London. Whatever the reason my card was full and I had no need to fear the shame and humiliation of sitting out alone for dance after dance. It was pleasant to be admired and complimented and to dance with good-looking and gallant partners. I danced a quadrille with Philip Paige, and as I had half-expected and dreaded, he stumbled and floundered his way through the intricate, stately movements. I felt a deep pity for his agonizing embarrassment as he made mistake after mistake and did my best to console him afterward when he looked so downcast. Perhaps, I thought, it was as well that he had no chance to partner Eweretta—she would not have spared his feelings in the least. I saw that she was dancing constantly with Lord Alfred and that he looked increasingly besotted by her as the hours went by. Later, he came to claim me for the waltz and talked of her incessantly.

"She's the loveliest girl I've ever seen," he told me ecstatically. "What an enchanting, delicate creature. . . ."

He continued to sing Eweretta's praises as we waltzed round and round the ballroom and I smiled to myself, thinking that they would probably do very well together. Apart from the occasional momentary hesitation as Lord Alfred paused to admire himself in one of the huge mirrors on the walls, we whirled across the floor as though we floated on air. My partner might be excessively vain but he danced wonderfully well and the waltz was my favorite. Once, as we turned, I caught a brief glimpse of Miles Metcalfe standing leaning against one of the pillars and watching us. His face looked as white as the plaster behind him and his hooded eyes as black and inscrutable as the night. Distracted for a moment, I missed a step and might have fallen but for Lord Alfred's steadying arm. And then he was lost to view as we spun away into the thick of the dancers. I had been surprised to see him standing there alone instead of with Catherine Benton, who had monopolized him for most of the evening. On our arrival she had put her arm through his in a possessive fashion and looked up at him in a way that clearly stated her renewed feelings for him. . . . I had turned away quickly, not wishing to watch her triumphant expression, and has assumed that their reengagement might even be announced that evening. Why then was he alone? And then, the simple explanation came to me. *He* was quite unable to dance and *she,* as hostess, had been reluctantly obliged to leave his side to partner her guests. I looked about me and saw her waltzing by in the arms of a very handsome young subaltern, icily beautiful in her frothy, white gown. Miles must have been watching her all the time from beside that pillar, and no wonder he had done so with such pale intensity of expression—it must be torture, I thought, to be hideously crippled and to have to watch the one you love dance by with another. . . .

We left the ball soon after midnight. The contessa was fatigued and insisted on returning home although Eweretta protested long and fiercely. For myself, I was content to go. I had enjoyed the evening but it had been marred toward its end by having to endure Lord Benton as a dancing partner. He was odiously oily and I had listened to the overfamiliar compliments that streamed from his wet lips with disgust. I disliked and distrusted him and knew him to be harsh and cruel; however much he smiled and bowed, he would be a dangerous man to cross. . . .

Eweretta sulked in her corner of the coach, furious at having been dragged away from the ball, but her pettishness was wasted on the contessa, who, lulled by the swaying motion, slept soundly as we rumbled homeward through the night.

It was not until later, when I lay sleepily in bed thinking over the events of the evening, that I realized that my silver locket was missing. I sat up instantly in the fourposter—wide awake and dismayed. Thurza had waited up to help me undress and I knew I would have asked her to help me undo the difficult clasp and yet I had no recollection of her struggling with it and the locket was certainly not still round my neck. I lit the candle and began a thorough investigation of the room: bed, dressing table, drawers, washstand, table, chair, and even the floor, which I crawled across on my hands and knees to grope and probe in every corner. The locket was nowhere in the room. I tried to think clearly and calmly. It had been safely in my possession on our return from the ball—I was sure of that because the contessa had remarked on how well it suited my gown, as we had sat for a while in the drawing room where Unwin had served a tray of refreshments. Therefore, the locket must have fallen from my neck somewhere in the house. I had sat on a small, velvet chair near the fireplace and I remembered fiddling idly with the silver chain as the contessa had aired her astringent views on the evening in general. . . . Undoubtedly the locket had dropped somewhere near that chair—the clasp had always been unreliable and now I reproached myself bitterly for not seeing that it was properly mended. To return to bed and to sleep while the only memento left to me of my parents was still lost was unthinkable. I *had* to go downstairs and find the locket. . . .

There could be no disguising to myself the plain fact that I was terrified. I dreaded the prospect of making the long journey through the dark and silent house, all alone. But I could not rest until I had retrieved my most precious possession and to hesitate would be to lose all courage. I grasped the brass candlestick firmly in my hand, and holding it high and bold, set off down the passage from my room. I had not waited to put on robe or slippers and shivered with cold as well as fear as I moved swiftly onward, the candle's flame stabbing the blackness ahead with a feeble, wavering light. The shadows around me were weird and distorted—stretching like long fingers along the walls and ceiling as I hurried on. And when I came to the head of the staircase the back of my neck tingled with terror as though it knew that someone stood close behind me, waiting to push me to a violent death. . . .

The stone steps were cold beneath my bare feet and drafts caught at the candle flame so that it flickered badly and I had to shield it with my hand. At the bottom of the long staircase the small light steadied enough for me to see my way across the great hall. I opened the drawing room door quietly and slipped inside.

The remains of a fire burned dully on the hearth and there was a tiny hissing noise and a splutter of sparks as an ember shifted and settled down into the ash. I lifted the candle high and looked about me, reassured by the familiarity of the room. The chair where I had been sitting earlier was beside the fireplace and I went at once toward it, and bending down, began to search the ground around it.

"Is this what you are looking for?"

The voice spoke in the semidarkness from somewhere behind me and I leaped to my feet in panic. The candlestick flew from my grasp to roll away across the carpet, its flame snuffed out. Blackness surrounded me. My heart raced, urging me to flight, and yet I felt too paralyzed to move. And then I began to run— blindly and stumblingly—in the direction of the door, and as I did so, I felt my arm caught and held tightly. The ruffled sleeve of my cambric nightgown tore and ripped as I pulled and struggled frantically to free myself, but it was hopeless. My captor was too strong.

The voice spoke again—slurred, amused, lazy: "Don't run

away just yet, Miss Chell. I rather like the idea of your company. You always amuse me, you know. There's a tinderbox on the table near your right hand. Find the candle and light it again."

I had recognized his voice but it had done nothing to steady the pounding of my heart. "I cannot, unless you let me go."

"Only if you promise me not to run away."

"Very well."

"You promise," he insisted.

"I promise," I replied, thinking that this was one vow that I would not hesitate to break if need be.

He released my arm then and I found the tinderbox and, eventually, the brass candlestick. With fingers that still shook, I lit the flame.

He was sitting slumped in a tall-backed leather chair near the fire, and I saw at once that he was very drunk. His hair fell in wild disorder across his forehead and there was a bright flush on the normally pale face. The loosened cravat, the rumpled green velvet coat, and the near-empty decanter of brandy on the table beside him, all told their tale, and I knew that he was in a black and devilish mood by the glitter in his eyes as his glance raked me from head to toe.

He said again: "Is this what you were looking for?"

He held the silver locket by its chain in his long fingers and swung it idly to and fro in an arc in front of him. "A pretty thing . . . and, if that is your mother's portrait inside, then she was indeed beautiful. What a pity *you* are not beautiful like her, Miss Chell, although you came very near to being so at the ball tonight. . . . You surprised me, yet again. I had always thought of you as very plain but now I'm not so sure. . . ." He looked me over with insolent appraisal and I felt near-naked in my flimsy nightgown. The locket twirled and spun round and round in a silver blur. He went on: "I found this on the floor over there. I knew it was yours, Miss Chell, and intended to return it to you in the morning. You have saved me the trouble by arriving in person. Here you are. Take it."

He held out the locket toward me, dangling it tantalizingly within my grasp. My hand stretched out and then dropped back to my side. I did not care at all for the drunken glint in his eyes and to take the locket would mean that I was once again within his reach. I hesitated.

"Come on, Miss Chell. Take it quickly. It's what you came for, after all."

But still I hesitated and, at last, he shrugged his shoulders with apparent indifference and dropped the locket carelessly into his pocket.

"I do believe that you are afraid of me, Miss Chell! I thought you had more spirit. Very well, I shall keep it until you find the courage to take it from me." He seemed very amused and refilled the glass at his elbow, and lifting it to his lips, watched me mockingly over the rim. "Tell me, by the way, what do you think of Miss Benton—she looked exceedingly beautiful at the ball, don't you agree?"

"Very beautiful," I said woodenly.

He turned the brandy glass round between his hands, watching the liquid gleam amber in the candlelight. "She is prepared to marry me, after all, it seems. She has quite got over her aversion to my crippled state—she told me as much this evening. What do you say to that?"

"I congratulate you."

"You don't care for Catherine do you? You don't like her at all. I can see it in your eyes and hear it in your voice."

"It cannot surely matter what I feel for her, sir. It is no concern of mine."

"Oh, but it is in a way, since this is your home now and I should inevitably bring my bride to live here at Aysgarth. So you must give me an honest answer—a plain yes or no. Do you think I should marry Miss Benton?"

"No."

"Ah! Now we have the truth! And why not?"

"Because she would not make you happy, Mr. Metcalfe."

He laughed at that—and it was a bitter, hollow sound. "My dear Miss Chell, no woman could do that now, I fear. I am long past happiness . . . happiness has abandoned me—or I it—to hell with happiness!" He raised his glass and finished the rest of the brandy in a single gulp.

"I should like to return to bed now, sir, if you will have the goodness to let me pass unhindered."

He said nothing but let his eyes wander slowly over me. "It makes me very sad, Miss Chell," he remarked after a moment of close study, "to see that you are still afraid of me. You are positively shaking with fright."

"I am very cold!"

"No wonder when you are only wearing that thin nightgown. You looked beautiful in that violet gown that matched your violet eyes . . . but did you know that you look even more pleasing to me in that plain and prudish thing you are wearing now, all buttoned up to your chin, with your hair falling over your shoulders. . . ."

I did not wait for more of his drunken compliments. I made to pass the chair and escape, but he moved swifter than the devil. In a flash his long fingers had reached out to seize hold of my nightgown as I ran. There was a rending noise and the fastening at my neck was ripped apart, and as I pulled frantically against him, the thin material began to tear open down the front. To have run on would have risked being left completely naked with my gown in shreds about me. I had no choice but to stop, and pitilessly and inexorably, he drew me backward until I stood before him.

He took my hands and held them fast in his. "Do you know the story of Beauty and the Beast, Miss Chell?" he said in almost conversational tones.

I must humor him and wait my next chance to escape. "Yes."

"Then you will know that to save the poor, ugly Beast from dying, Beauty kissed him . . ."

"I believe that is so."

"Then since you are so like Beauty this evening and I, as usual, am very like the Beast—will you not kiss me, just once, to save me?"

"You are not dying. So let me go at once!"

The heavy lids drooped over his eyes and he turned his head away. "But I am, you know, Miss Chell. Little by little, moment by moment, hour by hour, I am rotting slowly away . . . and do you know why?"

I said nothing.

"I am sick to my very soul," he said in desolate tones. "Once I had life and vigor and hope. Now there is nothing but pain and frustration. . . . You do not understand what it is to be a useless, grotesque cripple."

He let go of my hands suddenly to grope for the brandy, and finding both glass and decanter empty, hurled the glass into the fireplace where it splintered into tiny fragments. The embers spluttered briefly into pointed flickers of flame and then died away. . . .

I said quietly into the silence that followed: "You are not in the least grotesque, sir. I do not find you so."

He lifted his head to look up at me and I saw the unguarded, black despair in his eyes. It was the same wretchedness that I had seen on Dobbin's face and I responded to it instinctively. I stretched out my hand to comfort him, and before I could speak another word, he had seized it and pulled me roughly down into his arms, crushing me hard against him so that the breath was knocked from my body. For a second I was aware of his face close above me—dark, intense, frightening—and then he kissed me savagely, forcing my head back against his arm with a relentless, brutal pressure. I struggled frantically but he only held me the tighter. He was immensely strong and his arms encircled my body so fiercely that I was helpless to move. "Alice . . . Alice . . ." He murmured my name low, again and again, and his lips traveled over my hair, my eyes, my cheeks, my throat, as though he would devour me . . . His dark head bent to kiss the bare shoulder that protruded from my torn nightgown and then, with a violent, impatient movement, he ripped aside the fragile cloth still further and I felt the cool touch of his fingers over my naked body—so gently caressing and so insidiously persuasive in their practiced skill that, for a moment, I ceased to fight him and lay quite still. . . . And then I regained my senses. I struck him. I hit him hard across the face and he released me as abruptly as if I had stabbed him with a knife.

I ran from him then, stumbling and blundering blindly through the dark house, clutching my tattered gown to my body. And as I ran, the tears of shame and mortification flowed down my cheeks.

CHAPTER IX

I would have to leave Aysgarth. When morning came and I rose, still red-eyed and with a heavy heart, I knew that I would have to go. I could not stay on in this house after what had happened last night. I felt a terrible humiliation. *"You always amuse me . . ."* I could hear his voice speaking those words again. He was going to marry Catherine Benton but that had not prevented him from amusing himself with me with drunken brutality. In all probability he was still laughing about it this morning to himself, in his arrogant, cold-blooded way . . . Well, I would not give him the chance to mock at me any longer. I would depart from this hateful place at the first opportunity, just as soon as I could find employment—*any* post, *anywhere,* so long as it was far, far away from Aysgarth.

It is a truth of life that one quickly forgets one's own troubles if occupied with those of others. Suddenly, in the midst of my bitter brooding, I remembered Dobbin. I had promised him help and I had failed him, and I had been so preoccupied of late with my own feelings that I had quite forgotten his. I had not even been back to see him, and for all I knew, his uncle might have taken him away already and Dobbin might, at this very moment, be working down in some distant deep, black mine—sitting alone and terrified in pitch darkness for interminable hours and perhaps crying tears as bitter and desperate as any I had shed through the night. I hurried from the house, full of remorse, and set off on the long trek across the fields.

Mrs. Cropper was outside the cottage. She stood there with arms folded across her chest and watched my approach with unmistakable hostility.

"Come to interfere again, have you, miss?"

"Interfere, Mrs. Cropper? I don't understand."

"That's what I said, miss!" She stared at me defiantly. "I reckon it was all due to your fancy ideas that my Dobbin ran off instead of going with his uncle like he was told to. He said *you'd* promised you'd try and stop it . . . that's what he told me. Not that you've done much, it seems after all, but Dobbin has. Oh yes, he's in *real* trouble *this* time!"

I felt sick with guilt. "What do you mean, Mrs. Cropper? Where is he? What's happened to him?"

"He's been arrested, that's what!" She said it almost triumphantly.

"But whatever for?" I could not believe what she was telling me.

"Poaching a hare. He ran away so he wouldn't have to go back with my brother when he came to collect him. Stayed out in the woods for days—you know what he's like—and then he got hungry and stole the hare to eat."

"Mr. Metcalfe would never have him *arrested* for such a thing. I'm sure of that."

" 'Tweren't on Mr. Metcalfe's estate. Dobbin ran right away from here—he was that determined, the little devil. The hare belonged to Lord Benton. 'Twere *his* gamekeeper that caught him."

I stared at her in dismay. Dobbin had stolen from the one man who would have no compassion or mercy. I remembered the contessa's words: *"It is quite usual for him to sentence poachers to seven years transportation. . . ."* But surely not a child . . . not a little boy of seven whose only crime had been to fear being sent to work down a coal mine?

Mrs. Cropper was watching me and her eyes were hard. "Well, what are you going to do for him now, miss? How are you going to help him this time? You can do what you like—*I* don't care what happens to him. I've washed my hands of him!"

"Lord Benton may be lenient with him when he learns the circumstances," I said, with very little hope in my heart.

"Lenient!" She laughed bitterly. "The likes of *him* lenient with the likes of *us!* His lordship's not known in these parts for his soft heart!" She shrugged her shoulders helplessly. "There's nowt to be done. Dobbin brought this on himself with his wicked, disobedient ways and now he'll have to take what's coming to him. He'll be lucky if they don't hang him!"

The baby began to cry from the cottage—a thin, demanding wail. Mrs. Cropper turned her back on me and went inside without another word.

I ran all the way back to Aysgarth and my mind felt frozen with fear for Dobbin. I could not think clearly beyond the fact that he was in great peril and that I was, in some measure, to blame. I thought of his tear-stained, tragic face when I had last seen him up in the horse chestnut tree. How much more destitute must he be now—alone, defenseless, and terrified in the power of a man like Lord Benton! If I had not given the little boy any hope but had persuaded him instead to accept going away to the mine as inevitable then he might not have run away and would not have been forced to poach to survive. I had failed Dobbin when he last needed help; this time I must not do so.

"Contessa! Where is Mr. Metcalfe? I *must* find him and I've searched everywhere. . . ."

The contessa raised her lorgnette to stare at me in surprise. "Whatever's the matter, my dear? You look as though you had seen a ghost—which would not be unlikely in *this* house. Sit down and tell me why you want to see my great-nephew so urgently—you usually try to avoid him, not seek him out!"

I forced myself to sit calmly and repeat Mrs. Cropper's story—adding my own feelings of guilt and terrible anxiety for Dobbin.

"You cannot take the blame for this affair on your shoulders, Alice, that would be absurd and nonsensical. The boy would have run off in any case, whether you had spoken to him or not —I'm sure of that. He clearly has plenty of spirit in him and would have fought to the last ditch to escape from a fate so abhorrent to him. The guilt is not yours—it belongs to us all— every single one of us. So long as these children are permitted to work in factories and mines, ill-treated and abused, and thrown into prisons for stealing to keep themselves alive, then we are all to blame. . . ." She paused and patted my hand comfortingly. "As to helping the child now—Miles will do all he can, no doubt, but it may not be possible to extricate him. . . . I told you that Lord Benton is ruthless where poachers are concerned. We must just pray that something may be done." She frowned thoughtfully and twisted the heavy rings on her fingers. "It is most unfortunate that it should have been *him* of all landowners—what a vile creature he is. I think I dislike him more than anyone I have ever known. You must find Miles immediately, my dear, and tell him what has happened. You will have to seek him out in his room in the east wing—he was in great pain again at the ball last night—I could see that—and he may not appear for several days. We cannot wait for that!"

"I daren't disturb him there," I said, with a sinking heart. I could feel a deep blush spreading across my cheeks. My worry for Dobbin had caused me momentarily to forget my last encounter with Miles Metcalfe. Now the memory returned all too plainly and I found I lacked the courage to face him again.

The contessa eyed me sharply and with a gleam of amusement. "Nonsense, child! You're not afraid of him, I hope. I thought you had more pluck than that. If you want to help that boy you must brave the lion's den! Come, I will send for Thurza to show you the way or you may lose yourself there a second time."

And so, once more, I found myself in that strange maze of cold, dim passages in the very oldest part of the house. Theseus must have felt far braver as he sought out the Minotaur than I as I followed Thurza.

"This is the room, miss. I'll wait for you outside." Thurza watched me worriedly as I tapped at the oak door. Big iron hinges gave the door a prisonlike aspect and I imagined that beyond it lay something resembling a monk's cell—small, dismal, and dank. There was no sound from inside or any answer to my knock, and after some moments' hesitation, I opened the door.

To my surprise I saw that the room was large and airy and seemed pleasant enough—so far as I could tell in the dim light. Heavy curtains were drawn across the windows and it was a while before my eyes accustomed themselves to the darkness and could see shapes and outlines around me: a table, a chair, a large wardrobe, a chest . . . and, against the far wall, dominating the room with ponderous magnificence, an immense half-tester bed.

I could make out the ornate, molded head which rose fully eight feet or more above the floor level, jutting out in a curved canopy from which dark silk curtains fell, looped back by thick, tasseled cords.

I listened intently and heard the sound of steady breathing. He was sprawled across the bed, fully dressed in the evening clothes he had worn to the ball, one arm extended at his side, the other bent across his face. I tiptoed closer, and stretching out my hand, shook his shoulder cautiously. He grunted and stirred irritably, flinging his arm out straight, but remaining deep in sleep. I stared down at him uncertainly. Should I shake him harder—but might that harm his back in some way? I wished that I were far away from this room and far away from this man. . . . Only the thought of Dobbin persuaded me to remain rather than slide quickly and silently away, in cowardly fashion, before he did waken.

The curtains were of heavy velvet and they rattled back loudly on wooden poles as I dragged them open to let in some daylight. He groaned but his eyes stayed stubbornly closed. I looked at the dead-white face, the deeply furrowed lines on his brow, the long, black lashes that shadowed his cheeks, and the thin mouth —twisted derisively even in sleep. His hand extended outward over the edge of the bed, long fingers lightly curled, and the sight of them rekindled the memory of their touch . . . with an effort I looked away and back at his face. His eyes were wide open and he was staring at me as though I were an apparition.

"In God's name—I must be dreaming! What are you doing *here?*"

He reached out to touch me as though to establish that I was real and I stepped back hurriedly.

"I am aware of the impropriety of the situation, sir," I said coldly. "I need your help urgently—or rather someone else does. The contessa said I should find you here. We could not wait . . . else I should never have come here."

He said wryly: "It must be a matter of life and death to bring you to the ogre's lair!" He closed his eyes and passed a hand wearily across his face. "Be so good as to shut the curtains a little, Miss Chell."

I did as I was bid and when I turned back to the bed I found that he had levered himself into a sitting position with his legs swung downward to the floor, and was hunting about him for something.

"My stick, Miss Chell . . . I can't seem to find it. I'm helpless as a kitten without it. I must have thrown it down somewhere last night—how careless of me!"

It was lying near the foot of the bed, and without a word, I picked it up and handed it to him. He took hold of it and looked up at me in silence for a moment or two. I turned my head away to avoid his gaze.

"I owe you the deepest apology, Miss Chell," he said at last. "What happened last night must have been extremely distasteful to you and I behaved in an unforgivable fashion. I have no excuses to offer you—except to say that I was very drunk and scarcely knew what I was doing. . . . I can remember little and I would ask and hope that you will forget it too. It shall never be referred to again, I promise."

If possible, it seemed to me that his face had gone even whiter and there was an anguish in his eyes that I had never seen before.

I said more calmly than I really felt: "I am only too anxious to forget it, sir, which is why I have decided it best to leave Aysgarth and go away."

"I was afraid you might say that—and you have every reason to feel that way. I suppose you are quite determined and nothing I can say will change your mind?"

"Nothing."

"You are abandoning us in our hour of need then, Miss Chell? Where shall I find another housekeeper half as efficient as you? There is one excellent argument for your staying . . . don't you agree?"

"When you marry Miss Benton and bring her to live at Aysgarth, she will naturally employ her own housekeeper. I shall not be needed much longer in that capacity."

"That's true. And if I asked you to stay just for yourself alone —never mind your excellence as an unpaid housekeeper?"

"I should reply that it is far better that I go. You have been generous indeed in giving me a home here, sir, when you had no obligation toward me whatever, but you will recall perhaps that

when first we met I proposed finding a post as a governess instead of remaining here as a burden to you. . . . That is what I
shall do now and should have done in the very beginning."

"Yes, I do remember you telling me some such notion. . . ."

"You said I was plain enough to be an ideal governess," I
reminded him.

"Did I really say that? Well, I have changed my mind about
your looks, Miss Chell—either I was mistaken or they have improved remarkably. And I have told you once before that I do
not consider you to be a burden . . . surely you will not desert
us all. Say you will stay!"

But I shook my head fiercely, unaccountably close to tears.

He sighed heavily: "You are very stubborn, Alice Chell. At
least promise me one thing, if you are determined on this course
of action: let *me* find a post for you. I am not without some connections still in the country and could make sure that you go
somewhere where you will be happy and well treated. You owe
me that much. Do you promise?"

"Yes."

"Very well—thank goodness that at least is settled. And now
you had better tell me what life and death crisis has brought you
to my bedroom."

I told him—leaving nothing out from Mrs. Cropper's tale—not
even her scathing attack on me, although I feared that he would
be angry to learn that I had been foolish enough to promise
Dobbin help. I expected harsh words of criticism but, for a moment, he said nothing at all but twiddled the silver knob of the
stick beneath his hand and appeared to consider the matter carefully. At last he said: "You were unwise, Miss Chell, to interfere
in the affair—especially when you had no real prospect of hope
for the boy. However, you could not know that this would happen. . . . The child is wild, I know, but has never stolen before.
Your only fault is to have a compassionate, if somewhat impulsive and rash, nature . . ." He tapped the silver knob thoughtfully to his lips. "When last you asked me to help your small
protégé I could do nothing for him; I doubt I can do better this
time but I will try. I shall go and speak to Lord Benton on his
behalf and see if I can persuade him to drop the charge against
him—will that satisfy you? Here . . . take my handkerchief and

dry your tears. I can see several in your eyes. . . . I wish I could think that just one of those is for me!"

He offered me a silk handkerchief from his pocket and I hastily mopped away and returned it to him.

"Now," he said, "if you would be brave enough to give me your arm, the sooner I stand up and leave for Benton Castle the better."

He grasped my hand and levered himself stiffly from the edge of the bed to stand, swaying slightly and deathly pale. Beads of perspiration stood out on his brow and he looked very ill. Suddenly I was conscience-stricken.

"I don't think you should be doing this . . . you must be in great pain . . . I had not realized. Perhaps I could go in your place?"

"And perhaps you could not!" He shook my arm away almost brusquely. "Lord Benton would eat you alive, my dear girl, and he is most unpleasant when thwarted in any way. No, I shall manage very well . . ." With an effort he smiled at me, but it was painful to see the tormented twist to his lips. "You always do me good, Miss Chell, as I have told you before I believe. When you are around I feel considerably better. By the way, before we part, I still have something of yours to return."

He fumbled in the pocket of his green velvet coat and produced my silver locket, dangling prettily on the end of its chain. I felt my cheeks flush scarlet at the mere sight of it and held out my hand to take it quickly from him.

"One moment," he said easily. "I promise to behave in a manner above reproach, Miss Chell, but please allow me to fasten the locket round your neck. I have observed that the clasp is a difficult one to secure properly—so, if you would turn round and bend your head down a little, I shall do it for you so that it is not lost again."

Unwillingly, I did as he asked and was dismayed and embarrassed to find that I trembled and shook at the touch of his fingers on the nape of my neck. If he noticed my agitation, he gave no sign of it. When the locket was safely fastened, he took hold of my shoulder lightly and turned me round to face him again; and reaching for my hand, he took it gently in his and lifted it to his lips. He kissed the tips of my fingers and looked down at me for a moment, his eyes very dark and unfathomable. "There—that is the worst you need fear from me!"

He turned away abruptly, leaning heavily on the ebony stick. "Send Unwin to me will you, Miss Chell. I need his help to dress for battle with his lordship! I shall leave as soon as possible—you had best pray for that boy's sake that I am successful."

I hurried from the room.

"Are you looking for my brother, Alice?"

I started as Eweretta came up behind me in the great hall. She looked at me uncertainly, her blond head tilted questioningly to one side. I was surprised to notice that the customary glint of malice was absent from her eyes; altogether she seemed softer and more friendly. She even smiled a little at me and added: "I saw you from the gallery—you have been waiting here a long time. . . . I thought it might be for Miles."

I waited for some waspish comment but none came. Instead she fiddled distractedly with her ringlets and finally said in careless tones:

"Tell me, Alice, did you enjoy the ball?"

"Very much, thank you."

"I believe you know Lord Alfred Witherspoon well?"

Ah, I thought, now we are coming to the point of this conversation.

"I used to know him well but have not seen him for a long time. I had no idea that he was even in Yorkshire."

"Mmmm . . . He is extremely handsome and sophisticated— don't you think? And so elegant and stylish?"

"Oh, extremely."

"And very charming too?"

"Undoubtedly."

"Tell me, Alice, is it true that he is also exceedingly rich?"

"*Exceedingly*, Eweretta. He is worth a fortune!"

She blushed prettily and gave a nonchalant little trill of laughter. "How *very* interesting! He says he will call on me here—if he does then I think I shall definitely see him."

"Perhaps he will ride back from Benton Castle with your brother."

"But Miles returned an hour or more ago—he tried to find you but you were nowhere to be seen. I suppose you were buried away in the kitchens as usual, or something like that. He gave me a note to give you—I have it here and nearly forgot all about it. He left in a great rush and fury I can tell you."

"But where did he go?"

"To York. Don't ask me why. But I've never seen him look so angry. He was quite frightening!"

I took the single sheet of paper from her. It had been folded crookedly over on itself and the few lines were scrawled untidily in the bold, black script that I remembered well from the letter Mr. Pendleton had shown me in London. The message was brief: *Eweretta will give you this. Lord Benton will not give way unless a certain condition is met. I am leaving immediately for York because of this—the contessa will explain everything. Remember your promise and do not leave before my return.* His signature was scribbled hastily at the end.

Eweretta was eying me curiously. "What is it all about? Do tell me, Alice."

I stared down at the letter. "I don't know, Eweretta. I just don't know. . . ."

◎◎◎

The contessa was fast asleep in her chair with Topaz, the cat, curled comfortably on her lap. He opened his yellow eyes and inspected me lazily, blinking a little and stretching out a sharp-clawed paw. The gentle movement woke his mistress. She smiled at me brightly.

"Did you hear, my dear, that Miles has gone dashing off to York?"

"But why, Contessa? What happened with Lord Benton?"

"It's extremely simple, child. Lord Benton flatly refused to let the boy off the charge. It was a heaven-sent chance for him to revenge his daughter."

"Revenge? I don't understand."

"No—you wouldn't, my dear. I'm certain Miles wouldn't have told you a word about it—he's very reticent where you are concerned."

"He left me a note to say that you would explain everything."

"Well then, that leaves me free to speak. He told me that Catherine Benton made up her mind that she would like to marry him after all. Apparently she had decided that he wasn't quite so repulsive as she had feared. She said as much at the ball and suggested that their engagement be announced with a grand flourish at midnight. Unfortunately, she had neglected to consult her prospective bridegroom before planning all this. . . ."

"You mean he refused to marry her?"

"Exactly!" The contessa chuckled at the thought and with great relish. "And what's more he told her that he was eternally thankful that he had not married her before his accident and that he had no intention of offering his hand and heart ever again!"

"I can't believe it! She is so very beautiful!"

The contessa looked at me sharply. "Beauty, my dear child, lies in the beholder's eye and my great-nephew's were long since wide open so far as Miss Benton is concerned—thank goodness. No, the only drawback to the situation is that Lord Benton was furiously angry at having his daughter rejected by an impoverished cripple—as I believe he termed it. He refused utterly to have that boy released and swears he'll have him deported to Australia or, better still, hanged if he can possibly manage it."

"There was some condition—he mentioned a condition?"

"I am coming to that, my dear. Patience! Lord Benton said that he would only agree to drop the charge if the debt owed to him by Miles's father was repaid within three days."

"Did he owe him a great deal?"

"He owed *everyone* in the country a great deal," the contessa said dryly. "Most of them have been repaid but the debt to Lord Benton was so large that Miles has only been able to return part of it—a good portion is still outstanding. Naturally, Lord Benton has a right to expect it to be repaid, but not this way—not wagered against the freedom of a child. He is even more loathsome than I expected." She patted the cat soothingly as his pointed ears twitched at the note of anger in her voice. "But don't look so alarmed and upset, Alice. All will be well in the end, I promise you. The money will be returned and Lord Benton will be honor-bound to have the boy released."

"How *can* it be? It's impossible if the sum is a large one?"

"It's easy, my dear. I've given Miles my rings—as well as one or two other trinkets. He has gone to York to raise the money and will be back before the three days are up. You may rely on him."

I looked in dismay at her bare fingers as they stroked the cat's soft, gray fur. "But your beautiful jewels, Contessa! They meant so much to you."

Tears glistened in her blue eyes but she smiled at me and shrugged her shoulders defiantly. "Pooh! What use are rings on old hands like these? Look at them, Alice. They are all gnarled and veined and wrinkled with age. Once, long ago, I had beautiful hands—when I was a young girl like you—and then perhaps there was some point in decorating them with rings . . . but now, what does it matter? It's far better, I think, that they are put to some good use and what better one than to outwit that vulgar, cruel little man and save that poor child. Besides, Miles refused to sell them outright—I had the greatest difficulty in persuading him to take them at all. He is only going to pawn them so perhaps they may be redeemed one day. . . ."

Her voice trailed away brokenly and a single tear began to trickle slowly down her old cheek. I ran to her, and kneeling down beside her chair, put my arms around her and hugged her tightly.

CHAPTER X

I knew what I had to do. I knew one way, however impossible it might seem, to reclaim the contessa's jewels, and at the same time, to save Aysgarth. I had thought about it often, and again and again, the same deep, driving conviction persuaded me that there was a slender chance that *I* might be able to find the legendary Cross of Aysgarth.

I remember no clear reason in my mind why I thought that I could succeed where others had failed for so long. Perhaps I felt that because I was an outsider—a stranger to the house and family—I might perceive something that had eluded those more acquainted with the place by its very familiarity. Perhaps I even felt that in some unknown way destiny had brought me to Aysgarth for that very purpose. . . . At all events, I was going to try. If only I knew where to begin.

I began in the study—in front of the Abbot Haby's portrait. I stood for a long time in the dimness of that room, staring searchingly up at the complacent, corpulent monk as he sat at the table with the glittering cross before him. His gooseberry-green eyes looked down steadily into my own. *Tell me, I begged him silently, tell me where the cross is hidden. You know the secret and took it to your death at Tyburn . . . guide me somehow to find it. If you loved the Metcalfes, as I know you did, you must help me now to help them.* . . . My fingers closed over the little amber rosary bead from the abbey ruins, that I kept in the pocket of my dress. I held it fiercely as though it were some magic charm, closed my eyes, and prayed for inspiration and help. None came. There was no blinding revelation, no ghostly, hollow voice, no flash of truth; only the steady ticking of the clock on the mantelpiece, the faint creak of the paneled walls, and the pattering of the rain against the windowpanes. I opened my eyes and the abbot gazed impassively down at me, trapped forever in his gilded frame. It had been foolish to expect mere paint and canvas to be my ally.

The rain continued to pour down from heavy, gray skies. I wandered haphazardly about the house, examining the old walls, peering into cupboards, poking into deep, dark recesses, in the vain hope of finding some clue or irregularity that might lead me to a hitherto undiscovered hiding place—a secret niche, a sliding panel, or a hollow space. The housekeeper's keys were still at my waist and I decided to brave once again the locked, empty rooms that Signorina Frugoni and I had inspected so reluctantly. I had been stupidly nervous even with company; now, completely alone and with the increasing gloom of the rainy afternoon casting dark, dismal shadows around me, I felt my heart begin to beat fast as I selected each key to open the stiff, creaking doors . . . I forced myself to persevere with the task, searching painstakingly through the rooms from floor to ceiling, scrutinizing beams and plaster minutely, and brushing away thick curtains of cobwebs to run my fingers carefully across old stonework, ledges, and crevices. I crawled on my knees to peer up the chimneys, prodding and probing among the sooty bricks until I was as black as any sweep.

At last I came to the room where Signorina Frugoni and I had discovered the portrait. I hesitated for a moment: somehow it seemed wrong to peep and pry again at something that I had never been meant to see. But I knew I had to look in that room. I unlocked the door and pushed it gently open, fully prepared, this time, for the painted figure that would be staring at me from its dusty corner. I was ready to confront those eyes without fear . . . but there was no need. The young Master of Aysgarth no longer looked across the empty room. The golden frame still stood, propped in the corner against the wall, but the canvas inside it had been slashed and rent to ribbons. . . .

I did not wait to relock that room. I slammed the door behind me as I ran, fleeing in panic down the long, dark passages through the house until I reached my room and sank, terrified and exhausted, on my bed. All my fearful imaginings of before had returned to haunt me once again but this time the evidence of evil was too manifest to ignore or explain away. That portrait had been deliberately ruined—viciously mutilated with a hideous violence. But who had done it and why? I remembered the missing keys and knew that whoever had taken them from my room that night had also destroyed the painting. Who hated Miles Metcalfe so much that they could not bear the sight of his painted image? Or had he perhaps cut it to pieces himself in a terrible passion of frustration and despair? I knew no answers, but I was afraid. . . .

At last I calmed myself, washed my sooty hands and face, and went downstairs. I could not stay forever in my room, cowering and fearful—that would help no one. I went into the library in search of a book that would distract me. It was a peaceful room with a mellow, soothing atmosphere about it. I looked around, averting my gaze from the blank space on the wall above the mantelpiece where the darker outline left by a large picture still showed on the white plaster. *"It used to hang in the library,"* Signorina Frugoni had said. Now the portrait would never hang there again.

I began to look along the rows of finely bound leather volumes, reading their titles at random. One shelf seemed devoted to local history: *The Dales of Yorkshire, A History of Middleham Castle, The Yorkshire Moors, Benton Castle*—I grimaced at that one—*The Ancient City of York, The Story of York Minster, The Metcalfes of Aysgarth* . . . I picked out this last one and began to read, idly at first and then with growing interest until I became completely absorbed.

The book had been written by some local squire ten years previously, and it was a fascinating, detailed account of the long history of the Metcalfe family. I turned page after page with eager interest. There had been Metcalfes at Aysgarth since the eleventh century. For seven hundred years the ownership of the house and estate had been handed down from father to son until the present master. They had been a prominent and important family in the North—loyal to the Crown, friends and councilors of kings, brave soldiers in battle, rich, respected, and trusted by all. The original stone dwelling had been enlarged and enhanced by each succeeding generation until, gradually, it had evolved into the house it was today. . . .

The author of the work began to write of the founding of Aysgarth Abbey and its close link with the Metcalfes. He mentioned the arrival in the twelfth century of the monk Hugh de Quincy, bringing with him a fabuolus jeweled cross, and the granting of land by the Metcalfes to the monks. There followed a description of the abbey itself, its building and growth over the years, and the life of the monks in that peaceful little valley. A further paragraph caught my eye:

The Metcalfes maintained a long and intimate association with the abbey throughout the centuries, contributing greatly to its wealth and prosperity, sending their sons to be taught by the monks and traditionally preserving a close friendship and trust between the head of the family and the incumbent abbot. This fellowship was never stronger than that between Abbot Haby of the sixteenth century and Miles Metcalfe of that time. The two men were loyal friends for many years and, during that time, some fine additions were made to the abbey buildings through the generosity of the family, including the vast traceried window of nine lights to be found in the north wall of the church, and bearing the abbot's rebus at its head. . . . This Miles Metcalfe died in 1537, only two days before his old friend was arrested by the King's men and taken away to imprisonment at the Tower, and thence to Tyburn. Despite his probable preoccupation with his own personal danger at that moment, the abbot insisted on arranging for the immediate burial of Miles Metcalfe in the chapter house of the abbey—a privilege hitherto reserved for the abbots themselves. He declared, it is said, that the abbey owed the Metcalfe family an eternal debt of gratitude which might never be repaid but at least, in this way, they would be fittingly honored. It was his final act as abbot of Aysgarth before being dragged away and put to death. . . .

I read and reread the last lines on the page and as I did so I saw that my prayers had, after all, been answered. I now knew, without any doubt, where the Cross of Aysgarth was hidden.

The rain had stopped but a thick mist had drifted down from the moors, swathing the house in a blanket of opaque white. It was cold and I shivered as I closed the door behind me. I had run straight from the library without a word to the contessa or anyone about my intuition—there would be time enough to tell them when, and if, I was proved right. Until then I would say nothing, save to Philip Paige, who would be working at the abbey ruins and whose help I needed.

As I hurried along the narrow pathway through the thicket, I pictured to myself the archaeologist's delight at my discovery: I was so certain that I was right, so certain that he would share my conviction with equal enthusiasm. The mist became more dense and I had difficulty in seeing the track more than a few feet ahead. The clammy dampness in the air was making my hair cling wetly to my forehead and my feet felt soaked through in their thin slippers. I thought I heard the sound of footsteps somewhere behind me and stopped to listen—but there was only the dripping of water from the leaves and a faint rustle of twigs as though a bird moved in the branches close by.

The ruins rose eerily from swirling skeins of mist that disguised the crumbled walls and fallen roofs so artfully that for a moment I fancied I saw the ghost of the old abbey before me— intact and alive as it had once been long ago. . . .

I stumbled a little now and again over the stones that lay hidden everywhere in the grass, as I walked among the ruins calling to Philip Paige. The white mist hung thickly about me as I turned this way and that in complete confusion. I had no idea where I was—no door or archway or window seemed at all familiar—everything was blurred and nebulous. I called his name louder and more urgently, feeling a cold unease begin to take hold of me. What if he were not here at all? I had taken for granted that he would be working at the ruins as usual but he might well have returned to the house because of the mist—if so, then I was quite alone in the abbey. There was a noise close at hand: the patter of stones falling when dislodged, and a strange guttural, wheezing sound as though someone were breathing stertorously. . . . I thought of the footsteps on the path behind me and my flesh froze in terror.

"Who's there?" I cried out into the whiteness all around me. "Who is it?"

"Why, Miss Chell! Whatever are you doing here?"

I could have wept with relief at the sound of his calm voice and the sight of his slight, familiar figure as it materialized suddenly in front of me through the mist. Philip Paige stared at me, utterly bewildered by the spectacle of me cowering cravenly against a wall—damp, dripping, and petrified. His pleasant, homely face seemed the most reassuring thing in the world to me at that moment.

"I thought I heard someone calling me," he said, "but then I felt sure I must be mistaken. You shouldn't be out in this weather, Miss Chell. You're cold and wet and will make yourself ill. I will take you back to the house at once."

"No—wait!" I put my hand on his arm in agitation. "I have something very important to tell you."

"There can be nothing so important that it cannot wait until you are warm and dry again," he said reasonably.

"But it is—I assure you. Mr. Paige—I *know* where the Cross of Aysgarth is hidden."

I had blurted the words out like some impulsive, silly schoolgirl and I saw from his face that he considered I was talking hysterical nonsense. He looked polite but completely skeptical.

"Please don't think I'm being deliberately discourteous about this, Miss Chell, but I wonder if your vivid imagination has been at work again. You seem very overwrought."

I shook his arm, unable to restrain my impatience. "It must seem so to you, but you must listen and believe me this time, Mr. Paige. I know I am right—I know exactly where to find the cross and I need your help."

He was uncertain and embarrassed, shifting his feet uneasily. "Perhaps you'd better tell me all about it then so that I can judge for myself."

I told him what I had read in the book in the library. "The Miles Metcalfe who was head of the family in 1536 was a great friend of Abbot Haby. He died two days before the abbot was arrested for treason and Abbot Haby insisted that he be buried in the chapter house—even though this had never been permitted before. He spoke of a debt owed to the Metcalfes and I remember Mr. Metcalfe telling me that Hugh de Quincy had pledged that the cross be given to the family if ever the abbey were disbanded. . . ."

"Yes—I remember that."

"Well then—it's very clear to me. Can't you see what the abbot did, Mr. Paige? Think of yourself in his position three hundred years ago. The abbey was in great peril and so was he. The cross was the most precious, the most sacred possession of the monks—the symbol of everything they believed in. . . . If it were buried with Miles Metcalfe in that coffin, then it would be safe from pillagers and thieves should disaster strike the abbey. If all went well it could always be restored to its rightful place on the high altar—if not and the abbey was destroyed, then the cross was exactly where it had been pledged—with the Metcalfes. It was the wisest and safest thing he could do."

I watched his face and saw the gradual dawn of belief in his eyes. "It's possible," he murmured, almost to himself. "It's just possible. I told you though, Miss Chell, that legendary stories are rarely based on any real facts. The story in that book you read is probably only inaccurate hearsay. There are thirteen abbots known to be buried in the chapter house and I have examined and accounted for every tomb—there is no other grave that I know of."

"There is a fourteenth," I told him. "There *has* to be—I know it!"

He smiled at me indulgently. "It has waited three hundred years, in any case, Miss Chell, so it will wait a little longer. You must go back to the house now before you are chilled to the bone—I can see you shivering. If you like I will look round the chapter house later on, but I must confess I hold out very little hope."

"I'm sorry, Mr. Paige, but I refuse to go back now. I couldn't possibly rest until I have searched for myself. Please—help me look now and if we find nothing within half an hour then I promise to return to the house with you."

He hesitated and then shrugged his shoulders good-naturedly. "Very well, Miss Chell. If nothing less will satisfy you then I can see we shall have to go and look round the chapter house together. But I fear we shall find no other grave than those of the abbots. It is much more probable that you will catch pneumonia from being out in this damp and inclement weather."

He offered me his arm and guided me through the mist until

we came to the octagonal-shaped place that I remembered well. I looked about me.

Philip Paige said indulgently: "Look, Miss Chell, there are only thirteen tombstones here—you can count them all quite easily. As you can see I have cleared away the grass and moss from them so that they can be seen very clearly. There is no trace of any other grave."

"But you weren't looking for one," I pointed out, desperately determined to convince him. "I know it is here somewhere."

He handed me a small trowel. "Here, take this then and we can carry out a rough search—if that will please you. If you should strike any hidden stone beneath the grass then you should hear the metal ring against it. I'll search on this side and you stay here—in that way we shall cover the ground systematically."

He began to make a perfunctory exploration of the earth and I saw, with despondency, that he still gave little credence to my theory. I started to probe at the grassy floor of the chapter house with infinite care. I knew that it looked a hopeless task but I dared not despair. I thought instead of the contessa's tears, of the man who had ridden to York to save a small, unimportant urchin, despite his own great pain, and I thought of the rambling, dilapidated gray-stone mansion that had become a part of my life and somehow a part of my heart. . . .

It was I who found the grave and I shall always be glad of that. Quite suddenly, when I had begun to give up hope, I heard the sharp clang of metal against stone as my trowel drove deeply into the earth and hit something hard. I was working at the eastern end of the chapter house, only a few feet from the gap in the stone bench where the abbot had presided over the meetings in his chair. I dug further, tugging and tearing at the coarse grass and scratching away at the soil beneath. A small circle of limestone appeared. With growing excitement and a fast-beating heart I uncovered it more, working painstakingly until a large section of stone was exposed—muddy and smooth beneath my fingers.

I called to Philip Paige, who was at the opposite end of the chapter house, and seeing my face, he hurried across to my side and bent down to examine the find. "Miss Chell," he said at last, "I'm beginning to wonder if you could be right. It certainly *looks* like a gravestone—rather a simple one, I think, not nearly so heavy or impressive as the abbots' tombs, but then, if your story *is* true, then the burial would have been a hasty one. There was no time for anything but a very plain grave. Let's clear away some more earth and see—"

We worked on together and the damp mist hung heavily above us, chill and meancing. I no longer felt cold. I thought only of what might lie beneath us. My hands were black with dirt, my fingernails torn and broken, by the time the complete rectangle of limestone was revealed. Philip Paige knelt down and carefully brushed and blew away the earth that clung damply to the surface, and as he did so, faint indentations of lettering became visible—words chipped out crudely in the stone as though the mason had hurried over his task.

"*Hic jacet Miles Metcalfe,*" Philip Paige's finger's traced the characters lightly. "*A cruce salus*—salvation by the cross." His voice had an odd, incredulous note.

I said quietly: "The only clue the abbot dared leave. Now do you believe me, Mr. Paige?"

He turned to me, eyes gleaming behind the lenses of his spectacles. "I must confess I scarcely credited a single word of that account—let alone your idea—but now . . . I think it's just possible that you may have guessed correctly. We must open the grave and discover that for ourselves."

I hesitated, oddly reluctant to do so. "Shouldn't we leave that for Mr. Metcalfe? Now that we've found it and know that it does really exist—somehow I feel *we* have no right to disturb it."

He swept my objection aside impatiently. "But of course we must examine it now, Miss Chell. How can you suggest otherwise? I have Mr. Metcalfe's full consent to excavate these ruins."

"But a grave of one of the Metcalfe family . . ."

He smiled thinly. "You are too sentimental, Miss Chell. I cannot afford to be. We shall open up the tomb immediately. It was *you*, after all, who insisted on this treasure hunt. . . ."

I waited uneasily while he fetched a heavy crowbar and began to lever away at the corners of the limestone slab. It was deeply embedded in the soft earth, and at first, he could scarcely move it more than an inch. Perspiration streamed down his forehead as he worked away doggedly, wielding the iron bar this way and that against the stone until, at last, it shifted a little in the ground. Grunting and gasping, he pitted his slight weight against the solid slab until it gradually lifted sideways, pivoting against the bar so that he was able to slide it across the wet grass to expose the raw earth beneath. He flung down the tool and began to scrabble at the soil with his bare hands.

The lead coffin seemed very small. I looked down at it with surprise and misgivings. I did not want the Miles Metcalfe who had died in 1537 to be disturbed so rudely in this way. He had lain peacefully in his grave for three hundred years and it did not seem right to break open his coffin with the indifference that Philip Paige displayed as he forced the crowbar under the lid and wrenched at the edges. . . .

In silence we stared down into the interior. The coffin seemed to contain no more than a thick layer of gray dust and earth. Carefully, respectfully, I stretched out a hand to sweep aside the dirt. A gleam of white bone appeared—a skull with empty, staring eye sockets and wide, grinning mouth, and then more bones, the curve of ribs, the delicate bones of a hand, and beneath it, encrusted seemingly not with jewels but mud, lay a large, heavy object in the unmistakable form of a cross. I lifted it out, and with my finger tips, gently brushed away the coating of dust and grime. The faintest gleam of gold began to show . . . the cold glitter of a diamond, the warm fire of a ruby, the blue sparkle of sapphires . . . it burdened my arms with its weight but I held it tightly against my body, and closing my eyes, thanked God. . . .

"Give it to me, Miss Chell." Philip Paige smiled at me pleasantly and held out his hands.

Instinctively, I clasped the Cross of Aysgarth protectively, not wishing him to touch it.

"If you please—" he repeated, and moving toward me, prized it from my grasp.

"The contessa will be so pleased," I murmured, still almost unable to believe in the discovery.

"The contessa will never see it," he replied in matter-of-fact tones.

"What do you mean? Of course she must see it at once. I shall show it to her straightaway. I must take it back immediately."

"It is not yours to take. The cross belongs to me."

Had he gone mad? I stared at him, bewildered. "You are teasing me, Mr. Paige! The cross belongs to the Metcalfes—you know that perfectly well."

"In theory, yes, I believe it does. But in practice, Miss Chell, I intend that it shall be mine." He stroked the outline of the cross caressingly. "Do you recall me telling you that my father was ruined by the Metcalfes? The money owed to him was never repaid and I was denied my rightful inheritance. It is only just that I should take what is lawfully mine! I came to Aysgarth to find the cross and I had given up all hope. . . ."

I stared at him. "But you said you didn't believe the cross existed. You told me so many times."

He smiled. "I have always believed that it did, Miss Chell, but I pretended otherwise. I heard the legend from my father—unfortunately he misled me badly—he believed it to be hidden somewhere in the house. I had not thought of the abbey. . . ."

I looked at his pale, twitching face. "Then it was *you* who stole the keys from my room?"

He nodded, pleased with himself. "Of course. I had searched everywhere else at night, but there remained those locked rooms. . . ."

"And the portrait? Did you destroy the portrait?"

I felt sick to see his satisfied expression as he answered. "He was too handsome, too proud—I didn't like to see that. The Metcalfes have always been too proud—they deserve to crawl in the dust forever. Don't you agree? I've always wished that I were handsome—his sister might not have made such fun of me if I were rich and handsome, don't you think?"

My throat was so dry I could scarcely speak. "And Mrs. Silver? You said it was an accident—"

He looked at me sideways, tilting his head whimsically so that the glass in his spectacles glinted confusingly, concealing his eyes.

"You always wondered about Mrs. Silver, didn't you? No, I didn't kill her, Miss Chell, It wasn't necessary. She saw me that night when I was searching for the cross. She followed me down the staircase and tripped in the darkness—I heard her fall. She never cried out but she was quite dead, you know, when she reached the bottom step."

He placed the cross carefully on the grass beside him and picked up the iron bar.

"Unfortunately, Miss Chell, much as I have liked and admire you, I realize now that you stand between me and everything I have set out to achieve. The cross is worth a huge fortune, you know, and only you and I know of its discovery. When you are dead I shall be able to dispose of it as I wish and be rich and respected for the rest of my days . . . You can understand how I feel, Miss Chell. Your imagination will help you to see that I have no alternative. . . . I can put your body in the coffin, rebury it, and no one will ever find you. They will think that you have simply run away from Aysgarth—which would not be unlikely would it?"

He came toward me, smiling, and I could not move. My legs refused to take flight to escape the terrible danger that threatened me. He lifted the iron bar high above him and I screamed and ducked sideways as it hissed down, fanning my cheek as it clove the air viciously. Again, he raised it, and as I turned to run at last, the iron caught my shoulder with a stunning blow so that I fell helpless to the ground. There was no hope. I lay waiting for death as he stood above me, his face white, distorted, and demented. As in a dream I watched that iron bar hurtle downward, and then, dimly, I was aware of a shadowy form leaping forward from the mists. The bar jerked sideways, deflected at the final moment, so that instead of crushing my skull like an eggshell it glanced off my temple and I slid away into black oblivion.

CHAPTER XI

"I suppose you are going to make a habit of this?"

I opened my eyes slowly at the words and looked around me. The embroidered silk hangings of my fourposter bed floated above my head in a misty haze of colors; beyond that everything was blurred and indistinct.

"How many more times are you going to be carried into this house unconscious, I ask myself?"

The voice spoke again—dry and insistent. My vision cleared into sharp focus. The contessa sat, straight-backed and regal, beside my bed, her hands folded neatly in her lap, her blue eyes fixed on my face. "At last, child! I was beginning to think that you would never wake up."

My head was aching badly and I was finding it difficult to imagine what had happened and why I should be lying on my bed in this confused state. With an effort, I forced myself to think. It was something to do with the abbey ruins . . . some words in a book . . . a grave . . . the Cross of Aysgarth . . . and Philip Paige holding an iron bar in his hand and then raising it above his head. . . . I recoiled instinctively where I lay. In a terrified flash of comprehension I had remembered it all with dreadful clarity.

The contessa leaned forward quickly to take my hand in hers. "You must forget everything, my dear. Don't even think about it any more. Thanks to Daniel Duck you are safe and that is all that matters."

"Daniel?" I asked, puzzled. I had no recollection of him in my nightmare.

"He saved your life, Alice. Were it not for him you would not have escaped with just that bruise on your forehead."

"How was he there?"

"When you left the house Thurza tells me that he saw you and followed you. He was afraid for your safety in the mist—very foolish of you, by the way, child, those mists can be treacherous. When you went to the ruins he went with you and waited nearby to see that you were all right. It's as well that he did. . . ."

I remembered now the heavy, menacing breathing sound that I heard and the footsteps behind me on the path—not some fearful monster of the mists but poor, anxious Daniel who had deflected that iron bar and saved my life. I was ashamed to think how he had once so disgusted and frightened me.

"I don't understand what happened, Contessa. Philip Paige was always so gentle and kind—I trusted him completely. But suddenly he seemed to become like a maniac—he raved on about how the cross belonged to him to repay the debt the Metcalfes owed to his father—"

The contessa shook her head. "There was no debt, my dear. Not in this case. Not one single penny was ever borrowed from his family."

"He said that his father died ruined."

"And so he did. His father died a violent lunatic in an asylum and every farthing had been spent on doctors' bills. He had been an old and good friend of Miles's father before the madness took hold of him—which is why Miles was kind to his son, Philip. But the insanity had been in the family for generations. I thought it had missed this one—and so did Miles. Poor boy—in a way one cannot help feeling sorry for him."

"Where is he now? What happened to him?"

The contessa hesitated. At last she said quietly: "A tragedy, I'm afraid, my dear. He deserved it, of course, for what he tried to do to you. . . ."

"Tell me please, Contessa! What happened?"

She sighed. "When Daniel attacked him to save you he ran away into the mist toward the moors. Daniel would have followed him but he was far more concerned about bringing you safely home. So he let him go. The moors can be quite merciless in bad weather, you know. He must have wandered about, lost in the mist all night long. . . . A shepherd found his body early this morning near one of the old stone huts."

We were both silent. For my part I could feel no vengeance toward Philip Paige, even though he had tried to murder me. I felt only pity for his crazed mind and sadness at his lonely, miserable end.

"We must not dwell on it," the contessa said firmly and with bright determination. "We must thank God, instead, that *you* are safe. Miles would never have forgiven me if anything had happened to you in his absence."

"Contessa—the cross! Is it safe? I had almost forgotten all about it."

She smiled. "I have it in my room and it is quite safe, child. I find it highly amusing and intriguing that after so many have searched for it for so long, you should come to Aysgarth, a complete stranger to the house and family, and succeed so cleverly where all the others failed."

"Tell me, Contessa, what is it like? I could scarcely see it properly—it was so covered with mud. Is it *really* like the one in Abbot Haby's portrait?"

"It is even more magnificent, my dear! I tell you that I have never seen such jewels in my life—and I have seen some of the finest in the world in my time. There is a diamond in the center that alone must be worth a king's ransom. And the gold is exquisitely worked. It's the most beautiful thing you can possibly imagine!"

I smiled contentedly. "I'm so glad to hear you say that, Contessa. Then you will be able to redeem your rings and there will be money enough to begin to restore Aysgarth."

I had expected her to look delighted but instead, to my surprise, I saw that her eyes were full of tears. "Contessa—I thought you would be so pleased. . . ."

She dabbed at her face with a lace handkerchief. "And so I am, my very dear Alice. And I am deeply touched by what you have done for us. It only makes me wish the more for something that I have long hoped might come true—"

"And what is that?"

"To see you become a Metcalfe—to see you married to Miles. Wait!" She held up her hand as I opened my mouth to protest. "I know it is something that you have never even considered or dreamed of. Perhaps you find him repulsive and unpleasant—he is hardly every woman's picture of an ideal husband—at least not now. But did you realize, my dear, that he has been in love with you ever since you first came to Aysgarth?"

"You must be quite mistaken, Contessa."

"But I assure you that I am not. I have known it for a long time. I have seen it often in his face when he has been watching you and you were unaware of it. I know my great-nephew and I know that he loves you very deeply. You two would be so perfect for each other, you know. You are everything he needs in a woman—courageous, unselfish, humorous, and you love Aysgarth as much as he does . . . And he—if only you knew him better, as I do, you would know what he is not as arrogant and cold as he seems. Pain and the dread of pity have made him so bitter and distant with others—but he is capable of great love and gentleness if only you were able to return it. Tell me, Alice, is there any chance that, one day, you might come to love him?"

I could not answer her. I did not know what to say. All manner of thoughts and emotions were confusing my mind . . . so, I remained silent, my head averted from the contessa's shrewd gaze. She took my silence for denial and sighed heavily.

"It was unfair of me to ask you such a question, my dear. Please forgive me. Of course, it would be impossible. After all, he has not treated you very well . . . forget I spoke of it. I'm just an interfering old woman."

She stood up and went to the door and paused with her hand resting on the handle, looking back at me with a gentle smile. "Miles will return from York tomorrow. Perhaps when you see him again you may find that you feel more for him than you imagined—who can tell? What a pity he is such a proud man— he might persuade you himself but he would never speak unless he had reason to think that there was some hope."

The door clicked shut and she was gone, leaving me alone with my thoughts.

Fresh air would cure my headache, I decided in despair the following day. I had promised to stay in bed for a while but the room seemed as oppressive as a prison and I longed suddenly for the freedom and open space of the moors where fresh, cool winds might help to clear my mind of its confusion and erase the haunting memory of that nightmare by the grave.

"Are you sure you're all right to ride out, miss?" Garrick had saddled up old Melody for me—but with great reluctance.

"Perfectly, thank you, Garrick."

"I ought to come with you." He shook his head doubtfully. "The master wouldn't like it."

"I shall be quite all right, I promise you, and I should prefer to be by myself this time."

He looked after me anxiously as I left the stable yard. It was a gray, cloudy day and the rooks cawed noisily in the elms, flapping their black wings clumsily as they perched, swaying, on the topmost branches. I cantered steadily up the slopes toward the moors. Melody was as smooth and comfortable to ride as an old rocking chair, and although I missed the speed and fire of Seraphim, a quiet ride suited my thoughtful mood that day. An outcrop of black rock stood silhouetted jaggedly against the skyline high above me. I urged Melody upward across the heather toward it, and when we had reached its lee, I reined in the old horse and allowed her to crop contentedly at the short grass. The moors stretched out below me—wild, desolate, and beautiful and somewhere nearby a curlew called its mournful, eerie cry. The wind that touched my face seemed to carry with it the very smell of the North: the earthy scent of heather and wet grass, of misty rain, cold streams and dikes, and ancient hills—all as old as time itself. Unaccountably, I remembered the fat Yorkshire man who had journeyed with me in the stagecoach from London. *"Take a good look at that, lass. . . . That's Yorkshire out there and 'tis the best place on earth."*

A flash of movement far below caught my eye. I watched and saw a black horse and rider moving fast up the slopes in my direction. It was Seraphim: no other animal could gallop with such power and grace. He seemed to float across the moorland and his rider's cloak streamed out behind him like a banner. Beneath me old Melody stirred restlessly, raising her head from the grass to whinny softly in greeting.

He pulled up Seraphim within a few paces of where I sat, motionless, beneath the crag. He looked white and utterly exhausted and his black locks blew in a wild tangle round his face. He was breathing heavily and stared across at me in silence for a moment. Then he dismounted, and moving to Melody's side, looked up at me. I felt stiff and shy with him and turned my head away.

"Will you come down from your perch for a few moments, Miss Chell? I cannot see you well enough up there to be sure that you are truly recovered."

"You have heard—"

"The contessa has told me everything that has happened—just now on my return to Aysgarth. It is as well for Philip Paige that he is not still alive for me to deal with. I should have killed him myself for what he tried to do to you—but far less mercifully than the moors. . . ."

I shivered at the violence in his voice. He took my hand in his and said quietly:

"But for your sake we shall not speak of it any more."

"And the cross—does that please you?"

He laughed dryly. "It does indeed, Miss Chell, but only because your life was not lost in its discovery. What use would a hundred crosses be to me if you were not there to amuse me . . . ?"

"And you will sell it? The contessa says it must be worth a great deal."

"I must. I should prefer that it did not have to leave our family, but Aysgarth can be restored with the fortune it will fetch. And the contessa's jewels shall be returned to her. All in all, I think the abbot would approve—don't you agree?"

"I'm sure of it."

"I shall be forever in your debt, Miss Chell. Do you realize that?"

"But that's nonsense. You have more than repaid anything I did by saving Dobbin. Have you news of him?"

He nodded. "I have come straight from Benton Castle. When I repaid the debt Lord Benton was owed, he had no alternative but to agree to drop the charge as promised. The boy has been sent home to his mother."

I felt the tired tears of relief come to my eyes.

He smiled wryly. "What! Not more tears, Miss Chell! You are forever weeping when I am around. I must be very bad for you." He tugged a little at my hand, which he still held in his. "Come down from that horse, as I asked you. My neck is aching with talking to you like this."

I slid from Melody's broad back and he caught me in his arms and held me for a second, touching the bruise on my forehead lightly with his finger tips, before he set me down on the ground away from him. "Leave the horses to graze—they won't wander far. I have something else to speak to you about."

He leaned tiredly against the rock that sheltered us, his face half-averted from me. "While I was in York," he said quietly, "I found time to consult some newfangled surgeon who has set up shop in the city. He's been working in Germany with doctors there and people swear he can cure almost anything . . . hopeless cases like mine have been treated with success—"

"And what did he tell you?"

His face was still turned from me. "He told me that if I put myself in his hands there is no reason why I should not be cured of most of this lameness and pain that afflicts me—the spine could be straightened, muscles and sinews repaired . . . who can say if he is right or not, but at least there is some hope where before I had none. . . ."

I said gently: "I am so glad to hear that."

I watched the black, wind-swept hair, the head stubbornly averted still, the hunched shoulders, the long fingers that gripped the rock fiercely beneath them, and I knew that I loved this man. I did not care a farthing that he was bitter, bad-tempered, and altogether impossible—nor did I care that he was a cripple. But, for *his* sake I wished with all my heart that the surgeon in York would be proved right—with all my will I prayed that he could be cured.

The contessa's voice returned to me, whispered on the wind: *"He is such a proud man . . . he would never speak unless he had reason to think there is some hope."*

I said to the back of his head: "I wonder if you also found time to look for a post for me while you were in York? You said you were not without connections and promised me to do so."

"I'm sorry," he replied stiffly. "I had no time. I shall find you employment with some respectable family as soon as possible."

"Because I was going to tell you," I continued brightly, "that, in fact, I have changed my mind. I should like to stay on at Aysgarth—that is, of course, if you will have me. . . ."

He turned his head slowly then and stared at me. And he seemed unable to credit what he must have read in my face. I think I held out my hands toward him—or perhaps he moved first toward me. I shall never be sure because what followed obliterated all clear thought and memory. One moment we stood apart by that moorland crag, and the next I was in his arms, crushed against him as though he would never let me go. Somehow I managed to extricate my hands and to slide them up around his neck so that I clung to him as tightly as he held me. And, all the while, he murmured my name over and over as he kissed me with infinite tenderness and passion.

"Alice, my darling, lovely Alice . . . I can't believe this. . . . I never dared to hope for one moment that this could ever be so. I love you more than life itself. Tell me that you love me too or I shall think I am dreaming!"

I did so and was rewarded with an embrace that left me breathless.

"And you will be my wife?"

"On one condition only."

"Any! Name it at once!"

"That Dobbin is allowed to come and work in the stables at Aysgarth. He will be safe and happy there."

He groaned. "That boy—not him again! Very well. I promise. And now, say that *you* promise to marry me, and when you have done that, tell me once more that you love me."

And so I did as he asked, and after that, it was a long time before I could speak another word. Much later, he said:

"By the way, there was something else in that grave you discovered. Garrick found it when he was helping Daniel to rebury the coffin. He gave it to me just now at the stables."

He groped in his pocket and held out a small object between his thumb and forefinger. It was Abbot Haby's ring: a small circlet of dull gold with an egg-shaped ruby in its center.

"So he gave it to his friend . . ." I said, wonderingly.

"As I give it now to you," Miles replied. And he took my hand in his and slid the ring on to my finger. It fitted perfectly. "With the abbot's blessing and full approval, my darling, you are now a true Metcalfe and will be mine forever."

And some time after that we rode back together down the hill toward the house.

ENVOY

I have written this story sitting at my desk by the window in the library.

There have been many changes at Aysgarth. The farms on the estate flourish now with good crops and thriving stock, and the house is no longer the gloomy, dilapidated place that I described to you. It has been restored to its former beauty and is full of light and laughter.

A new portrait hangs behind me on the wall, in place of the one that was destroyed, and in it my husband is standing straight and tall, his face no longer ravaged by suffering since his miraculous cure at the hands of the surgeon in York. I am painted sitting beside him and on my lap I hold our first-born—a daughter, Louisa.

The contessa is very frail now in body but her mind is as lively and caustic as ever. Eweretta has married Lord Alfred and is as blissfully content with her fine jewels and carriages in London as Dobbin is with his simple life in the stables.

From the window I can look out on to smooth green lawns that slope gently away beyond the terrace. There are neat flower beds and carefully raked gravel paths, and I can see the beautiful new rose garden that Daniel has made for me, sheltered from the winds that blow down from the moors to Aysgarth.

Author's Note

Readers will be interested to know that a Miles Metcalfe did live at Aysgarth in Yorkshire in the fifteenth century. He was a loyal friend of King Richard III, who often rode to meet him from nearby Middleham Castle. Miles later became Recorder of York, dying in 1486.

The Metcalfes in this story, however, like all the other characters, exist only in my imagination. But Nappa Hall, where the family lived in the fifteenth century, still stands at Aysgarth.